I0562963

THE CASE OF THE COSMOLOGICAL KILLER

Endings and Beginnings

STEPHANIE OSBORN

Enigma House Press

Enigma House Press
Goshen, KY

www.enigmahousepress.com

Copyright © 2018 Stephanie Osborn
Second Edition
ISBN: 978-1-940466-80-4

Cover art by Darrell Osborn

Contents

A Different Game is Afoot

Skye was sleeping peacefully in their bed in Gibson House, and Sherlock was deep in her hyperdimensional equations, reviewing them with all the grey matter he possessed, when a whiff of ozone reached his nostrils.

"Good day to you both," he said into the air without raising his head. "How are matters progressing?"

"We have hopes," his own voice came back to him. "The experiment devised by the firm of Chadwick & Chadwick, Limited, looks to prove successful." Holmes' voice was tinged with humor. "Or perhaps I should say, Chadwick & Chadwick-Holmes, Limited."

"I am glad to hear it," Sherlock said softly.

"Speaking of Skye, where is she?" Chadwick wondered. "I wanted to give her the experimental setup and double-check for updates. We told her we'd come back at this time."

"Oh, I am sorry. I am afraid she did not mention that," Sherlock raised his head and shot a regretful but firm glance in the direction of the voices, knowing the other Holmes would read his thought in his expression.

"She is in bed, soundly asleep. She worked most of the night and barely ate at all today. I finally convinced her to take tea with me, and then discovered she was too inflexible to even stand upright. She permitted me to manipulate her musculature sufficient to release the kinks, but by the time I had done so, she was in a deep sleep. She is nigh exhausted."

"Damn," Chadwick breathed.

———

"He has a point, Chadwick," Holmes observed quietly, referring to the refusal to awaken Skye he had noted in the other man's face. "It does us no good if she exhausts herself on our behalf, and falls short of the mark when her body and mind cannot take any more."

"I know," Chadwick agreed with a sigh. "That's what I meant, not, 'damn, she didn't get the work done.' She's me, remember? And she's pushing herself as hard as I do."

"It appears so," Holmes agreed. "And that is saying quite a bit."

———

"Is that her work you were looking over?" Chadwick asked Sherlock.

"It is," Sherlock admitted.

"Can you make anything of it?" Holmes wondered.

"I can," Sherlock confirmed. "And it looks good, insofar as it goes. But it is incomplete. And as I have not been in this continuum as long as you have been in yours, I do not have sufficient knowledge of the science as yet to consider even attempting to complete it for her."

"You are the expert here, Chadwick," Holmes admitted somewhat grudgingly. "What do you wish to do?"

"Might I make a suggestion?" Sherlock offered.

"Please," Chadwick said.

"Dial back in around noon tomorrow," Sherlock advised. "It will not delay your experiment overmuch; for you, it is a matter of minutes. And this will give Skye time to 'catch up' her sleep—she has slept scarcely more than ten or twelve hours total in some three days—and I will see to it that she eats properly whenever she awakens. Then she will have the morning to complete her calculations here," he waved the notebook at them, "and she can give them to you at noon, then eat lunch."

"Ha! I know what you are doing," Holmes discerned with amusement. "Just as I—just as we—once managed Watson's finances to ensure he did not come to ruin, you are taking control of her schedule to ensure she obtains adequate rest and nourishment. I have been known to do that once or twice with Chadwick, here."

"And, I would suspect," Sherlock retorted with the faintest hint of a smile, "she has likely done the same with you, on more than one occasion."

"She has," Holmes admitted, and this time Sherlock did not hear begrudging in the other man's tone. "We four can become amazingly single-minded when need drives us."

"Indeed," Sherlock nodded.

There was a brief silence, and Sherlock could picture Chadwick gazing at Holmes with a sort of grateful, wistful expression. *Open your eyes, man, and see the treasure you have in front of you, before it is too late,* he thought with some vehemence. Eventually Chadwick spoke again, and this time there was a soft smile in her voice.

"That sounds like a plan, Mr. Holmes, and we'll follow

it. Tell Skye we'll see her at noon tomorrow. Meanwhile, you take good care of her, okay?"

"As much as in me lies," Sherlock nodded.

"Which is considerable," Chadwick chuckled.

The air crackled, another surge of ozone wafted through the room, and they were gone.

———

The other continuum checked in the next day, and a refreshed Skye had some refined numbers for them. Then they disappeared for a few days, during which time Sherlock insisted that Skye rest more than usual. She still spent time jotting alternative theories and equations into her notebook, however. This meant that Sherlock was, to some extent, bound to Gibson House to ensure Skye didn't dive head-first back into her calculations, but took at least some rest, and ate properly and on time.

Finally, after about three days, Chadwick and Holmes returned.

"Well," Chadwick noted immediately to the married couple, who were seated in the kitchen eating lunch, "you don't have to look for anything else, Sis. We got instant, fast electrons and to spare, with quantities increasing exponentially with time. Probability oh point nine eight four that we had the tail end of Higgs boson decay."

"Then we've almost certainly got tachyon condensation," Skye announced, before drawing a deep, somewhat shaky breath.

"Which is bad," Sherlock noted in a slightly querying tone.

"Which is bad," Chadwick confirmed.

"So now," Holmes added, "we must start looking for

the precise source of the tachyons in the tesseract, and correct it."

"I really think we've probably already found it," Skye decided. "I think if you re-order the string sequencing, and tighten the beam configuration, you'll eliminate the tachyon condensation, and certainly get 'em out of the brane."

"Yeah, but I'd really like to double-check the calcs before we actually start making changes," Chadwick admitted.

"We can do that," Skye said. "Gimme a chance to finish lunch here or Sherlock will pitch a fit—"

"And rightfully so," Sherlock fired back. Skye shot him an *I won't argue* smile before continuing.

"...And then we'll go in the study and work together on the blackboard."

"Deal," Chadwick agreed.

"In that case," Sherlock decided, "I will be of little help, so I may perhaps run over to the McFarlane estate and see what may be seen."

"Sounds like a plan, Hon," Skye nodded. Then she put a hand on his shoulder. "And don't worry. I'll be here when you get back."

Sherlock gazed solemnly at her. "As I said once before, Skye: Do not make promises you cannot keep."

Three acknowledging sighs were his only answer.

2

Unpleasant Discoveries

While Skye worked with their counterparts in the other continuum, Sherlock headed for the McFarlane farm. He had no preconceived notions about what he might be looking for; he only knew he needed to look around. In this way he hoped to determine what was causing so much attention.

Upon arriving at the farm, he parked the car out of sight and meandered into the fields. He located a slight rise that would give him a reasonable view of most of the farm, then found a chalky limestone outcrop for a seat. He settled down and gazed about.

Off to his left lay the homestead: the house, stable, garage, and a few small sheds. *Not unlike our ranch in Colorado,* he thought, *saving only that the stable is for cattle rather than horses.* He watched the cows meander out of the stable and into the fields, counting as they emerged from the stable. When the last had emerged into the sunlight, he turned and surveyed the landscape in general, wrapping his muffler closer about his throat as a chill wind whipped the hilltop.

The McFarlane pastures were somewhat rolling, with some flatlands as well as a few hillocks such as the one on which Sherlock sat. The cows spread over the pastures, locating their favorite grazing spots. This, in turn, drew the detective's attention to the various features of the terrain. Absently, he drew out his gloves and donned them against the cold, blustery winter day. He shoved his cowboy hat down further on his head.

He had been there for two hours, forgetting the cold in the intensity of his scrutiny, when he suddenly noted that there were fewer cows in the fields than before. He stood and counted swiftly, then spun to look back at the stable.

There were no signs of cattle inside.

A short jaunt on his long legs took him to the stable to verify its emptiness; the sleuth returned to his rock perch, and resumed his seat. Once again he counted cows, coming up with a different number than before.

"Hm..." he murmured under his breath. "First there were eighteen missing, now three have returned."

He kept counting, over and over. "Two more have disappeared," he noted softly, watching carefully, "over near that hill beside..." Sherlock's breath caught. "Of course!" He rose and headed swiftly down the hill toward the area of the two most recently missing cows. "In the corner nearest the air force base! I have patently failed to use the brains with which I am blessed!"

Moments later, he spotted the two missing cows, as well as three more, emerging from an opening near the base of the hill.

"A cave. Of course! They go into the cave for shelter— from cold or heat, wind or rain...or unduly playful dogs."

Holmes circumspectly avoided the cave entrance, giving it a wide berth for the time; but he cautiously approached one of the cows that had just emerged.

An ulcerated sore, not unlike a kind of blistered sunburn, and free of hair, was plainly visible on the cow's flank. He circled the cow, noting one or two other similar sores, then moved on to study the other cows from the cave. Each had at least one sore on it.

Sherlock nodded to himself, then embarked on a hike toward the far pasture.

———

When he arrived there, he carefully scanned the cattle, even doffing his gloves and feeling the hide through their hair.

"Most telling," he told the air. "Not one sore."

The detective turned and looked back at the hill containing the cave, a thoughtful, distant focus in the grey eyes.

"It seems I have made quite the unique find. Two mysteries have been solved. The question then becomes, is this the answer to the third, and most important, mystery? More pertinent, if it is, why are they in search of it?"

He nodded to himself.

"This wants looking into. But perhaps it would be best to consult an expert before embarking upon a detailed exploration."

Holmes turned toward the McFarlane house and his car.

———

The tesseract was active and Chadwick and Holmes were reviewing Skye's work from their console in the Chamber, and she, theirs, at the desk in the study, when Sherlock came in. Abstractedly, the three listened to him move through the house: Leaving muddy Wellingtons at the back door, hanging his coat and hat on the rack near the door, washing up in the mudroom, moving to the bedroom to replace shoes and pullover sweater—a "jumper," in modern British terms—with slippers and dressing gown. Skye and Chadwick smiled absently, affectionately; Holmes noted the similarity in the expressions of the two women and grew thoughtful.

———

"Skye?" Sherlock called from the bedroom.

"Yeah, Sherlock?" Skye called back in a preoccupied manner. She never looked up from the calculations she was reviewing on the pad in front of her.

"Just checking."

"Okay."

"I have news," he confessed from the other room as he changed.

"Oh? What's that?" Skye devoted more than half an ear to that statement; if Sherlock offered news, it was generally worth hearing.

"I found the source of the beta burns on McFarlane."

"Oh. That's good. I—" Skye's head snapped up. "Oh, dear God."

———

In the Chamber in the other spacetime, Holmes and Chadwick straightened up in sudden anxiety. They shot a dismayed glance at each other, eyes wide.

"Oh, shit," Chadwick whispered, horrified.

"Indeed," Holmes murmured, shocked. "Surely he would not have..."

"Dunno," Chadwick shot back. "He hasn't been there as long as you've been here. He might not have learned enough yet to know better."

"She is about to run to him."

"Yup. And with good reason. Defocus and track subject."

"Defocusing, track initiated," Holmes agreed, promptly entering the appropriate commands.

———

Skye leaped to her feet with a panicked cry and spun for the door of the study, completely forgetting the tesseract.

"Sherlock!" she shouted frantically as she ran into the hall. "Sherlock, where are you? Where'd you go?! SHERLOCK!"

———

Hearing the urgency in her voice, Sherlock emerged from the bedroom door to stand in the hall, his dressing gown loosely draped about his lean frame, the belt not yet tied.

"HERE, Skye! What is wrong?!"

"Where? Where?" She launched herself at him, grabbing him and scrabbling desperately. "WHERE? Where is it? Show me! How bad?" she chattered frenziedly.

Sherlock stared in confounded amazement as his distraught wife pawed him, grabbing his hands and looking at their palms and backs; she even shoved the sleeves of his dressing gown up his arms and scrutinized his forearms. She cupped his head in her hands and stared at him, inspecting his face and neck with intent, almost wild eyes. Then she snatched at his dressing gown, holding it open and staring at his shirtless body. Her hands followed quickly, searching furiously.

"SKYE! Skye, calm down!" he exclaimed, worried. "What is wrong, my dearest?"

"WHERE ARE THEY!?" Skye wailed, nearly in tears. "Show me! How bad are they? How close did you get to it??"

"Where are what? Get close to what?" Sherlock wondered, trying to sort out her rapid-fire and nearly incoherent babbling. He caught her frantic, trembling hands and held them tightly in his own, to still their frenetic explorations.

"Your burns!" Skye said, coming to a halt and gazing up at him with wide, despairing eyes. Her lower lip quivered as she fought to avoid bursting into tears.

"What...? Ah," he suddenly understood. "NO, no, no, my dear wife, calm yourself. I should never do something so rash as all that. You need have no fear, for I have no beta burns...or any other kind of radiation burn. I am completely unharmed. I suppose I should rather have said that I deduced the source, rather than that I found it; the statement would have been more precise, so, and frightened you less. I now know where it is, but have not myself approached it as yet."

"OH!" And suddenly Skye flung her arms around him, kissing him vehemently.

The detective wrapped his arms around his badly frightened wife, holding her close and returning her kisses as he soothed her.

"Hush, hush, my dear," he murmured against her face. "Settle down, my bonny Skye. All is well."

With a suddenness that took his breath away, Skye's knees gave way and she sagged against him; Sherlock quickly pinned her against his body or she would have fallen.

"Oh dear," her voice said plainly.

Sherlock blinked, then stiffened. He had been looking directly into his overwrought wife's semiconscious face when the statement was made, and knew she had not spoken. It was therefore obvious that the tesseract was active; and as he had not smelled ozone, it had been active since some time before Skye had come in search of him.

They saw everything, he realized, schooling his visage into a bland, neutral expression, even as heat rose in his face. *Private, intimate moments I thought I shared only with my wife.*

"Relax, old chap," Holmes' voice murmured. "No one here sits in judgement. Please forgive us. We did not mean to intrude, but we were almost as concerned as your spouse, when we heard your statement."

"We sure were," Chadwick added vociferously. "Radiation sickness is nothing to mess with. We'll unfocus so you can see to Skye. Looks to me like she needs to get horizontal for a few."

Sherlock remained standing stiffly for several more seconds before he was able to convince his offended sensibilities to ignore the situation. He swept Skye into his arms and carried her into the sitting room, where he laid her on the sofa. One pillow went beneath her head and several beneath her feet; in a few minutes she stirred.

"Skye?" he murmured, kneeling beside the sofa. "Are you all right?"

"I...yeah," she whispered, staring up at him with huge azure eyes. "Are you sure you're okay?"

"Positive. Calm yourself, my dear. All is well. I have no

plans to investigate the source of the radiation for a few days yet."

"You mustn't investigate it at ALL! At least not by yourself!" Skye exclaimed, lunging upward. Sherlock caught her shoulders, keeping her prone with some effort: It was patently evident to him that the tension she had been under for days was manifesting, and her reactions were greatly adrenaline-enhanced. "PLEASE, Sherlock! PROMISE me you won't investigate it alone!"

"Why?" he wondered, astounded at her vehemence.

"Mr. Holmes, what do you know about radiation?" Chadwick's voice asked softly, as the other woman aided her alter ego.

Sherlock shrugged, turning in the direction of the voice. "By 'radiation' I assume you mean that which is due to radioactivity, given the circumstances. Isotopes of certain elements may have their nuclei spontaneously break apart, emitting one or more of three different types of radiation: alpha particles, beta particles, and gamma rays, in order of increasing penetrative ability." He paused, then added, "The initial research was going on during my day, but I have not been idle since arriving in this time-frame. The very first book Skye loaned me was a modern physics text; I desired to better understand the tesseract theory, and picked up considerable knowledge of particle physics and quantum mechanics in addition."

"Do you remember the section on radiation sickness?" Skye asked quietly, watching him. Sherlock glanced back at her.

"I do," he remarked grimly. "And once I realised your train of thought in the morgue, I myself recognised the symptoms in McFarlane's body, if you will recall."

"Then you should know why your wife does not desire you to approach a radiation source strong enough to create beta burns of the severity observed upon your murder victim," Holmes remarked.

"It must be done sooner or later." Sherlock drew a deep breath, somehow combining concern, frustration, and determination in the same action. "Whatever it is may be found within a cave on McFarlane's property. And as the cattle are still experiencing beta burns, and we know that whoever killed McFarlane is likely looking for a way into the underground base..." Sherlock allowed his voice to taper off, knowing that he did not have to explain the implications to any of the three listening to him.

"Fine," Skye said, grabbing his arm. "But call Ryker and have his unit bring in proper protective gear. Don't go in off the cuff and get yourself irradiated! Please, Sherlock. I can't lose you. I CAN'T." She pulled herself up until she gazed into his startled eyes. "Don't you understand?" she whispered, ardent love shining from the despondent blue eyes. "I...I can't live without you." And she buried her face in his chest.

His grey eyes widened, then slid closed. No longer caring about the two observers—even though the observers were themselves—Sherlock gathered his bride close and held her tight.

———

Holmes' identical grey eyes narrowed in defense against the nearly palpable feeling radiating from the couple in the other continuum and which threatened to affect him deeply. Sparing a glance at his own companion by way of diversion, he nearly did a blatant double take.

For Chadwick watched the other couple with a soft, open, pensive smile, and the sapphire eyes he knew so well sparkled with unshed tears. She looked at them for long minutes, while the light of memory flickered in her eyes. An unconscious sigh escaped her lips then, and the smile twisted, becoming wry and bitter.

———

Beside her, pain flashed through dark grey eyes at the disillusioned expression upon Chadwick's face.

But she was gently understanding when she announced, "The two of you need a few minutes to yourselves. We'll come back in an hour."

Then she shut down the tesseract and stood.

"I'm going up to the office to get something to eat before I keel over," Chadwick told Holmes curtly. "Either the continuum will collapse while I'm gone, or it won't. So...wanna come along?"

———

"I—" he began. He had been on the point of refusing, but suddenly changed his mind. "Yes, I should like that...Skye."

The blue eyes blinked at the unexpected mode of address, then warmed. "Well, come on," she told him, waving him to her side with a smile. "Let's go. I'm starved."

———

The faint sizzling pop and whiff of ozone told Sherlock and Skye their doppelgangers had departed, though they cared little by that point. He did take the opportunity to ease into position on the couch and pull her fully into his lap, but otherwise they simply sat and held each other. Skye eventually calmed down, relaxing into Sherlock's arms, cheek pillowed against his bare chest. Long, nimble fingers picked loose her braid, then tangled themselves in the golden mass. She sighed, a long shuddering breath, before looking up at him.

"You won't do it by yourself, will you?" she whispered.

"No, Wife. I give you my word, I will not. I did plan on consulting you, as the subject matter expert, regarding the best way to approach the matter in any event, and in fact to ask if you might be available to assist. On your advice I shall most assuredly contact Ryker and request appropriate equipment. Will that satisfy you?"

"Yes," she breathed in relief. "It sure will. Thanks, Hon."

―――――

"You are overwrought, my dear," he murmured, concerned. "You push yourself to the utmost, and are losing your self-restraint."

"I know. But we're SO close to a solution, and their continuum's destabilization seems to be accelerating."

"I have an idea. But it may seem counter-intuitive to you..."

"Shoot."

"Given the tesseract's considerable, though admittedly not total, ability to negate gaps in time," he observed, "I should like to recommend that you take some time away from your figures, and assist me in the last throes of my little investigation. It should only be a matter of a day to ascertain what is in the cave, once Ryker arrives with whatever equipment is needful. Then we should know why McFarlane was murdered. It would be a great favour to me, and would allow your mind a break as well. A break I suspect it sorely needs."

"Ooo, not bad," she decided, raising a considering eyebrow. "I like the idea. It gives me time away from the equations, but I still have to keep using my noggin. That way I won't get rusty, and I stay fresh. Yeah, I think it's a plan. I'll see if Chadwick and Holmes are okay with that when they get back."

"That is acceptable. In the meanwhile you are going to lie here and rest, and allow your husband to hold you and soothe you."

"That's acceptable, too," Skye grinned, "as long as some of that soothing lands right here." She tapped her lips with her index finger.

"I should not think of neglecting so effectual a method," Sherlock noted, eyes crinkling as he bent his head to hers.

————

February 9

My bonny comrade in arms, The Woman, My Wife, Lady Holmes, my dear Skye, The Woman I Love. So many names I have for this one being, this one woman I know so well—and yet today she still found a way to shake me to my centre.

For I never dreamed as capable a woman as she would ever utter the words now branded in my memory: "I can't live without you." Five simple words—whose import means the world itself. In the three seconds it took her to utter those words, my life was changed forever. She has a way of doing that, my Skye.

I wonder if she knows she is not the only one to have considered the truth of that statement.

————

Holmes and Chadwick strongly agreed Skye needed a

break, and Sherlock promptly contacted Ryker with a coded message and request for assistance. The next morning the MI-5 agent arrived with the military part of his unit, ready to go.

"Righto! You two ready?" he called as their deuce-and-a-half truck pulled up to the door of the cottage. "Got your level 4 MOPP gear already in the lorry. Get your bums into the back with the rest of my mates and the HazMat team from Porton Down, and we'll help you get into the gear once we get to the site."

"MOPP gear?" Sherlock murmured, shooting an inquisitive glance at Skye, as they stood in the front door.

"Mission Oriented Protective Posture. Special HazMat —er, hazardous material—suits designed to protect against nuclear, biological, and chemical agents."

"Ah," Sherlock nodded, and headed toward the truck. "Excellent. Come, my dear Skye. It is high time. We must ascertain the nature of this situation and contain it."

———

The experienced units were soon in position outside the mouth of the cave on McFarlane's farm; an additional covert guard was stationed around a small perimeter centered on the cave, to prevent unwanted spectators. A quick sweep of the area with a Geiger-Müller counter verified Sherlock's deductions. The exploration team suited up in full Level 4 MOPP gear with the assistance of the decontamination team, and Ryker himself served as squire to Sherlock and Skye, assisting them into the extra suits the unit had brought for the couple's use. Grey eyes twinkled with amusement as the detective peered out of his gas mask while Ryker taped down the openings in their suits.

"I shudder to think what 'my' Watson would make of

this outlandish getup," he noted with a chuckle. "It would likely give him nightmares for a week. Still, if it prevents us becoming ill, it will be well worth it."

"Only as long as you don't get too close," Ryker warned, affixing dosimeters to a patch of Velcro on the left breast of their suits. "The suits will only handle so much. Too much radiation will still injure or even kill, despite the suits. Remember that. If what's in there is what I suspect, if it's what we discussed, this team is trained for it and will take care of it ourselves. You two will stay back, stay out of our way, and watch. By rights we wouldn't normally be letting the two of you even come with us. But as you're the government's principal investigators on the case, we're bringing you along to make sure you get the data you need."

"And we thank you." Sherlock somehow managed to execute a graceful bow, even from within the bulky environmental suit.

"But you DO AS WE SAY," the captain added sternly. "You are NOT in charge here, not this time. I am. So we do it MY way. That means: NO heroics, NO wandering off, NO leaving the group, NO inquisitive hands on ANYthing. EITHER of you curious buggers. Is that ABSOLUTELY CLEAR?"

———

Sherlock blinked at the other man's vehemence, then glanced at Skye, seeking her reaction. The blue eyes peering through the gas mask were extremely sober as she nodded immediate and unequivocal assent to the MI-5 officer.

"That serious?" the detective wondered softly.

"Worse," his scientist wife responded quietly.

"According to the documents we saw, we might not even reach the central source, or we might have only minutes to observe it before having to leave."

"Min——?" Holmes breathed, astounded.

"Seconds," Ryker corrected, cutting him off. "Potentially, at least. Remember, for this one time, I'm the superior here, and I give the orders. If I say stop, you stop immediately, right in your tracks. If I say retreat, you turn around and go back. If I yell run, you haul ass out of there. Now let's go. The two of you, stick with me. I don't want either of you out of my sight. I'll not lose two good mates, nor have it said that Sherlock Holmes and Dr. Skye Chadwick-Holmes were lost on my watch."

———

Ryker turned and set off toward the mouth of the cave, signaling his exploration team to get into position with hand gestures.

Immediately behind him, two detectives—one of whom was also a physicist—hurried obediently in his wake.

———

Inside the cave, the Geiger counters clicked faster; some two hundred yards inside, as they slowly descended a gradual slope, the clicking became a continual chatter. They rounded a bend in the open tunnel...

...And were met with an eerie blue glow. It reflected dimly off the damp walls of the cave, and filled the far passage with a soft azure mist.

"Cherenkov radiation," Skye said aloud, awe in her voice. "I've always thought it was so...beautiful."

"You and Madame Curie," Sherlock murmured, a hint of affection in his tone, his smile hidden by the gas mask.

"All halt," Ryker ordered. "Readings?"

"Still within limits," Wang replied, checking the meter on his counter. "Recommend slowing forward speed, however."

"So ordered."

"Sir! There's an opening in the cavern floor ahead!" Huggins called from his position only five feet ahead of Wang, on point. "About... mmm...twenty metres away, I'd say. Looks like the blue light comes from it."

"Huggins, hold your position. Wang, join him," Ryker ordered. "Stay with him. Get a reading."

Wang hurried forward, keeping an eye on his instrument. When he'd reached Huggins' side, he scanned the other man carefully, then turned toward the opening.

"Skirting the line, sir," Wang reported. "I'd recommend halting here."

"Blast and damnation!" Holmes exclaimed in frustration. "So close, and yet unable to see our goal!"

"Sherlock," Skye said sternly. "No freakin' way."

"Skye! It is right there! You cannot tell me you do not wish to see it yourself!" Holmes stared in fascination at the dim blue mist ahead, as if hypnotized.

————

Skye shot a meaningful glance at Ryker, warning him of her intent. When he met her gaze and subtly acknowledged her signal, she addressed Sherlock.

"Fine. I'll go to the edge and look in, and tell you what I see. Then, no matter what happens, you can still finish the investigation." She turned toward the two men in the lead, determined to prove a point.

But before she could take a step, a tall body material-ized directly in front of her. Strong, gauntleted hands gripped her shoulders gently but unyieldingly.

"Your point is made, Skye. But you are not so foolish as all that, my dear," her husband said quietly from above her, "nor am I. You misunderstand; I am merely frustrated. Let me remind you that frustration does not equal fool-hardiness."

"Good. Let's get out of here," Ryker ordered.

The rest of the team, which had frozen at the pair's reactions, took deep breaths and began to pull back toward the cave's mouth.

"Don't worry, Holmes," Ryker told the detective. "We came prepared for this possibility. I think I can get you your look at what's in that hole."

———

Soon they were outside, and the decontamination team was checking out the exploration team, ensuring that no one had been unduly irradiated, nor had they come back contaminated.

"Everyone's clear," Murphy called. "You can shed your suits now."

"Good," Ryker decided, then ordered, "Gear off. Huggins, you and McGregor get the remote up and in place as soon as you've ditched your gear."

"Yes, sir!" McGregor acknowledged.

Five minutes later Skye and Holmes watched as a squat, tracked robot, bristling with cameras and sensors, trundled its way into the cavern.

"C'mon over here," Ryker waved them across to the cab of the truck. "We've got a video monitor set up to watch." Sherlock and Skye joined Ryker by the monitor.

"Um, how long is that gonna take?" Skye wondered, waving a hand at the screen. "I mean, to get to the opening where the radiation is."

"Oh, probably a good twenty minutes, maybe as long as a half hour," Ryker estimated. "Ol' Tin Can was made for manoeuvreability, not speed."

"Uh, okay," Skye said in a mildly strained tone, glancing around the area in search of a likely clump of bushes. Holmes eyed her with amusement.

"The house is a short walk over that rise, my dear," he murmured in her ear, nodding his head in the proper direction. "In this locality, it is never kept locked. The, ahem, 'little scientist's room' as you call it, is down the hall, second door on the left. I told you not to drink that third cup of coffee at breakfast."

Skye shot him a rueful grin. "I'll be back before the probe gets there," she informed them, then scurried for the top of the hill and the McFarlane homestead beyond.

———

To her surprise, Dr. Victor was wandering around inside when she arrived.

"Oh, hello there," Skye greeted the man warily. "I didn't expect to see you here. Is everything okay?"

"Oh, yes," Victor smiled back. "I came by to make sure James' things were being taken care of, and to see if there was anything I could do to help. But it seems the neighbours have matters well in hand. Is your husband's investigation proceeding well?"

"I guess so." Skye shrugged, pretending ignorance. "I've been following him over half the farm today, seems like. I finally told him I had to come up here and, uh, use the facilities."

"Ah. It sounds as if he's much like his namesake—very fixated and single-minded."

"Sometimes, I guess," Skye grinned, trying not to dance by this time. "Um, if you'll excuse me?"

"Certainly. When nature calls, we can only answer. I'm afraid you won't find any linens," he called after Skye as she hurried down the hall. "The local ladies seem to have taken them all off to wash, or something. But I have a handkerchief you're welcome to dry your hands upon when you're done…"

———

After her bathroom break, Skye did indeed make use of Dr. Victor's handkerchief to dry her hands.

"Thank you," she told him politely, offering the damp cloth back to the physician.

"You're more than welcome, Madam," he replied courteously. "And now I think I shall depart. I have an appointment in an hour, and I shall just have time to return to my office and prepare for my patient."

He held the front door for her as they exited together, then Victor walked around behind the house. As Skye made her way through the fields, deliberately meandering in an aimless way as if looking for Sherlock, Dr. Victor's Cooper Mini emerged from the back of the McFarlane house, sped down the drive, turned left onto the road, and disappeared.

Skye watched him out of sight, then headed for Ryker's unit.

———

Skye was back in plenty of time to see Tin Can approach

the pit in the floor of the cave, though she made a point of telling her spouse in detail about her encounter with Victor. Then she, Holmes, and Ryker huddled over the monitor in the truck cab, while the rest of the unit viewed either the monitor which the remote controllers were using to guide Tin Can, or another, linked video display in the back of the truck.

Huggins and McGregor skillfully maneuvered Tin Can into a position as close as they dared to the opening, then extended a boom camera out and tilted it to look down. Sherlock's eyes narrowed, Ryker let out a long whistle, and Skye muttered, "Sonuvagun."

"That is NOT what I expected," Ryker noted.

"I can tell it is some very large aeroplane," Holmes observed, "but what is in its aft, and why is it glowing so?"

"It's one of the old nuclear test aircraft, I think," Skye decided. "That's the only explanation I can come up with, anyway."

"Righto," Ryker confirmed. "It's a Convair X-6."

"I thought those never made it off the drawing board," Skye said, surprised. "They really built one?"

"They did here, back in the late 50's," Ryker nodded. "Unfortunately they also had a reactor breach. Killed the crew. I knew that was one of the classified little things 'downstairs,' but I thought it was a lot further that way," he made a furtive hand gesture in the direction of the Bent-waters base. "I guess they wanted to get it out, away from the functional part, for the safety of the base workers. I wonder if they realised they'd placed it under private lands. I'm betting not, based on the files I saw."

"A bit more explanation, and a bit less speculation, please," Holmes remarked testily. "Are you trying to say this aeroplane was powered by a...what is it called again...nuclear pile?"

"Exactly, Hon," Skye nodded. "A nuclear reactor. They were looking for a way not to have to refuel the aircraft all the time. But the shielding was a problem—it was a trade-off, the weight of the shielding for the usable payload."

"They got it to work, on this aircraft," Ryker explained. "But it turned out that the materials they used for shielding degraded in the radiation environment a lot faster than they expected. After the containment shield cracked on its fourth flight, and the crew voluntarily sustained fatal exposure in order to land the plane safely on the tarmac at Bentwaters, the project was put to bed—literally. The crew...from all accounts, it was a nasty death." He shook his head, expression grim.

Skye's face crumpled in sympathy, and she surreptitiously slipped an arm around her husband's waist. Upon receipt of the very private message, the detective pressed his arm against her hand. She drew a deep breath, noting, "It looks like they built a containment sarcophagus around it."

"Yeah, I think they did," Ryker agreed, "if I remember the report aright. But it doesn't look to be in good shape now..."

"No, it looks like the Chernobyl sarcophagus," Skye decided. "If not worse, and probably for the same reasons. Judging from the condition of the aft part of the fuselage, there was a partial meltdown, probably after the onboard cooling system died. So the exposed nuclear fuel is aging the construction material of the sarcophagus at an accelerated rate, and I'm sure the dampness of the cavern above isn't helping the matter. Looks like the roof just...caved in. Take a look over there." She tapped the video screen. "Isn't that a pile of roof debris?"

"It does appear so," Sherlock agreed.

"Sherlock," Skye considered, "the instability waves that

come through the tesseract when it's active...are they felt outside the core?"

"I cannot say, Skye. I have felt them when I was with you inside the core, certainly; but I have not noted any earthquakes when I was investigating here and you were at the cottage, working. That does not argue that there were none, merely that I could not detect them."

"I can check seismic stations, if we need to, Boss," Ryker offered to Skye. "Is it important?"

"Potentially, very much so. If a decent-sized quake came through, it might bring the rest of the sarcophagus down around that mess."

"Ew," Ryker grimaced. "THAT would be bad."

"Very bad," Skye agreed firmly.

"I'll check," Ryker decreed.

"Good. This is certainly not the sort of thing that should be left to lie, in any event," Sherlock observed. "Especially if our faux heirs know of it. If they are in search of the radioactive material, that could be 'very bad,' as well."

"It sure could," Skye agreed. "They could be spies looking for an energy source, or terrorists looking for toxic material, or anything. But then again, that presupposes a knowledge of the situation that we didn't even have."

"True," Sherlock noted. "If even Ryker, who checked the records before coming out for this little sortie, did not know this was here, how would someone not privy to the records know?"

"They couldn't," Ryker declared. "They had to be looking for something else."

"But what else could they think was in there?" Skye wondered. "I mean, even if they're...I dunno, scavengers or something, they have to have SOME notion of what they're looking for!"

"That is the question," Sherlock averred. "But regardless, we must take action. As I said, it cannot be left so."

"No," Ryker confirmed. "It'll have to be sealed up again. The question is how best to do it..." He paused, then picked up his radio. "Huggins, have Tin Can get samples and readings."

"Roger," Huggins' voice responded.

They spent the rest of the day watching as the agile little robot wormed its way around the sarcophagus collapse, taking readings and obtaining samples for analysis. It was a chilly winter's sundown by the time they left the area.

———

Upon delivering the Holmeses to Gibson House, Ryker followed them inside that evening, intending a brief discussion regarding how best to proceed. It was necessary to handle the matter delicately to permanently seal off the damaged containment sarcophagus without revealing the truth about Bentwaters. He and Sherlock were deep in a discussion of the matter as they entered, and neither man noticed Skye's flushed face, or the slight shivering wracking her body as she crept about the house, turning on the lights.

"I think we should consider the matter carefully before taking the next step," Sherlock noted. "Handled incorrectly, the whole truth comes out. Yet we cannot afford to wait too long; we know another is intent on finding his way into the sarcophagus."

"Whoever it is can't possibly know what's in there," Ryker pointed out. "It's a death warrant to go in any farther than we went today."

"That is likely so. Still, it is just possible that they are after either exposing the base, or obtaining the radioactive fuel for their own nefarious purposes. In the which case, they will know how to approach the deadly material contained within. Wife, you have been uncharacteristically silent on the matter, and you are the scientist specialising in the subject. What say you, Skye?" he addressed her as she re-entered the room.

"Um...what, Sherlock?" Skye glanced up at them with a blank expression. "I'm sorry, I'm afraid I...wasn't listening. I'm kind of tired." She shivered. "Honey, could you start a fire in the fireplace? I'm freezing."

"I'll get it, Holmes," Ryker offered, moving to the fireplace in the sitting room and kneeling. "You go ahead and catch her up on what we've been saying. Can't say as I blame you, Boss; it's been a stressful day, and I'm tired, too. Not to mention the wind was pretty stiff out there in the field, and you're smaller than the rest of us."

"Certainly," Sherlock agreed. "And you do have a point, Ryker. Poor Skye is probably half frozen; I should have considered urging her inside the lorry, out of the wind, instead of standing about with us. My dear, we were discussing how to proceed with the reactor and the damaged containment sarcophagus. We are trying to find some happy medium between acting with all due haste to prevent a calamity, and preventing word of the underground base from leaking."

———

Skye struggled to listen to her detective husband as a chill went through her frame; she was exhausted beyond reasonable explanation, and only wanted to lie down and sleep. Momentary dizziness gripped her, and she fought it down to answer Holmes.

"I think maybe we need t-to...sleep on it," she murmured wearily. "Leave the guards on it tonight and decide what to do tomorrow. Maybe slap a guard perimeter around it..."

"But if we put a lot of guards on it, then anyone watching will KNOW something's up," Ryker observed, having laid the logs on the grate atop the kindling. He struck a match and held it to the kindling. With a cheery crackle, it lit.

"After today's exercises, they will likely know in any case," Holmes said, watching the logs catch and the flames leap up. "Guards are definitely in order, and I am glad for tonight's detail, but they should—"

Another wave of dizziness, far stronger than the first, assailed Skye, and this time she could not fight it off. She staggered, stumbled, then fell to the Persian rug.

———

With an exclamation of distress, Holmes spun, leapt the coffee table and knelt beside his wife, laying a hand on her shoulder.

"Great Scot, she's burning up! Ryker, is your unit still outside?"

"Yes, sir! You want me to fetch Dr. Wilder?"

"Please. Make haste. By the feel of her, Skye is quite ill." The detective lifted his wife and laid her on the sofa nearby as Ryker sprinted out the front door.

Two minutes later Ryker was back with Dr. Wilder. The physician moved immediately to the couch with her medical kit and knelt. Holmes eased aside to allow access for the medic as she took Skye's vitals. After a few more anxious minutes, the physician raised her head.

"It's a nasty case of influenza," Dr. Wilder diagnosed,

and Holmes tensed, feeling the blood drain from his face. "Looks to be the very strain we immunized for this year, which is surprising. Did Mrs. Holmes not take a flu shot this year?"

"No," Holmes sighed, dismayed. "She reacts rather violently to them, I have it to understand. So, as she was not working on the base this past autumn, and in fact interacting little with the populace as a whole, she opted not to take it."

"She still should have had it before flying over here," Wilder pondered. "Vaccinations like that are de rigueur for international travel these days."

"The good Lord knows, she had everything else," Holmes noted with distaste, despite his anxiety. "Roughly a week prior to our wedding, my poor wife was made a miserable pincushion—which is something I have experienced firsthand myself. It must have been an inadvertent oversight. I wondered, at the time, why she submitted to them. I did not know we were coming, as the trip was a gift, or I might otherwise have made more certain that all was properly done."

"Have you had the shot, Mr. Holmes?" Wilder pressed.

"Yes. I did do some consulting on the base in the autumn, so I was required to have it, as well as a few others. I am quite up to date on my vaccinations."

"Well, that's something," Wilder decided with relief. The group fell silent as Wilder tended the sick woman.

———

Influenza, Holmes thought, clenching his jaw against the roiling sensation in his gut. *The same thing that made Watson nearly despair of me in the Russian outbreak. The same thing that killed a million people around the world, only a couple of years before*

I came to this continuum. And my wife has the damnable stuff. God, help me. God, help HER.

———

"How serious is it?" Holmes finally asked the physician in a distinctly subdued manner. "Will she...survive?"

Dr. Wilder blinked in surprise, then suddenly remembered to whom she was speaking: A man who had lived through at least one deadly pandemic long before the advent of modern antiviral medications, and for whom the term *influenza* was not to be taken lightly. His experience gave him reason to be concerned, she concluded.

"Not to worry, Mr. Holmes," she reassured him. "Influenza is much less serious nowadays than it used to be —at least this strain is, though there are a few potentially fatal ones out there. Mrs. Holmes is in no danger, unless her fever runs very high. Some tender loving care, and she'll be fine in a few days' time."

———

Thank God, Holmes thought, relieved. He closed his eyes briefly and nodded silently. "What needs doing?"

"Oh, I'll give her an antiviral here in a moment, and some decongestants for use later. Then it's a matter of keeping an eye on her fever. If it spikes up around 39.5° or so, start giving her lukewarm sponge baths. Other than that, acetaminophen and plenty of fluids are the rule. Keep her in bed and make sure she rests."

"Thirty-nine and a half degrees...centigrade?" Holmes verified.

"Oh, that's right. You're probably used to the old Imperial System of units. Yes, that would be around, uhm, 103° or 104° Fahrenheit. Do you have a thermometer of some sort?"

"Not here, no."

"Okay, I'll get you set up," Wilder offered. She extracted an electronic oral thermometer from her medical kit and demonstrated to Holmes how to use it, then set it aside on the coffee table and turned her attention to her patient. "Mrs. Holmes? Are you awake?"

"Mmh," Skye groaned, rousing from her fever-induced lethargy. "Yeah."

"Brae, go fetch a glass of water," Wilder ordered, and the captain was off to the kitchen, returning seconds later with the requested drink. Taking the glass, she addressed Skye again. "Mrs. Holmes, you need to take some medications, love. Can you sit up for me?"

With an effort, and a certain detective's supportive arm at her back, Skye pushed into a seated position. Wilder handed her the glass of water, then got out several different tablets and capsules from her kit.

"This is an antiviral, and this is acetaminophen, and here's a decongestant," the doctor explained, handing over each medicine in turn. "Down the hatch, now."

Skye popped the pills into her mouth, washing them down with a mouthful of the water. She started to set the glass aside, but the medic stopped her.

"Drink it on down, dear," the physician urged. "I want you properly hydrated."

"I'm freezing," Skye murmured, obediently sipping the water.

"I know, love," Wilder said sympathetically. "Your fever's around 38.5° C. I expect you feel like someone's beating on you, too."

"Yeah," Skye sighed, setting the empty glass aside and leaning back. "I ache all over. And I've got concrete setting up in my head."

"Yup, that'll be the flu," Wilder nodded confidently. "Mr. Holmes, get your wife to bed; I'd recommend stripping her down and keeping a sheet and maybe a light blanket over her tonight, but no more than that. If you have to sponge her down to lower her fever, concentrate on areas where there's lots of blood vessels. That'd be areas like—"

"The throat, the wrists, the underarms, backs of the knees, the feet," Holmes nodded knowledgeably. "And other, more private areas. I have some knowledge of anatomy, doctor; thank you most kindly."

"Do you need any help, mate?" Ryker queried, as Holmes bent over his ill spouse, placing his hand on her forehead to feel her temperature, before allowing it to slide down and cup her cheek for the briefest instant. The affectionate gesture was barely noticeable, but Skye looked up at him gratefully.

"Not at the moment, Ryker," Holmes decided. "But I thank you."

"Brae and I'll pop back by in the morning to check on her, Mr. Holmes," Wilder noted. "Would you like a nurse tonight? I can arrange for Mrs. Holmes to have one for the next several days. That way, you can continue your investigation."

"I..." Holmes paused, torn. *There was a time when I would not have hesitated to accept,* he thought. *She should be in no danger; yet, if her fever rises too high, I fear it could damage that delightful intellect. And therein does lie danger. For she is needed to help stop the deterioration of the other continuum, and by extension, possibly our own. No, I cannot leave her in the hands of a stranger, even one of the*

Secret Service. Too much is at stake. Still, I may need the assistance of a nurse, if Skye becomes very ill.

"Let us see how the night goes, Doctor," Holmes decided. "Not for tonight, not unless she grows worse—in the which case I shall contact you at once. Tomorrow, if she IS worse, I may need a nurse's assistance, for I fear I am no nursemaid. But for now, I shall endeavour to tend my own wife."

"What about the cave, Holmes?" Ryker wondered.

"We left a clandestine guard on it overnight. It might be wise to set up a shift schedule, sufficient for several days. I dare not leave Skye until her fever has gone down—the matter of the other continuum takes higher precedence than the murder case and the cave." He scooped up Skye and headed for the hall.

"How do you figure that?" Dr. Wilder wondered, surprised.

Holmes paused and turned back to look at them. Skye's head lolled tiredly against his shoulder as he observed, "It is my understanding that, if the other continuum collapses, it would likely take a number of continua with it, almost certainly including our own. I cannot speak for you, Dr. Wilder, but in my estimation, the dissolution of our entire reality trumps the potential exposure of a secret military base."

Then he turned and carried his wife to the bedroom, as Ryker let himself and Dr. Wilder out.

———

Sherlock carried Skye into the bedroom, got her undressed and tucked into bed. She lay there miserably, shivering violently, even after he pulled the covers over her and tucked her in. He frowned as he watched her by the light of the bedside lamp.

"Skye, would you like some dinner, my dear?"

"N-no," she murmured despondently. "Not hungry. Just wanna lay here and die."

"Come now! Let us not use such morbid language, Skye."

"'Member how you felt after all your vaccinations last spring?" Skye reminded him somewhat tartly.

"Yes, I do indeed." Holmes winced, recalling.

"Okay, then. Lemme 'lone."

My, someone gets grumpy when she feels unwell, Holmes decided in fond amusement. *Not, I suppose, that I have room to talk. If she can deal with my fiendish temper, I can certainly deal with hers. She is starting to sound distinctly congested, also.*

He considered for a moment, realizing he was hungry, then suggested, "Would you mind if I ate?"

"No, go 'head," Skye agreed affably, turning to face him and curling on her side in an effort to feel warm. "You've had a long day, too. Go eat, an' I'll just lie here an' try to rest. 'Ventually that medicine's gotta kick in. Then maybe I c'n go to sleep."

"Very well. I will return shortly. In the meanwhile, do try to rest." He left the bedroom and returned several minutes later with a sandwich in hand. Sitting on the bedside, he ate it silently, resting one hand lightly on Skye's blanket-swathed hip as he did so. She sighed.

"That feels good," she observed quietly.

"What does?"

"Your hand. Just to know you're there."

That clinched Holmes' decision. *It is quite early,* he considered, *but if it helps her to feel better...* He polished off the last of the sandwich, then disrobed.

"Move over, my dear," he murmured, sliding in beside

her. "There. Now, come here." Gathering her close, he lifted her until he could cradle her in his arms, bringing his knees up on either side of her body to complete the effect. "How does this feel?" He settled the covers over them both.

"Ohh," she sighed, relaxing against him. "Warm and comf'ble."

"Good. Now settle back and try to sleep, my dear wife."

"Okay..." Another sigh escaped Skye, and she snuggled against him, falling into a fitful sleep within minutes.

Holmes' smile grew deeper. He himself relaxed, under the influence of comfort, a bellyful of food, the nearness of his mate, and the warmth of her fevered body.

Five minutes later, he too was asleep.

———

He woke several hours later. The alarm clock read 11:04. The bedside lamp was still on. Skye was squirming restlessly and had managed to work her way off his limp slumbering form, though she had not herself awakened. His hand to her bare skin told the tale: Holmes rose in haste and went in search of the thermometer Dr. Wilder had left.

Returning with it, he sat on the bed and gently shook Skye by the shoulder. When her eyes finally opened, he murmured, "Here, my dear, let me take your temperature," and promptly stuck the device into her mouth. Sixty seconds later it beeped, and he read the tiny screen, then took a deep breath. "104.3°. And not yet time to take more of the prescription febrifuge. This is not good." He gazed down into glazed azure eyes, adding, "Stay here, my dear. I will be right back."

She nodded weakly, and he laid the thermometer on the nightstand, stood and headed for the bathroom, coming back with a bowl of lukewarm water and a washcloth.

"Now it is my turn to return the favour of last spring," he smiled at her, dipping the cloth into the water and wringing it out.

Gently Holmes tugged the covers away and wiped the damp cloth across his wife's skin, moistening her throat, shoulders and breasts. Her breath caught as he skimmed the cloth over her left breast, and her eyes widened in alarm as she stared up at him.

"I...where am I?" she whispered, peering at him with eyes that wouldn't quite focus. "What are you doing?"

"You are in our cottage in Suffolk, my dear," Holmes explained, disturbed by her confusion. "You have a bad case of influenza, and your fever is quite high. I am trying to lower your temperature."

"You're...I'm...who are you?" Skye asked, and Holmes froze.

"You...do not know me?" he breathed, shocked.

"You..." Skye shook her head. She glanced down the length of her nude body, then looked up with troubled eyes. "I should know...no, I don't know." She blinked slowly, then scanned his naked form. "I'm cold, and I hurt. And I'm scared. Are you a doctor? Why aren't you...?" She gestured jerkily, indicating his unclad state.

Oh, dear God, he thought in horror as a shudder ran through him. "I am your husband, Skye," he murmured, trying to jog her memory. "I am Sherlock. Your 'very own Sherlock.' Can you remember? Try hard, my dear."

Her forehead creased, and she frowned.

"Mama," she said finally. "I want Mama. Is Mama here?"

Holmes swallowed hard, pain filling him. Not only did he feel rejected by the plea, but he knew he could not possibly remind his wife that her mother was dead while she was in her current condition.

"No, Skye, Mama is not here. But I will take good care of you, this I swear."

Does she remember nothing of the last year? he wondered in dismay. *Nothing of our marriage, of my arrival in this continuum, even of her parents' horrific deaths?* Then another thought struck him with the force of a sledgehammer, and he grew alarmed. *"I want Mama" is a CHILD'S CRY...*

By this point, the detective was in a state of agony. *Skye does not know me. She is afraid because we are both nude and she does not recognise the man whose hands are upon her body. Good Lord, if this does not resolve itself upon lowering her fever, she is lost to me. And if she has suffered irreversible brain damage, if she truly has reverted to a childlike state, then our universe and many others are lost, as well.*

He temporarily set aside the bowl and washcloth, reaching for his dressing gown to help alleviate Skye's fear, but by this time she was delirious, unaware of her surroundings, and murmuring incoherently about handkerchiefs and insects. Nevertheless he donned the garment, cinching it closed, before returning to bathing her.

Long thin fingers, used to ferreting out clues, trembled as they gently swabbed Skye's body. *Dear God*, he thought, almost desperate, *in Your tender mercies, do not take her from me; I shall have nothing. And our world, and many like it, may very well collapse.*

The telephone rang just then. Holmes set aside the bowl of water, throwing the washcloth in its general direction, before sprinting into the sitting room to answer the instrument.

"Holmes," he barked as he held the receiver to his ear.

"Mr. Holmes, it's Dr. Wilder," the voice on the other end announced. "I hope I didn't wake you. I know it's late. I wanted to check on Mrs. Holmes."

"If at all possible, come over right away, doctor. Her fever is quite high—over 104°—I cannot get it to subside, and she is delirious."

"I'll be there in five," the doctor answered swiftly, and hung up.

3

Remembrances

The doctor was as good as her word. Not only did she arrive in record time, but she brought Ryker and a small guard contingent to keep watch on the house.

"With The Boss that sick and you tending her, Holmes," Ryker explained as Wilder bustled past them into the bedroom, "we weren't gonna let you stay alone."

"It may all be moot, Ryker," Holmes admitted with a sigh, his mood decidedly subdued. "She remembers nothing."

"Nothing?" Ryker stared at the detective, stunned.

"Nothing," he whispered, raising pained grey eyes to meet those of the operative. "Ryker, she does not know me."

"Oh, Holmes," Ryker murmured sympathetically, tentatively putting a hand on the other man's shoulder. Holmes tensed, but permitted the contact. "Surely she recognizes you."

"I fear it is worse." The detective shook his head. "Skye has been calling for her mother. I believe she has reverted to childhood memories."

Ryker's jaw dropped in horror, and Dr. Wilder's head shot around to listen in astonishment and dismay.

"But that would mean...the tesseract work..." Ryker whispered, shocked.

"If her memory does not return, she cannot finish it." Sherlock nodded. "She will not remember sufficient science to do so."

"Good God," Ryker breathed. "That's..."

"Disastrous," Holmes finished the other man's comment. "There is no one else in over seven hundred continua capable of helping complete the work. How very unique is my wife..."

He glanced over his shoulder at Skye. She was clad in one of Holmes' own button-front shirts, having been so dressed by Holmes himself before the arrival of the doctor and the guard contingent, and was now lying on the bed, tended by Dr. Wilder.

————

"I can't believe this is happening," Ryker muttered, agitated. "Of all the awful coincidences—what rotten timing!"

The detective's head suddenly snapped around to stare at the agent.

"No...there is no such thing as coincidence, Ryker," he murmured, eyes growing hard and distant even as his expression became taut with excitement. "No, this was no coincidence. I should have seen it before."

"What is it?"

"It is a delaying tactic. Skye did not merely 'happen' to contract this. She has not been around anyone who has been ill, and it struck her down far too quickly to be a normal mode of contagion. No, she was deliberately infected."

"But how? How did she catch this nasty little bug, if not through normal means?"

"What did you say?" Holmes barked, staring at Ryker. "A bug?"

"Yeah. Modern terminology for a germ."

"But I thought it referred to either an insect, or a computer software error."

"It means those things, too. It's kind of...well, it means any tiny thing that can be a nuisance or worse."

———————

"Of course!" Holmes exclaimed, suddenly grasping the whole situation. He spun toward the bed, gazing at his unconscious wife. "Skye, my dear gem! Even in your delirium, you were trying to give me clues! Ryker, she has been going on for some time about handkerchiefs and 'bugs!'" he explained. "I assumed she referred to insects, and that it was merely the nonsense babbling of a fevered mind, but she meant this damnable influenza virus! A virus on a handkerchief! And that is a trail which leads us directly to Dr. Victor, who offered his handkerchief to dry her hands at McFarlane's house today, when she walked up to use the facilities!"

"But why? Why would he do something like that?"

"To deliberately infect her, my dear fellow! And possibly transfer the contagion to me as well. By doing that, he knew he could ensure that we would be off the case for at least the duration of her illness. Ryker, there are several things that want doing, and you, my dear chap, are in a position to do them."

"Tell me what they are, Holmes, and I'll do 'em,"

Ryker said instantly.

———

In a matter of minutes, Ryker was off to comply with Holmes' requests. The detective returned to the side of his stricken wife. Dr. Wilder spared him a brief glance.

"When's the last time she had any acetaminophen?" the physician queried.

"I gave her the next scheduled dose shortly before you arrived. Tell me what I may do to help."

The doctor pondered for a moment, then told him, "Answer some questions for me. I need to know some things so I can determine what antipyretic she can tolerate."

"Of course."

"Is she pregnant?"

Holmes' eyes grew wide, and he felt his cheeks grow hot, but answered the doctor's questions forthrightly, recognizing the need to obtain information.

"No, not to my knowledge. She is on 'The Pill,' she has told me, so it is unlikely."

"Is she an asthmatic, or allergic to any anti-inflammatories?"

"No."

"Does she have ulcers, kidney problems, or is she on blood thinners?"

"No, she was quite healthy until contracting this confounded disease. A bit run down, perhaps, from too many long hours spent working this blasted hyperspatial problem, but I watched over her and attempted to prevent her becoming unduly fatigued or malnourished."

"Okay, good. In that case I'm going to give her a hefty dose of ketoprofen and see if that doesn't bring her fever down. If it doesn't, we'll have to resort to some serious measures. Help me sit her up, then go get a biscuit and some water."

Together the detective and the physician got Skye into a seated position. Then Wilder took the other woman's blood pressure while the detective hurried to the kitchen, returning with a packet of crackers and a glass of water.

"Here," he said, placing them on the bedside.

"Feed her a couple of biscuits, Mr. Holmes, while I get out the ketoprofen. It shouldn't be taken on an empty stomach," Wilder noted.

Holmes extracted a cracker and sat beside Skye, who appeared to be sleeping sitting upright. He laid a gentle hand on her shoulder, and she opened bleary eyes.

"Here, my dear," he murmured, offering the cracker. "Can you eat this?"

"Um...a cracker?" Her head wobbled, and she looked at the object in his hand, trying to focus on it.

"Yes, Skye," he said with a smile. "It is time for more medicine, and you must have something in your belly before taking it, else it may make you ill."

"Ugh," Skye grimaced, "'M sick 'nough awready. Gimme."

But instead of taking the cracker, she opened her mouth wide. Holmes' eyebrows rose, but he gingerly stuck the cracker into her mouth. She bit down and munched slowly, swallowed, then opened her mouth for more. When the last of the cracker had gone down, she croaked, "Water?"

Wilder nodded, waving a hand at the glass of water on the bedside, and Holmes held it steady while Skye took several sips, moistening her dry mouth. Sherlock fed her two more crackers, each followed by water, before Wilder stopped him.

"That's good," the physician said. "Here, Skye. This will make you feel better very fast, love. Down the hatch." She popped the capsule into Skye's open mouth, and Holmes held the glass for Skye to wash the capsule down. "Good girl," the doctor added.

"Want Mama," Skye murmured, her Southern dialect thick. "C'n I lay down now?"

"Yes, dear, you can lie down now," Wilder soothed, and Holmes helped Skye settle back into a prone position. "Just rest. I'm afraid your mum can't be here now, but this nice man is going to give you a bath and help bring your fever down, okay?"

"Husband-man?" Skye surveyed Holmes consideringly.

"That's right," Wilder nodded. "He loves you very much, and wants to help."

Holmes felt himself flush again at the doctor's words, but gazed steadily at Skye, who returned the look with as much interest as her exhausted, fever-confused mind could manage.

"Hokay," Skye agreed, closing her eyes and flopping her arms out wide. "He looks nice. He's cute."

Dr. Wilder choked back a snort, and Holmes' lips twitched despite himself.

"Well, her opinion of your looks doesn't seem to have changed, at any rate," Wilder muttered under her breath to the detective, stifling a giggle with effort. "Though I'd bet you've never been called 'cute' in your life."

"Not as an adult, I can promise you," Holmes agreed with amusement, glancing at the door to ascertain Ryker had indeed closed it when he left. The detective unbuttoned the shirt covering Skye's nakedness and slipped it from her shoulders, discarding it, then reached for the bowl of water and washcloth. Testing it with his fingers, he decided it was still warm enough to use, and wringing out the cloth, he began swabbing his wife's body.

"How does that feel?" Wilder asked the sick woman.

"Mmm," was the only answer she got. But it was a satisfied sound, so Wilder nodded approvingly at Sherlock. Skye drifted into a light sleep.

For the next twenty minutes, Wilder monitored Skye's temperature closely as Holmes continued to sponge his wife. Her fever rose no further, and at the end of that time, began to drop markedly.

"Excellent," the medic sighed in relief. "It's coming down to something we can deal with now."

An hour later, Skye's temperature hovered around 100° F.

"Normally," Wilder offered in a whisper, "I'd be inclined to let her sleep. But maybe it's more important to know if there are any lingering memory problems..."

"Do as you think best, Doctor." Holmes glanced sharply at the physician, a hint of apprehension in the grey gaze. Wilder shook Skye by the shoulder.

"Skye? Wake up, love. We need to check on you."

"Mmph?" Skye muttered, groggily opening her eyes with some difficulty. "Oh...no more aches..."

"Good," Wilder smiled. "You feel better?"

"Yeah," Skye admitted with an effort. "Kinda limp, but better."

"Excellent. I have a very important question for you, Skye," Wilder continued.

"What?" Bleary blue eyes fixed themselves on the doctor's face.

"Look at this man beside you." Skye turned her attention to Sherlock, who sat on the bedside. "Do you know who he is?"

Skye drew a deep breath, but said nothing, simply lying

quietly, gazing at Holmes.

Wilder and Holmes exchanged concerned glances. Finally Holmes offered, using the deep, throaty tone he knew she had once loved so well, "My dear Skye, do you recognize me?"

Skye sighed, and her eyes closed. Holmes stared at the weary face in dismay. *It would appear she still does not know me. I have indeed lost her. The universe has lost her.*

But a small perception inserted itself into his consciousness: A warm hand had crept, unnoticed, across the sheets to slide atop his own. Weak fingers were trying to wrap themselves around his, and a small thumb gently stroked the back of his hand. His gaze dropped from her face to his hand, to find Skye prizing feebly at his fingers in an attempt to hold hands with him.

"Skye," he repeated hoarsely, "do you know me?" He turned his hand over, lacing his fingers with hers.

"Yeah," she breathed tiredly. "C'n I have a hug?"

"Not until you tell us who he is," Wilder pressed insistently. "And what he means to you."

Azure eyes fluttered open for a few seconds, badly startled.

"Musta been outta it, huh?" she muttered, closing heavy lids once more.

"Yes, you have been," Holmes agreed. "Now please answer Dr. Wilder, Skye."

Skye took a deep breath, strengthening herself for the effort, then murmured, "Love m' Sherlock." She squeezed his hand with limp fingers. Holmes shot an imperative glance at Wilder, who immediately rose and slipped out the door, adding, "I'll be back in a couple of minutes." As soon as the door closed behind the physician, Sherlock leaned forward, slipping his hands beneath his wife and lifting her into his arms.

"Here is your hug, my dear," he whispered into her ear. "And gladly given it is. I am...relieved...to have you back. I was beginning to think I had a serious dilemma on my hands."

She tried to raise her head from his shoulder; it lolled back, and he caught it in his hand, steadying it before she could injure her neck.

———

"I scared you," she observed, gazing up into his face and seeing the residual traces of his anxiety. "I'm sorry. I really didn't know you?"

"No," he breathed, taut lines of pain appearing around the grey eyes. "Not only did you not know me, you were frightened by me."

"FRIGHTENED?!" Skye whispered in shock. "Why??"

"We were both unclad, my dear, and I was bathing you to cool you. And you did not recognise me. Such circumstances were, naturally, a fearful situation for you. It was understandable, but...distressing."

———

He tucked her head under his chin, content merely to sit holding her, and she sighed, leaning heavily against him in her weakness. Holmes fully realized that she was still very sick, but suspected that the crisis had passed. A thought occurred to him.

"Skye, do you recall what you were doing, scientifically, before you fell ill?"

She was silent for a few seconds, then queried, "You mean the tesseract?"

"Yes." Relief shot through the detective.

"Yeah, I think I do, although at the moment I couldn't tell you where I'd gotten to in the calculations. I got cotton for brains right now."

"Perfectly understandable," Wilder's voice said behind them, as she opened the door and slipped into the room. "No, no, please don't," she protested, as Holmes released his wife and eased her to the mattress. "You've had an upsetting night, Mr. Holmes, and I just wanted to come in and check her temperature once more. I plan on spending what's left of the night on your sofa, but I wanted to see Mrs. Holmes once more before stretching out, myself."

———

"Certainly," Sherlock agreed, continuing to tuck Skye back into the bed as if the doctor had never said anything. He met his wife's eyes briefly, and she knew as soon as the doctor was gone, the embrace would return, so Skye didn't protest. "I am sorry we cannot offer you something more comfortable than the sofa, but the cottage is not equipped with a spare bedroom, I fear."

"Don't worry about it," Wilder smiled, tucking the thermometer into Skye's mouth. "The sofa in the sitting room is more comfortable than some of the cots in the teaching hospital where I did my residency. If you have a spare blanket, it might be nice, but I'll manage fine if you don't. Brae stoked the fire a couple of minutes ago, and the sofa is in front of it."

———

Skye gestured with her hand, making an out and around

motion, and Holmes nodded his comprehension of her improvised sign language.

"Linen closet down the hall?" he verified, and she nodded. "Very good. I shall be right back."

He strode out and returned, blanket in hand, by the time the thermometer could beep.

"Here you are, Doctor," he said, laying the blanket beside the medic as she removed the thermometer from Skye's mouth. "And how is my wife?"

"Fever hovering between 100° and 101° Fahrenheit," Wilder observed. "As long as it stays in that neighbourhood, I'm happy. Mrs. Holmes might still have the occasional body ache or chill, but nothing more serious. How is your congestion, love?" she asked Skye.

"I feel stuffy, but not real bad," Skye decided. "Didn't you give me something for that earlier?"

"I did," Wilder smiled. "Good, you do remember."

"It's kinda woozy, though."

"And no wonder. Your fever was around 105° when I got here. That'll make most adults pretty loopy. In a few days, your memory should be essentially back to normal, although you may never remember much about what happened while you were delirious." She rose. "Now, you and Mr. Holmes go back to bed, and try to get some sleep. I'll be in the sitting room if you need me, and we have guards around the house that I can call if we need something from the village."

As soon as Wilder left the room, closing the door behind herself, Holmes removed his dressing gown and slid under the covers. With a determined effort, Skye rolled weakly onto her side in an attempt to snuggle close to her husband. That worthy considerately drew her against him, leaned over and turned off the lamp, before settling down to resume his interrupted night's sleep.

4

Truth Will Out

Skye was still sleeping the next morning, and so was Dr. Wilder, when Sherlock dressed and slipped across the hall and into the study for a very important appointment. Shortly after his arrival, there was a crackling sound and a smell of ozone.

"Hello there, Holmes," Chadwick's voice said cheerily. "I see you're quite unharmed, and I hope the explorations went safely. Where's the Other Me? Did she get a nice break and some fresh air?"

Sherlock's brows knitted, and he pondered how to explain.

"What is wrong?" Holmes' urgent voice queried immediately. "What happened to her?"

"She has influenza," Sherlock admitted, "a serious case. She was delirious a good part of the night. We very nearly had a disaster on our hands."

"Oh no," Chadwick's voice murmured in distress. "How bad?"

"She did not know me, at one point," Sherlock

confessed, "and she was calling for her mother. I believe she thought she was a child again."

There was dead silence from the other end of the tesseract.

"Then we do have a disaster on our hands," Chadwick whispered in shocked dismay.

"Do, you don'd," an identical voice—though decidedly more nasal—came from the doorway.

Sherlock spun with a wordless exclamation. Skye stood there wrapped in his dressing gown, which, he assumed, had been handy. She was clutching at the doorframe and leaning heavily against it to keep herself upright.

"Defocusing. Get her!" he heard his other self exclaim as he lunged for his wife.

"Skye, my dear, what am I going to do with you?" Sherlock muttered, trying hard to sound annoyed and reprimanding, but not quite succeeding, as he scooped her up and carried her to the nearest chair. "You should be in bed."

"I dow, but I'b deeded here worse jusd daow," she murmured, allowing him to spread a lap rug over her. "Sis, are you dere?"

"Of course, dear," Chadwick replied. "I take it you remember, after all?"

"Yeah," Skye nodded. "Bud I'b jusd doo dired and headachy doo work on id righd daow. Doo bud id bludtly, I feel like dog poo. Add I'll probably be like dis for adother couple ob days. So I was woderig if you waded doo dake de nodebook add see whad I'b dode, den dry to pick ub where I lefd off, udtil I'b able doo cobe back doo id."

"You mean tag-team the calculations?" Chadwick wondered.

"Yeah," Skye grinned weakly, obviously exhausted

already. "You work od id for a while, add I resd add stubb, you dow, add ged bedder. Den you cad had back off doo me whed I'b a liddle more healthy, add I cad fidish dem ub while you sdard makig de chages doo de desseracd. Are you gabe? Add doo I ebed bake sedse, wid all dis sdot for braids?"

There was a long pause. *Evidently the other side of the tesseract is attempting to work their way through the effects of Skye's congestion on her speech,* Sherlock decided. *Even the other version of her is having trouble comprehending. "Snot for brains," indeed.* He stifled a snort. *Thank God I can understand her, or life would quickly become even more confusing than it is already, what with two of both of us.*

Finally Chadwick offered, "Sounds like a plan to me."

"Indeed," Holmes agreed. "It might even prove beneficial so, as we can see where you are going with your theories, and I can commence a more detailed planning of the modifications while Chadwick works on the calculations."

"Excelled," Skye sighed, relieved. "Sherlock, udlock de filig cabided add obed de middle drawer. The nodebook is od de dob of de sdack."

"I have it," Sherlock noted, going to the filing cabinet and doing as she directed. "Holmes, Chadwick, how shall I give this to you without risking...?"

"Hang on a second," Chadwick said. "We'll invert."

Slowly the room around them faded, revealing the pink granite of the Chamber in the other continuum. Chadwick waved with a grin from her seat behind the control console, and Holmes rose, moving between two of the monoliths, just outside the core itself, where Sherlock and Skye sat.

"Hand it to Holmes. But be careful," Chadwick urged. "If an instability wave comes through while you're both so close to the boundary, it could be catastrophic."

The two men, so nearly identical, nodded in unison as Sherlock moved to face his counterpart. Both men braced themselves firmly against any tremor, then Sherlock offered the notebook to Holmes, holding it gingerly by one end. In his turn, Holmes accepted it, grasping it in a similar manner.

"Thank you," the other detective murmured, stepping back from the core to increase the safety factor.

"You are quite welcome," Sherlock responded. He, too, moved away from the continuum interface, returning to Skye's side and standing behind her right shoulder.

"May I enquire as to how your Dr. Chadwick came to contract such an obviously virulent case of influenza?" Holmes wondered. "Especially as you are well, and she herself was fine yesterday morning?" He turned and walked to the console, handing the notebook to his companion. Chadwick accepted it, opening it and leafing through it.

"She was deliberately infected." Sherlock scowled. "I cannot yet prove it, but Dr. Victor infected her."

Chadwick's head snapped up. Holmes and Chadwick both frowned, glints of anger in grey eyes and blue.

"And you are pursuing the matter?" Holmes pressed.

"Of course," Sherlock replied grimly. "The issue is under investigation—and more—as we speak. I started Ryker upon that little matter last night, as soon as I realised the situation."

"Capital," Holmes nodded approvingly. "Precisely what I should have done."

"I'm glad you're doing better than last night, Skye," Chadwick added. "Your hubby said you were in a bad way."

"Thags, Sis. I coulde'd dell ya for sure aboud lasd dight, bud whad I do rebeber wase'd pleasad. Dod ad all."

"When do you want us to dial back in?" Chadwick asked. "Give yourself plenty of time, girl."

"Uh. Gibbe a couble days," Skye decided. "Aboud fordy-eighd hours, I thigk."

Behind her, Sherlock shook his head. He held up his hand, index finger and thumb separated by an inch or so; then he deliberately increased the spacing by a significant amount. Holmes' eyelids instantly fluttered slightly in acknowledgement; Chadwick's fluttered a scant second or two later.

"Well, let's give it a little longer, just to be on the safe side," Chadwick suggested smoothly. "We wouldn't want to load too much on you too soon, and throw you into a relapse."

"Indeed," Holmes agreed firmly. "I should say another twelve to twenty-four hours at the very least, wouldn't you, Chadwick?"

"Oh, hell yes," Chadwick nodded vehemently. "If she feels anything like I do when I have the flu, every bit of it. Maybe a couple of days more, even." Seeing her other self about to protest, she added, "It isn't like it's gonna hinder us, either way. It's only a matter of what numbers we enter into the computer."

"I'b so sorry aboud dis, guys. I dow de whole boid of by doig dese calculations was dat I could dake aboud as log as I deeded doo do dem widoud much dime havig bassed id your codinuum. Bud dis is a real bokey wredch id da works."

"No worries," Chadwick shook her head, throwing Skye a smile.

"Quite," Holmes agreed. "We had already anticipated at some point that Chadwick would need to do some of the calculations herself, to ensure everything was properly set up to compensate for any differences between your apparatus and ours."

"It's just happening earlier than we figured, which is probably good," Chadwick finished.

"Okay," Skye acknowledged, comforted.

"Now, may I suggest we depart," Holmes observed, "so the Other Me can get the Other You back into bed where she belongs, my dear Chadwick?"

"I think that's an excellent plan, Holmes," Chadwick grinned. "Let's go. Holmes—uh, the other Holmes—you get some rest, too, Hon. You look tired yourself. I'm sure you didn't get much sleep last night."

"I shall be fine, doctor," Sherlock replied calmly. "I am anticipating a report from Ryker sometime soon."

———

Chadwick raised a contentious eyebrow. Holmes saw it.

"I suggest you agree to rest if you become weary, old chap," Holmes offered to his other self. "The look in Chadwick's eye does not bode peace if you do not."

"I am no fool," Sherlock answered tartly. "I will do what is necessary to maintain my own health when it is needed, but not at the expense of a critical situation."

———

"That'll do. Catch y'all in a couple days." Chadwick looked mollified.

The Chamber faded, replaced by the study. The air sizzled, a whiff of ozone filled the room, and the other couple was gone.

Sherlock scooped up his wife and carried her back to bed, just as Dr. Wilder came looking for them to check on them.

———

February 11

Skye is considerably better today—in one respect—and rather the worse in others. Her fever is much lower, hovering around 100° F and staying there, for the most part; but her congestion is substantial, and she is quite weak. Weakness is normal after such a high fever, however, so it troubles me only in the respect of Skye being so very weak and helpless. It feels strange to be feeding my wife as if she were an infant, but there it is.

Dr. Wilder is staying close, and at least for the time being, so are the guards whom Ryker has set about us. I am still awaiting Ryker's report, however. I anticipate his arrival here soon, indeed at any moment, and it should be very interesting to hear what he has to say. I shall be surprised if he arrives alone...

———

But Ryker did arrive alone. However, he did not arrive without news.

"Well, I've intensified the guard on the cave," he declared, as Sherlock led him back to the bedroom so Skye could be updated as well, "and put most of 'em in camo. HQ knows what's in there now, too; I sent in a full report to the Director first thing this morning, and she was NOT happy. Oh, and no indications of any earthquakes in the entire UK anytime in the last five months, by the way, so we're safe there, I think. I checked with the Geological Service right after I reported in to the Director. Then I turned around and called her back and told her that, too."

"Good," came a firm, if nasal, editorial from the bed.

"We've initiated the process to buy the farm from McFarlane's nephew," Ryker continued. "He hates to do it, but we're giving him a real strong heads-up that there might be something there that he reeeeally doesn't want to deal with."

"Aid't dat de druth," a stuffy, pyjama-clad Skye noted from her sick bed.

"Yeah," Ryker agreed. "Of course, he'll be given all the personal effects, contents of the house, and such. But the government has told him it would be best for the land to be in our hands. The cattle will be vetted for health, the healthy ones sold off, and the proceeds given to the nephew. Any cows with serious radiation-induced illness will be humanely euthanized. A fair price for those will go to McFarlane, as well."

"Sobethig occurs doo be," Skye murmured. "Does adyone dow if dad cabe was used for adythig by de McFarlades?"

"As a matter of fact," Sherlock recalled, "I do remember in a chat during the drive to the McFarlane farm, Mr. Carver saying something to the effect that the couple used regularly to picnic in it during the summer, as a cool spot to have a pleasant outing. The Carvers even joined them once or twice, shortly before..."

———

Grey eyes abruptly widened in horrified understanding as Holmes' voice tapered away.

"Sherlock?" Skye queried anxiously.

"...Shortly before their infant child died," the detective finished grimly. "Of causes unknown."

"Aha," Skye nodded knowingly, growing sad. She sighed. "Dad's exacdly whad I was afraid of. Guys, I bed de McFarlades were udable doo habe kids at leasd pardly because of de radiation frob dis ding, seebing up through de cabe floor. Id fids, based od whad I read of Wadsod's medical repords. Add den de Carber baby died, probably frob oberexposure. Beig odly ad idfad, de lethal radiation dose would've beed a lod sballer..."

———

Ryker sent Sherlock a confused glance, and the detective translated Skye's stuffy English.

"The radiation likely sterilised the McFarlanes. 'And then the Carver baby died, probably from overexposure. Being only an infant, the lethal radiation dose for it would have been a lot smaller,'" he summarized solemnly, quirking his fingers around the quotation.

"Oh," Ryker said, subdued.

The three were silent for several moments.

"What a tragedy," Ryker murmured then. "All because of an underground directional error." He shook his head bitterly. "And there's no way we can even apologise."

"You can make some amends, however," Sherlock said sternly, "if you give young McFarlane an excellent purchase price for the land and buildings."

"True," Ryker agreed. "I'll call the Director and tell her our conclusions. I'm sure she'll agree." He thought for a moment. "We might even be able to arrange for the Carvers to be government suppliers of search dogs."

"That, my dear Ryker, is a capital notion. As excellent as are the Carvers' dogs, the benefit will be mutual, I can assure you."

"Whad aboud de sarcophagus idself?" Skye wondered, then hastily grabbed a tissue and sneezed hard into it. "'Scuze be."

"Headquarters is on it," Ryker assured them. "Ever since Chernobyl, some of our scientists have been working on containment methods for nuclear accidents, and they've developed some pretty good stuff. Sandwiched lead sheets, rebar, and concrete doped with lead powder, things like that."

"Leejade?" Skye queried intently, much too stuffy after sneezing to enunciate properly. She grabbed several more tissues.

"What?" Ryker wondered, no longer able to understand her at all.

"Leachate," Holmes repeated clearly. "Our physicist wishes to know about possible lead leaching from the containment materials. Which is a very valid concern."

"Thag you," Skye nodded at her husband, reaching for the tissue box. "Bigo."

"Oh," Ryker nodded. "Not to worry; they've developed a sealant that goes into and over all that stuff. No environmental contamination, according to the experts. Meantime, we're working on embedding a lead shield with a locked door for access. It'll be hidden inside the entrance, with a guard on it, so it's not visible from outside. But the cave is under majorly serious, clandestine guard now, and as soon as that's installed, it'll be locked down."

"Excellent," Sherlock decreed. "Now, as to the attack on Skye..." Skye pushed herself up in bed to listen alertly.

"Okay, first off, I verified Victor did have access to the influenza virus," Ryker ticked off his finger. "Not only did he have access, but he had access to the pure, concentrated strain, through some research he was doing at Suffolk New College, in the health care department."

"No woder id clobbered be," Skye sniffled, reaching for another tissue.

"Indeed," Sherlock cut in, scowling, seeming to grow taller. "And where is the miscreant now?"

"Popped by the house and the office," Ryker informed them, "but he wasn't at either place. Receptionist said he was off on an emergency house call. Something about a birth going too quickly to get to hospital. We followed up on that, and it's legitimate, so we didn't interfere. He, his house and his office are all being watched. We'll know as soon as he shows up at one place or the other."

"Good," Sherlock said coldly. "When he does, bring him here straight away."

———

Dr. Nathan Victor returned to his office around lunchtime, and was promptly, if clandestinely, taken into custody by Ryker's unit. They, in turn, brought him directly to Gibson House, under guard.

"We got the handkerchief from the laundry hamper at his house, Holmes," Ryker noted immediately. "Enid already pegged it positive." He handed him a note, and Holmes scanned it briefly.

"Excellent. Ah, Dr. Victor," Holmes said politely from his seat in the armchair next to the sitting room fireplace. "Won't you sit down?" He gestured imperiously at the chair across from him. Ryker and his men moved out to stand guard at each potential room exit.

"Um...certainly," a nervous and unsure Victor took the indicated seat. "May I inquire as to what this is all about?"

"It is no less than attempted murder," Holmes noted calmly, but letting a dangerous glint flicker in his grey eyes. "The deliberate introduction of the pure strain of Influenza Type A, serotype H7N7, to Dr. Skye Chadwick-Holmes, to be specific." He waved the note Ryker had handed him.

"At-attempted murder?" Victor stammered, paling. "She...did she actually contract the flu?"

"She did," Holmes noted, "and very nearly died of it,

last night. Aside from her importance to me, her death would have assumed catastrophic proportions in a matter which cannot be discussed, for reasons of—"

"National security," Ryker sternly finished for him. "According to my unit physician, her fever topped 40.6°C."

"Dear God," Victor whispered, horrified. "Hadn't she had the vaccine?"

"It seems to have been an inadvertent oversight in her vaccinations, before we travelled here," Holmes replied crisply. "Hence her extremely strong response to the pure strain."

"Oh, dear God. Oh, dear God," Victor groaned, putting his face in his hands. "Not that lovely, sweet woman. God, help me!"

"Tell us everything, and perhaps we can be His hands," Holmes suggested sternly.

"Yes! Yes!" Victor exclaimed, looking up in desperate appeal. "Please, I never meant to hurt her! I know how much you love each other! You have to understand! They told me to! I told them it probably wouldn't work, but they insisted. I never dreamed...I've been living in terror for weeks. I thought she'd need the pure strain for it to even affect her, because I assumed she'd been vaccinated before flying overseas. At most I thought she'd have the sniffles and maybe feel unwell. I was only supposed to delay your investigation for them. I SWEAR."

"'They' being the pair who killed McFarlane," Holmes deduced.

"Yes! How did you...?" Victor looked astonished.

"Never mind that. What hold do they have upon you?"

"They have my twin sister Mary," Victor moaned pitiably. "They've had her for weeks. Our parents are dead; we two are the only ones of the family left. They're using threats against her to force me to help them. Rape, torture, death; the good Lord only knows what they've already done to my poor sister! God help me! God help me! But I swear, I didn't help them with McFarlane! I swear! They asked me how to kill someone and make it look like a heart attack, and I told them—in order to keep Mary alive, you understand—that it would take potassium chloride, but I did NOT tell them how to DO it! I flatly refused! I swear! And I didn't give them anything!"

"How did they know, then?" Ryker wondered, and Victor shook his head miserably.

"They went to one of the local veterinarians and asked," he told them, obviously sick at heart. "I didn't think about that. Their story was that they wanted to put down a sick animal. It was Dr. Mark Peterson," he added, trying to help. "He can tell you more."

"Speaker mode, if you please." Holmes pointed imperatively at the telephone.

Dr. Victor submissively moved to the phone and dialed a number, hitting the speaker button.

"Dr. Peterson's office," a female voice answered.

"Is Dr. Peterson in, please?" Holmes inquired.

"May I say who is calling?"

"This is Special Investigator Holmes. I am looking into the death associated with the local UFO sightings. I should like to ask Dr. Peterson some medical questions, as I believe one or more of our murder suspects may have consulted him to obtain information to aid them in dispatching their victim."

"Oh! Right away, sir!"

There was a pause; then a male voice came on the line. "Dr. Peterson here. Is this Mr. Holmes?"

"It is," Holmes replied in a businesslike tone.

"What's...all this about a...a murder?" Peterson

wondered, voice betraying more than a hint of nervousness.

"Dr. Peterson, first of all, I wish you to understand that you are under no suspicion," Holmes noted more casually. "I merely wish to ask you some questions, and have you answer to the best of your ability. I have reason to believe two men approached you some time back—shortly before the death of Mr. McFarlane, supposedly of fright from a UFO sighting—and obtained not only information upon putting down an ill animal, but possibly pharmaceuticals and paraphernalia."

"Very well," Peterson answered a bit uncertainly. "Yes, I distinctly remember the two men who came in. It was unusual for several reasons, because they weren't any of my regular patients, and weren't even British. One was French, and the other sounded American. Short, dark-featured; and tall, medium-complected, respectively."

"That's them," Victor whispered, looking as if he might be sick.

"What are the other unusual circumstances, Doctor?" Holmes queried.

"Well," Peterson responded, not having heard Victor's remark, "most of the people around here that are my patients—clients, rather, I suppose—are farmers. Either they put their animals down with a gun, quick and simple; or they call me in to do it for them, if it's a large animal; or they bring a small animal to me. It's not very often I get someone coming in, asking how to do it themselves."

"I see," Holmes said, nodding to himself. "Pray, continue your most interesting narrative."

"They said they had an ill pet—it had cancer—and wanted to put it down," the veterinarian continued. "They also said they'd been told potassium chloride would do it, but didn't know how. I told them it would, if they injected it intravenously, because it would induce a heart attack, but there were a lot more humane ways of euthanising a pet. I told them if they'd give me the pet's weight and come back the next day, I'd have a euthanasia kit ready for them. They told me it was a large dog, a male German mastiff, around seventy kilos, and I gave them the dosage for several different drugs, including the potassium compound. And I had the kit ready for them, the next day, with a humane euthanising agent. But they never came back."

"I see," Holmes nodded to himself, steepling his fingers. "And did you give them any equipment?"

"No sir. I gave them nothing but information and options. But it wouldn't be hard to get what's needed from a local chemist."

"And were they charged?"

"A nominal fee for a consultation, but they paid in quid. So I'm afraid I don't have any paper trail you can track."

"Do you, perchance, still have the money? We might be able to obtain fingerprints," Holmes considered.

"No, sir. I'm afraid it's already long since been taken to the bank with the rest of our deposits. I'm sorry. It's not unusual for my fees to be paid in money, rather than cheque or card, so it didn't raise any red flags here at the office."

"I see. Thank you very much, doctor. You have been an immense help," Holmes said. "We may need a formal statement from you later."

"Anything I can do," Dr. Peterson agreed, and they ended the conversation.

———

"I'm on it. We'll see what we can dig up on any chemists'

purchases," Ryker offered, scribbling in a notepad, which went into his uniform pocket.

"Good," Holmes agreed. "Meanwhile, we must look at rescuing Dr. Victor's sister. Doctor, have you anything you can offer us as a clue as to where she might be?"

"I don't know," Victor moaned, terrified and grieving. "I know you probably don't think highly of me, Mr. Holmes, but I assure you, I AM a good doctor, and I DO love my sister. I didn't know what to do. They said...they said if I told anyone, they'd kill her outright."

"Do you know what they are after?" Holmes queried.

"No."

"...Where they are headquartered?"

"No. They either come by my home, or contact me by phone." The physician shook his head. "And they know exactly when to do which." He shivered, paling further.

Sherlock sighed in frustration.

"By PHODE," a hoarse, nasal voice floated out of the back of the house.

"Ah, of course," Sherlock sat up straight. "Do you have caller ID?"

"Yes, on both cell and office phone," Victor admitted. "But the ID is blocked. That's how I know it's them— they're the only ones around here who block their ID." He shivered violently, face paling nearly white.

"Hm. Were any of these calls with your sister, to ascertain her health?"

"Yes, there were two. I demanded to speak with her, and they put her on."

"Were there any unusual sounds in the background, whenever these phone calls were made?"

"Um..." Victor racked his brains, hands fisted in his hair, nearly ready to literally pull it out. Suddenly he sat bolt upright, staring at the detective. "Now you mention it,

I do remember a prolonged rumble once, which put me in mind of a train crossing. And twice I heard the distant sound of..." he shrugged, "I took it to be a boat whistle."

"But not a ship's horn?" Sherlock pressed.

"No," Victor shook his head definitively. "Too high-pitched. And not loud enough, either."

"Very good, Doctor Victor. I shall want a good description or possibly a photograph of your sister, and any other such information you think may be useful in her identification. Be patient, and trust me. Ryker, do you take him back to his office."

"What?!" Victor exclaimed, terrified. "Back to my office?! They'll kill Mary, then come after me!"

"On the contrary," Sherlock pointed out, "if you disappear now, they will most certainly know you have betrayed them, and your sister's life will not be worth a moment's purchase. But if you return and go about your business as normal—albeit with clandestine security," he glanced hard at Ryker, who nodded understanding, "it will give me time to scout your sister's whereabouts and perchance effect her liberty."

"At which time, we can whisk you both out of here and into hiding," Ryker added. "I promise you, you'll be safe, Dr. Victor."

The physician looked back and forth between the two men, then nodded.

"All right," he agreed. "I can see that. Let's do it."

The unit slipped out of Gibson House and returned Victor to his office, while Sherlock extracted his pipe and prepared for a prolonged smoke.

Skye, who had been listening in the bedroom, settled down for a nap.

Holmes pulled out maps of the area and surveyed them, then headed for the bedroom.

"Skye," he wondered softly, seeing her resting, "would I upset any apple carts were I to use the computer in the study?"

"Do," a drowsy Skye murmured. "Dod buch od de 'buter. Beed doig id all od baber add d' blackboard. Whadcha doid?"

"I intend to perform a search for a location where one might hear trains—possibly at a crossing—and boats at the same time. I have some preliminary areas ascertained, based on paper maps, but I need finer detail."

"Lookid' f'r Bicdor's sisder?"

"Yes."

"'Kay. Dad's good. I feel bad for 'eb. I could dell Bicdor was scared widless, all de way id here."

"Indeed. He was patently terrified, both for his sister and for his own life. And justly so, by the sound of it. May I take it you are not quite as antagonistic against Dr. Victor as you had been?"

Skye considered that for a moment.

"Do, I dod dink so. Sdress cad dake sdrage forbs."

"Indeed it can. From bizarre dreams to unwanted advances, one may assume from the experiences of recent months."

"Yub."

"So, I shall endeavour to locate his sister, using your computer and going onto the internet to ascertain possible locales."

"Souds good."

"And you?"

"I'b godda jus' sdooze."

"As you should, my dear." Sherlock nodded, pleased. "I

suppose I should request Dr. Wilder come watch over you, once I set out in search of the Victor woman."

Skye cracked a sleepy blue eye. It had a twinkle in it.

"I god a bedder idea."

"And that would be?"

"Call Wadsod."

"Capital notion! I shall do precisely that." A smile broke across Sherlock's face.

In short order, Watson had been contacted, had volunteered his assistance before Holmes could even ask, and was en route to Gibson House. Sherlock, meantime, settled down at the computer and began a map search for appropriate locations.

———

Within the hour, Dr. Watson was at Gibson House, dutifully and affectionately watching over a sleeping Skye, while Sherlock slouched before the computer in the study, poring over street-level maps and performing advanced searches for railroads and boat moorings.

By dinnertime, the sleuth had refined his search to three possible locations. Skye awakened, to be cheerfully greeted by Watson; and the two men repaired to the kitchen to prepare a bite. Dinner was a casual, congenial affair in the bedroom, in order to keep Skye company.

———

"Not to mention, I've a little herbal tea for you here, my dear," Watson said kindly, placing a cup of the brew on Skye's bed tray. "It will help those congested sinuses, while not interfering one whit with your prescription medications."

"Souds woderful," Skye said gratefully, picking up the cup and sipping. "Mm. Dasdes good, doo."

"I thought you'd like it," Watson grinned, his long years of experience as a physician enabling him to understand her perfectly. "And now I'm quite sure we'd both like to know how your husband's researches have progressed."

"Yes, we do," Skye agreed, turning to look at her spouse.

———

"I have three locales which meet the criteria," Sherlock decided, waving his fork in the air absently. "The first is southern Ipswich. It is fairly riddled with rails, and lies on an inlet of Harwich Harbour."

"Sounds promising," Watson decided. "Lots of people in which to lose three persons."

"True," Sherlock agreed, "but it is rather far off. I had the distinct impression from Dr. Victor that our suspects were able to keep a much closer eye on him than would be possible if their base were all the way out in Ipswich. Of course, that does not argue that the woman is not in Ipswich, imprisoned, alone. But I think it unlikely, moreso as the woman was available on the spot when Victor demanded to speak with her."

"Mm," Skye hummed. Blue eyes grew distant with thought. "Whad aboud de oder doo?"

"The next would be the Port of Felixstowe," Sherlock ticked off a finger. "This shows a bit more promise, but it is still rather far away, and it is right on the junction of the Channel and the Harbour. It is a major port city. That would argue for ship horns in addition to, perhaps in excess of, boat horns and whistles."

"Whereas Bictor said he neber heard any indications of shibs," Skye noted, slightly less nasally than previous.

"Excellent, Watson. Skye already sounds better."

"And she'll stay that way. I brought Bess with me."

"Bess?" Skye wondered, pulling a tissue from the box and wiping her nose.

For answer, Watson extracted the handle of a well-maintained revolver from his pocket.

Sherlock grinned knowingly.

———

"Cool," Skye grinned, congestion improving rapidly now. "Thank you, Doctor." She grabbed a tissue and mopped at her nose, then grabbed another when the first rapidly became soggy. Skye stared at the tissue box. "Oh boy. I'm gonna go through these like a baby through candy..."

"Come, come, I thought we were past formalities after my last visit," Watson upbraided her gently. "Call me John, or at least Watson. And I brought several more boxes of tissues; don't worry. I've had plenty of experience with the effects of my herbals. In fact, there's an entire case in the boot of my car."

"All right...Watson," Skye's grin grew wider. "So, Honey, what's the third location?" She reached for yet another tissue.

"That would be the village of Melton, within Woodbridge itself. It is well on this side of Woodbridge proper, and is now what might be termed a community within the larger municipality. But there is a major rail route through the area, and the River Deben runs through it, which has its outlet on the Channel. Too small for ships, but perfect for fishing boats and the like."

"Bingo," Skye nodded. She finally grabbed the entire box of tissues off the nightstand and plopped it on the bed.

"I should say you have it," Watson concluded.

———

"Indeed," Sherlock agreed. "Tomorrow I shall disguise myself and go to Melton and see." He turned to Skye. "I may be gone a few days, my dear. But I shall have my ciphered cell with me, and will attempt to contact you at least once per day."

"Oh," Skye said, seeming to wilt slightly.

"What about Valentine's Day?" Watson protested. "Surely you'll not leave your lovely wife alone on your first Valentine's Day as husband and wife?"

"Our first Valentine's Day ever," Skye murmured under her breath, eyes downcast. Quickly she hid her face in another tissue.

"Valentine's Day? When is it?" Sherlock blinked, nonplused.

"February 14th—two days' time," Watson pointed out.

"Ah," Sherlock said, finding himself somewhat at a loss. "Then I shall most certainly be back by then."

"Okay," Skye said, discarding her tissue, once more cheerful.

———

When the men had retired to the sitting room for a pipe— in Sherlock's case—and a glass of brandy for both, the sleuth turned to the physician.

"Watson," he said in a low voice, ensuring it did not carry beyond the room, "I am afraid I require your assistance."

"Then you have it," Watson answered simply, to the detective's gratification. "What do you need?"

Sherlock hesitated briefly.

"What will Skye be expecting for Valentine's Day?"

Watson's eyes widened in surprise, then narrowed in understanding. "Of course. You would never have celebrated it, in your own day. And you'd have no idea how it's celebrated now, in any case."

"Precisely," Sherlock sighed.

"Well, the usual types of things are chocolates and jewellery, as well as a special dinner, candlelight preferred, and that usually at a nice to expensive restaurant. Oh, and an appropriately sentimental greeting card. But knowing your reputation, you'd like it to be unique. Skye will be in no condition for an evening out anyway, not yet. So what, in your mind, would be a romantic gift? Whatever that is, that's what you should get her. And I'll do any preparation for a special dinner at home that you'd like, then clear out when you do get home."

Sherlock drew a deep breath, thinking. Suddenly an image of Skye in her favorite blue nightgown popped into his mind, and he knew what to get.

"I shall handle the gift, if you will set the table for a formal dinner for two—with candlesticks—and perhaps chop some vegetables for a curry."

"Curry is my speciality," Watson said, beaming. "My wife always said my curry was better than any restaurant's. Tell me how spicy, and what meat, and it'll be simmering when you get home, and the rice steamed."

"My dear Watson, you are priceless. Chicken, and of moderate heat. All the necessary ingredients should be in the kitchen already."

"Consider it done, my friend," Watson returned the detective's grin. "And I shall spend the night on the sofa with Bess while you are gone. I will not leave your dear wife incapacitated and alone."

"You are not as young as you once were, Watson. Are you certain a sofa...?"

"I'm a considerable way from the grave yet, young man," Watson retorted with asperity. "I'll do well enough."

"Dear God. How I have missed you," Holmes murmured, unaware he'd spoken aloud. Watson merely gazed at him for a long moment before recovering his power of speech.

"I have never been...more honoured in my life," he said quietly.

"Nor I, to have a second chance," Sherlock added softly.

They sat by the fire for long hours, simply chatting.

———

The next morning, Sherlock dressed as a rural resident, in worn jeans, battered work boots, a work shirt, and barn jacket. Eschewing shaving to ensure a scruffy stubble, and pulling a tweed newsboy-style cap on his head, he wrapped a muffler about his neck, clapped Watson on the shoulder, kissed Skye, and headed for Melton in a vehicle procured by Ryker for the purpose.

Sometime later, Sherlock entered Woodbridge's bedroom community of Melton in a beat-up, nondescript pickup truck and drove around, getting a feel for the overall layout of the streets, especially relative to the rail-road and the river.

Further information obtained from Dr. Victor had not only included a description and color photograph of his sister Mary, but also further data regarding the sounds he had heard. Whereas he had reported the rumble of the railroad had been very loud, almost enough to create difficulty in conversing with his sister, the boat whistles had been more distant, and occasionally changed pitch in mid-whistle.

"Doppler shift," Skye had declared, and Sherlock had nodded assent. "It was passing by."

So Sherlock avoided the docks proper and concentrated on the area around a rail spur down the river from the principal docks. After deliberately driving around randomly enough to be noticed by the locals, he pulled over at a fishmonger's shop, parked, and went inside.

"'Ello there," he remarked cheerfully to the clerk. "I 'uz wonderin' if ya might be able ta he'p me."

"Of course, sir," the friendly young clerk replied. "What may I do for you?"

"I live a good piece nor'west o' here," Sherlock answered, "an' my sister, she jus' moved back inta England wi' 'er 'usband from France. 'E an' 'is partner 'ave an import business, an' she writ t' tell me they were livin' 'ere, or had a shop 'ere, or summat." Sherlock winked drolly. "Sis never was real clear in 'er explanations. Ta beat it all, 'z if that weren't bad 'nuff, the postal got th' letter rained on 'r sumpin, an' th' bloody address is right unreadable. I knows they's around 'ere summat, but I ain't got a notion where, eezackly."

"My mother is exactly like that." The young clerk chuckled. "I learned years ago to get directions from my father whenever possible, if I didn't want to waste a tank of petrol. Have you a name?"

"Well, I think they 'uz usin' th' import company name, an' I'll be bound iffen I c'n recall it," Sherlock rubbed his unshaven chin. "But she's a bonny little tow-head of thirty-one," here he extracted the photo Victor had provided from his wallet, "'bout five an' a half feet tall, wi' hazel eyes. 'Er 'usband's a Frenchman, some shorter'n me, real dark complected, an' 'is partner is a tall American chappie. Mary's a stay at home type, so's ya might not see much o' her. But that husban' o' hers an 'is partner are real balls o' fire."

The clerk examined the picture intently, thinking deeply, then shook his head.

"I'm afraid I don't know the lot," he said apologetically. "I wish I could help."

"Thankee anyways," Sherlock said, nodding his head politely. "I reckon as how I'll jus' try some 'a th' other shops. Mebbe somebody's aroun' what knows 'em."

He was about to leave the shop when an elderly lady grasped him by the arm and pulled him behind a display of fish fryers.

"I seed yer sister's pichure. I know the couple ye're talkin' of," she declared, "an' if ye're a good brother, ye'll be a' takin' 'er outta there."

"Whazzat?" Sherlock said, pretending surprise and hiding his jubilation. "How do ya know 'em?"

"They moved in down th' street from me, few weeks back," the old woman explained. "Mebbe 'round the first o' th' year, mebbe a bit afore. An' I'll be bound she's bein' mistreated by that husband o' hers an' 'is partner, or my name ain't Martha Southern. An' my name mos' certainly is Martha Southern, as anybody 'roun' these parts 'll tell ye," she added, "so's ye c'n put y'r hat on't." She jerked on his arm with a withered, claw-like hand. "Wait 'ere whiles I git me dinner, an' ye c'n drive me home an' I'll show ye."

———

Ten minutes later they were en route to Martha Southern's

cottage. It backed upon the railroad, and some fifty yards of riverbank lay between the tracks and the River Deben.

Perfect, thought Sherlock. *It fits known conditions to a tee.*

"'Ere's me 'ouse," Martha said, pointing to a small but neat whitewashed cottage with cheery yellow trim. "Make a casual-like glance three 'ouses ta th' left, an' that's where y'r sister lives."

Sherlock glanced in the direction indicated without seeming to do so, and espied a cottage similar to the others on the street, saving that it was more unkempt. Whereas the others had tidy little lawns, pristine whitewashes, and painted trim, the house in question was faded and peeling and had large patches of mildew on the walls, with a scraggly yard filled with little but dead weeds.

"Don't look like such as a decent man 'd bring 'is beloved wife to, do it? Now, c'mon in, an' make haste abou' it," Martha declared, "an' I'll tell ye what I've 'eard. I c'n even tell ye th' comin's an' goin's o' th' place, so's ye c'n git 'er out."

"An' 'ow'd ye be knowin' all that?" Sherlock wondered, helping the elderly woman carry her groceries toward her dwelling. So anxious was the old lady to remain unseen with this stranger to the neighborhood, she fairly scuttled for the front door. She also refused to answer until they stood inside, behind that same closed door.

"I'm an ol' widder woman," she explained then, with a grin and a twinkle in her eye, "an' I ain't got so much t' keep me time anymore. So I watch me neighbors. Busy-body, some says what knows I does. But I don' meddle none, I just watch, leastwise 'til now. An' that lot," she nodded down the street, sadness filling her to overflowing, "makes f'r...interestin' watchin', b'lieve me. Comin's an' goin's at all hours, argymints an' raised voices..." The woman broke off for a moment, sobering further, "...and a woman cryin' in the night." She shook her head. "This is a quiet lit'le neighborhood, sir. Real quiet at night, special. So's a woman sobbin' 'er 'eart out in th' wee sma's..."

She met Sherlock's pained grey eyes.

"I ain't th' onliest one what's 'eard it, neither. Y' c'n ask 'most ennybody 'long the lane. You need t' git y'r sister out'n there."

————

Sherlock pretended to look perplexed.

"How'm I gonna do that? I ain't keenest 'bout goin' up 'gainst Jacques an' 'is partner both. Jacques is hot-tempered enuff as 'tis. An' me wif," he glanced around, then lowered his voice, "no weapons t' hand."

"He'p me put away me things, an' I c'n tell ye egg-zackly how." The old woman nodded knowingly.

————

Half an hour later a highly satisfied Sherlock left the Southern cottage with a complete plan of action, as described by an astute Martha. Once well out of the area, he pulled out his cell phone and called Ryker, explaining it to him. They agreed the plan was a good one, and would be executed the very next day.

Sherlock pulled into a hotel Ryker had recommended, and got a room for the night. He carried an overnight bag inside the room, emerging as a dapper, clean-shaven, casu-ally handsome man in jeans, cowboy boots, and a woollen turtleneck sweater—in other words, his usual self—some half an hour later. A short drive to a nearby shopping mall, and he was standing in front of a lingerie store.

Sherlock wandered past the store three times before gathering himself and plunging into the store, the colour in his cheeks heightened. But the manager, an older woman, spotted him and read the signs, waving off the younger store clerks, and took him in hand herself. Soon Sherlock was striding out of the store with a pink and white wrapped and beribboned package, and a satisfied gleam in the grey eyes.

He spent the rest of the evening wandering around the mall, window shopping.

———

The next morning around half past eight, Ryker and three of his unit members met Holmes along the railroad tracks, two blocks up the river from the house where the Victor woman was being held. The small group was hidden among several parked boxcars.

"Local law enforcement already knows," Ryker murmured in response to Sherlock's glance. "Everything's on the up-and-up. There'll be no interference."

"Excellent," Sherlock murmured. "Did you discuss the situation with the British Medical Association?"

"I did that, too. AND the General Medical Council. Both agreed to be lenient with Victor, under the circumstances. But the GMC says he'll be on probation for a year. No limitations on practice, though, given the fact that he was trying his damnedest to walk a fine line of 'do no harm' to his sister, or anyone else."

"Did you bring up Skye's case?"

"I mentioned it briefly. And also indicated there was a slip-up on the American end, in that she didn't get the inoculation. Had she had that, the committee's consensus was that she might not have even gotten sick, or at the worst, might have had a right good case of the sniffles." He shook his head. "Victor really was just obeying his blackmailers and trying to delay the investigation, and even that was a gamble."

"Right. Very good, then."

"I see 'em leaving, sir," Wang, staring through binoculars, reported. "Down the lane...onto the cross street..." He shifted position to peer around the corner of the boxcar. "Main street now...they're gone."

"Now we wait a good ten minutes," Ryker noted, glancing at his watch.

"Indeed," Sherlock confirmed. "It would not do to have them return for some forgotten item and stumble across our rescue attempt."

At that, Ryker checked his radio, turning on the wireless earpiece.

"Well?" Sherlock demanded.

"The tail is on 'em," he answered briefly. "All systems green."

The ten minutes ticked slowly by. "Aaaand...go," Ryker said, eyeing his watch.

The group started purposefully down the tracks.

———

The back door was locked, of course. But such things were little more than minor nuisances to Sherlock Holmes. He extracted latex gloves and his lock-pick kit from a pocket, knelt before the door, and silently and swiftly unlatched the door. Holding his arm back to keep the others behind him, he scanned the doorframe, searching for possible traps or security that could notify the kidnappers.

"It is safe," he decided, and pushed the door open, stepping forward. "But touch nothing." Ryker and his men were right behind, the rear guard holding their weapons at the ready.

"Miss Victor?" Sherlock called softly. "Miss Mary Victor? We are friends of your brother, Dr. Nathan Victor, and we are here to rescue you."

"I'm Captain Braeden Ryker, of Her Majesty's Secret Service," Ryker announced in a similar tone, "and this is Detective Holmes. We're here to reunite you and your brother, then take you to a safe house."

"Nathan told me to tell you, 'Tweedledum says hello,'" Holmes added. A closet door burst open, and a woman of about five and a half feet, with medium blonde hair and hazel eyes, tumbled into Sherlock's arms, sobbing nearly hysterically. A startled and decidedly taken aback Sherlock very swiftly handed her off to Ryker, trying not to show his discomfort.

"Oh, thank God! Thank God!" the woman cried. "I thought Nathan and I were both dead!"

They spirited her out of the house, locking the door behind them so her kidnappers would be baffled as to her means of escape.

————

Ryker led them to a safehouse on the opposite side of Woodbridge, then made a phone call. "The crow has Tweedledee," he murmured into the phone. "Time to shake the rattle and roll." Then he hung up.

"Your brother will be here shortly, Miss Victor," Sherlock said gently, easing her into an overstuffed armchair. "In the meanwhile, do you require medical assistance?"

"No—no, I'm fine," Mary Victor said faintly. "Well,

I'm not fine, but well enough, given the circumstances, I suppose. A few bruises where they gripped my arms too hard, and I could use a bit more to eat than cold cereal and milk..."

Ryker made a couple of finger gestures to his men. Murphy, the unit's emergency medical technician, immediately bent over the woman, examining her for injury and taking her vital signs. Wang headed for the safe house's kitchen and fired up the stove.

After several minutes, Murphy looked up at Ryker.

"It's as she said, Captain. She's got finger-mark bruises on her arms, particularly in the wrist and upper arm areas, but nothing further that I can see. Enid might see more."

"I'll have her examine the lady when we leave with Dr. Victor," Ryker agreed. "Or perhaps Dr. Victor himself would prefer to see to his sister."

"Miss Victor, if you do not mind my imposing upon you after what has been a most harrowing experience," Sherlock murmured, crouching beside her chair, "I should like to ask you a few questions."

"Y-yes," she said quietly. "I know you need to find these men and arrest them. I'll tell you all I can. Do you know what they look like?"

"I do. One is short, dark featured, and Gallic. The other is a tall American, with brown hair and blue eyes."

"Yes. Their real names, as far as I could determine from listening to their conversation, are Fereaud and Cunningham. Honestly, I think they must be madmen."

"And why is that?"

"Because all they could talk about was some stupid old cave. And whatever was in it."

Ryker and Holmes exchanged serious looks.

"They seemed to be some sort of scavengers, or maybe salvagers," Mary Victor explained. "Quite unscrupulous ones, though. They intended to gain control of the cave through whatever means necessary, and then get inside. That's why they kidnapped me; they wanted to use Nathan's medical knowledge to get around the land's owner."

"I'd say they managed that in spades," Murphy muttered under his breath. "'Stiff' is pretty easy to get around."

"Oh, NO! Is poor Mr. McFarlane dead?!" Mary exclaimed, distressed.

"Yes, ma'am," Ryker confirmed, shooting a cautionary look at Murphy, who grasped what had happened and became anxious. "I'm afraid so."

Murphy unassumingly reached for her wrist, checking her pulse. He looked up at Sherlock and Ryker and shook his head. "Agitated," he mouthed. "Sorry."

"Nathan didn't do it, did he? Please, tell me Nathan didn't do it!" Miss Victor cried, almost in tears.

"No, madam, your brother flatly refused," Sherlock soothed her. "He would not do the deed himself, even at the risk of both your lives. He did tell them a chemical that could be used, in order to save your life, but not how to use it. Unfortunately, they concocted a story and got that information elsewhere."

"He didn't do it. Oh, thank God," she breathed fervently. "Nathan's a good man. He has his faults—he tends to be a hedonist, and it's worse when he's stressed—but he's a good man at heart, I swear he is."

"Agreed, Miss Victor," Sherlock affirmed. "You have both been living in fear of your lives for quite some time, but that fear has ended at last, and you are both safe. Now, can you tell us what your captors wanted with the cave?"

"Yes. They seemed to think the government had hidden something valuable in there."

"What did they intend to do with the contents?" Ryker joined the inquiry.

"They had three options, as far as I could determine." Miss Victor shrugged. "One was to keep it for themselves; another was to ransom it back to the government; and the third was to auction at least part of it off to the highest bidder on the black market."

Another grave glance passed between Holmes and Ryker.

"Did they give any indication as to what they believed to be within the cave?" Sherlock asked.

"Yes," Miss Victor stated unequivocally. "Gold. Nazi gold."

"What?!" Holmes and Ryker both exclaimed, startled.

————

By lunchtime, Mary Victor and her twin brother, Nathan Victor, had been ecstatically reunited in the safe house. Dr. Victor and Dr. Wilder collaborated in an examination of Mary, and both confirmed Murphy's conclusion: No serious injury. Nathan joined Mary in her second proper meal of the day, then Ryker's unit whisked them away to safety; Fereaud and Cunningham had lost their plain-clothes police tail.

"What will the locals do for a physician?" Sherlock asked Ryker after the others had left. "Did you install a Service physician as a substitute?"

"No," Ryker grinned, "Dr. Watson agreed to come out of retirement, until you catch the 'blackguards,' I believe he put it. Then the Victors can return, and he'll go back to his retirement."

"Ha!" Sherlock exclaimed, delighted. "That could not be more like Watson."

"Oh, and he said this morning to tell you the Boss is doing much better," Ryker added, "and that the Boss, he, and...Bess...slept well all night, and he already has the...curry simmering?"

"Capital," Sherlock declared, mischievously neglecting to enlighten Ryker. "Shall we depart, then? I believe it is a holiday of sorts, and I do have a wife awaiting."

"Yeah," Ryker agreed, a sheepish grin spreading across his face. "Enid is planning a nice dinner at her flat tonight. Er, not her home flat; the one she's using while we're here."

"Ah," Sherlock said knowingly, only the twinkle in his eyes betraying his amused comprehension. "Well, I suppose it is good to know that the head of the modern Baker Street Irregulars has his own divertissements."

Ryker flushed, but grinned broadly.

They slipped out of the safe house, and went their separate ways.

5

Interludes

Watson and Skye were both waiting in the sitting room, she reclining on the sofa, he in the armchair, when Sherlock arrived at Gibson House. The smell of curry was in the air, and Skye was showered and wrapped in her robe, a hint of red lace peeking out between the robe's hem and her shearling house shoes.

"How did it go?" the two asked in unison. Skye's voice had no hint of congestion.

"Quite well," Sherlock announced, setting a shopping bag down at the end of the sofa. "We easily extracted Miss Victor, and she and her brother had a most touching reunion." He turned to Skye. "Per her testimony, I think we may indeed chalk up certain...indiscretions...to stress, as you suspected. Miss Victor swears she believed both she and her brother would die before these two men would release them. Dr. Victor has been living in fear since at least the first of the year, if not before."

"Oh, my," Skye murmured, blue eyes widening. "Are they safe now?"

"They are. And not even I know where they have been taken. Which is as it should be."

"And I fill in for Victor until this whole mess is over," Watson declared with satisfaction. "So I'll be handy if you need me, as well." He picked up the overnight bag beside his chair. "And now, since you are reunited, and it is a most special day, I shall take my leave and pop by tomorrow to see about Skye."

"Capital, my dear Watson," Sherlock said, taking Watson's free hand. "You are invaluable, in all your incarnations."

Watson laughed, shaking Sherlock's hand vigorously. Suddenly he dropped his bag, grabbed Sherlock's shoulder and drew the detective into an affectionate male embrace. Sherlock stiffened, then relaxed into it, returning it.

Watson next went to Skye and deposited a fatherly kiss on her forehead. "You behave, young lady," he said sternly, then his eyes twinkled. "But—given the day—not too much." He shot a mischievous glance at Sherlock, who felt his cheeks warm.

And he was gone.

Skye rose from the sofa, letting her robe slide off, revealing the red nightgown her husband had so favored on his birthday. She stepped forward and wrapped her arms around Sherlock's neck. His hands, in turn, automatically went to her waist.

"Welcome home, Sweetheart," she said with a smile. "Happy Valentine's Day."

Sherlock bent his head to hers.

———

The table was formally set for two; the curry and rice were in covered warmers on the table, ready to serve, and all that lacked was lighting the candles. Sherlock had retired to the bedroom to change into the gift Skye arranged for him long before: Rich, dark blue silk lounging pyjamas which matched the dressing gown he'd received for Christmas. Now he lit the candles, seated Skye, and sat down himself.

Watson had been right; his curry rivaled any Holmes had ever tasted, and the couple devoured it in enjoyment. When that was finished, Skye rose and prepared the dessert —a decadent double chocolate torte with hot fudge sauce. Where it had come from, Sherlock didn't know. *But it matters not,* he thought, savoring its richness, while watching the red-clad siren across the table from him. *It is almost as delicious as my wife.*

————

"You have a bit of chocolate sauce on your face, Skye," Sherlock observed when they'd finished eating. He stood and came around the table, offering his hands to help her to her feet.

"Oh," she said, reaching for her napkin. Sherlock snatched the napkin from her hand, tossing it back onto the table. She stared at him, confused. "But you said I had..."

"I know," he noted, a mischievous glimmer in his grey eyes. "I have my own plans for removing it."

He bent his head and covered the chocolatey spot with his lips, licking the sweet from her skin; then he pulled her against himself.

"Ohh," she whispered, wrapping her arms around his waist. "I missed you."

"I know," he murmured, following suit. "Would you like to see what I have for you?"

"Besides the obvious?" she answered mischievously, pressing closer, and he chuckled.

"Indeed. Feel honoured, Wife. Never before have I interrupted an investigation to obtain a gift, let alone a suitably...romantic one," his cheeks developed a dusky tinge.

He drew her into the sitting room, seeing her comfortably on the sofa before joining her. He pulled the shopping bag before them, and Sherlock extracted a small envelope, handing it to her.

Skye opened it to find a card in traditional red heart shape. Inside, the printed sentiment simply read, "You already had it, but I thought I'd give it to you again anyway." It was signed, "Your very own Sherlock."

———

Skye smiled, sapphire eyes glimmering with love. From beneath a magazine on the tea table, she produced another envelope and handed it to him. He extracted the card within, to find a night scene: A single black, silhouetted figure stared upward at a shooting star in a deep blue firmament. It read, "I made a wish upon a star..."

He opened the card, to find the identical image, saving the lone figure had been joined by a second, and they stood in a gentle embrace, still looking upward into the heavens. The remainder of the sentiment read, "...and then you were there."

It was signed, "To my very own dream come true, to the man I can't live without. Love, Skye."

Sherlock swallowed once.

"I love you," Skye whispered, gazing at him with adoration in her azure eyes. Sherlock met those eyes.

"And I love you," he breathed. Gently he placed a

small package wrapped and bowed in scarlet in her hands. "Here is the first of two. This one was not planned, but it caught my eye in a shop window, and...well."

He gestured for her to open it.

———

Inside the box was an oblong velvet box. Inside that was a ruby pendant, faceted in heart shape, hung on a white gold chain. *He wants to make sure I know his heart belongs to me,* Skye thought, and smiled, immediately donning the necklace.

"It's lovely, Sherlock. I've never seen anything like this."

"I rather liked it," Sherlock agreed. "And it looks...nice...there." He lightly fingered the ruby, in the hollow of her throat; then he handed the second package to her; this one was large and flat, wrapped and beribboned in pink and white. "And here is this."

Skye unwrapped the box, lifted the lid, and unfolded pink tissue paper. A handful of satin and lace emerged. Soon she was lifting out a pale blue babydoll nightgown.

"I can assure you, it is sufficiently appealing that your husband will most definitely keep you warm," Sherlock said with a straight face, but his eyes twinkled.

"Then let's go get warm," Skye grinned. They rose and headed for the bedroom.

———

The next day—very late in the morning—Watson stopped by to see about Skye. The babydoll and the silk pyjamas had disappeared many hours before, and had only recently been replaced by normal jeans and sweaters. Watson declared Skye fit to resume work, provided she took her decongestants and analgesics as needed, and rested when necessary. Then he returned to the clinic that was once his, and now was again, albeit temporarily.

After lunch, Ryker visited.

"Well, I think I know what the men are after, now, although where they got the idea is a bit balmy. Hi there, Boss," he greeted Skye belatedly. "Looks like you're feeling better."

"I am," she agreed. "A little weak yet, and if I wipe my nose any more it's gonna fall off, and I'm on my fourth, or, um..." she briefly reckoned on her fingers, "maybe that's fifth, box of tissues since Sherlock went under cover, but pretty good other than that."

"Fourth—FIFTH box?!" Ryker exclaimed, startled, as Holmes frowned.

"Yeah," Skye said ruefully. "I seem to average a rate of about one, one and a half, boxes a day. I feel like I'm blowin' my brains out, half the time. I didn't know I had that much room in my whole head."

"Wow," Ryker said, at a loss for words. Sherlock tapped his foot.

"So what are they after?" Skye returned to the original subject.

"THANK you, Skye!" Sherlock exclaimed in impatient frustration. "Please get on with it, Ryker."

Ryker grinned mischievously at Skye.

"No, don't do it," she warned, wagging her finger. "Bad Brae. Bad, bad Brae."

The two laughed, and Sherlock glowered.

"Sorry, Holmes," Ryker chuckled. "Okay, I had to do a hell of a lot of digging into the history of the bases, but here's the gist of it. In 1943, RAF Woodbridge was constructed as one of three airfields that were intended to accept damaged bombers or aircraft running short on fuel, returning from raids over Germany. In other words, it was expressly designed for emergency landings. That's why it has such long, heavy-duty runways, and is so close to the coastline. Its first name was actually RAF Station Sutton Heath," Ryker explained.

"All right," Sherlock nodded. "I comprehend so far. Pray continue."

"Okay. It seems that, in July of 1944, a Luftwaffe fighter on a North Sea night patrol accidentally landed at Woodbridge. The Nazi German crew only had a hundred hours of flight training. They were flying by compass heading, or so they thought; but they went exactly bass-ackwards."

"And they thought they were over their own airfield!" Skye exclaimed, eyes wide with amusement. "But they landed by accident on their ENEMY'S airfield instead!"

"Exactly right," Ryker grinned.

"Boy, I bet THAT was a helluva shock," Skye opined. "Talk about a woops." All three chuckled.

"Yup, a real FUBAR, that. Now, they had some experimental Nazi equipment on board, radar and such, so the aeroplane was taken into custody, the crew became prisoners of war, and the whole thing went classified while the Allies deconstructed the equipment and devised counter-measures," Ryker continued.

"But our two treasure hunters must believe that some of the purported 'lost Nazi gold,' of which I have read in Skye's historical tomes, was aboard," Sherlock theorized.

"That's my feeling," Ryker verified. "I've dug up some articles in the less-reputable 'historical' and treasure hunting journals proposing the notion. That seems to be the preferred idea among some circles for why the flight was classified, rather than war-critical technology. I'd guess our boys have been reading that junk."

"So," Sherlock considered. "Greed is our motivating factor."

"Looks like it," Skye agreed. "Enough greed to kill, kidnap, blackmail, forge documents, and a whole buncha stuff."

"How is the cave?" Sherlock queried.

"Temporarily 'sealed' under guard," Ryker declared, "while the experts back at HQ decide how best to enclose the contents permanently."

"Very well," Sherlock decided. "Clandestine guard, I presume."

"You got it," Ryker averred. "I called in another unit, because mine was spread thin, and the HazMat team is busy figuring out how to best close this thing up, but let's just say 'ghosts' protect the cave now. Don't worry; Gregory's unit is the local unit assigned for the area, and they're good. Really good."

"Great," Skye decided.

"And do we have surveillance on the house in Melton?" Sherlock pressed.

"We do," Ryker nodded, "from Gregory's bunch, but our marks haven't come back yet. Evidently it's not uncommon that they disappear for a couple days or more at a time, according to Miss Victor. She thinks they had nicer quarters somewhere else."

"Likely, from what I saw yesterday," Sherlock agreed. "I suppose I should next turn my attention to locating the 'somewhere else.'"

"But we don't have any clues for that," Skye protested.

"Agreed," Sherlock sighed. "Perhaps I can dredge up something in a return visit to the cottage in Melton tomorrow."

"That's a plan," Ryker concluded. "I can arrange for

the surveillance to give you a heads-up if they're seen returning and you need to clear out in a hurry."

"Then we shall do precisely that," Sherlock decided. He glanced at the clock. "It is nearly tea-time. Would Wiggins care for a bit of tea? Skye is, as yet, probably not up to preparing it, but if you do not mind tea, cold sandwiches, and tinned shortbread instead of Skye's home-baked, you are welcome to stay."

A huge grin spread across Ryker's face.

"Wiggins would love to stay, at least for a little while. We can coordinate things more, and maybe the Boss can fill me in on this continuum thing, too. All things considered, I'd like to understand more about that."

"Then do you stay and discuss wormholes with Skye, while I put the kettle on," Sherlock agreed.

————

The next day, well before dawn, Sherlock departed for Melton once more, fingerprints of Miss Mary Victor in hand for comparison. When he neared the village, he contacted the surveillance team via ciphered cell phone, to find that the coast was clear and nothing had yet been seen of their quarry. Sherlock parked near the railroad spur, choosing the back entrance as least likely to raise attention. He crept down the railroad in the pre-dawn light, donned latex gloves, and picked the lock once more.

Inside, he performed a detailed inspection of the entire cottage. It was a single-story dwelling, with no cellar due to its proximity to the river, so there was not much to inspect. The windows, contrary to outside impressions, had thick plywood nailed over them, with sufficient set- decoration on the outer side to fool a casual passerby; the external doors had been modified so that they only locked from without. He concentrated on doorknobs and any other items the men might have handled, looking for fingerprints; but those objects had been handled so much by Miss Victor that they were essentially rubbed clean of any other prints. Sherlock sighed and resumed his search.

He found a dilapidated bed with a single top sheet and blanket, and signs that it had been Miss Victor's, in the back room; the wardrobe held three changes of feminine garments. The kitchen had nothing in it but some stale dry cereal and a half-used carton of milk in the refrigerator. A single bowl, spoon, and cup rested in the dish drainer by the sink.

The bathroom showed signs of use, with a drinking glass and an abandoned toothbrush and tube of toothpaste; a hairbrush, with medium-blonde strands of hair woven into the bristles, lay on the vanity.

The front room had little in it save a rough wood table and two matching chairs, none of which was capable of sustaining prints. A deck of cards lay on a corner of the table, however, and this Sherlock appropriated, placing the entire deck into a forensics evidence bag.

"We may at least be able to lift some fingerprints from them," he murmured to himself, "possibly even DNA."

There was nothing else in the house, and Sherlock quickly checked with the surveillance team, ascertaining it was safe to go into the front yard. It was, and he slipped outside and looked around. No fingerprints were to be found on the outside doorknob either, presumably because the men had been wearing winter gloves. There were tire tracks in the gravel driveway, however, and he pulled a notebook and quickly sketched the pattern of tread, then sighed again.

"Not enough. We shall simply have to wait until they return, then follow them."

He entered the front door, locking it behind him. There he gathered Miss Victor's personal items, placing the smaller items into another forensics bag for safekeeping, and the clothing into an unused trash bag found under the kitchen sink, until they could be returned to their owner. Then he slipped out the back door, locking it, and headed down the rails.

Ten minutes later he was on the road back to Gibson House.

———

After Sherlock left, Skye moved into the study and began considering the last of the calculations needed to correct the tesseract focus. As if on cue, there was a pop and whiff of ozone.

"Hi, guys," she said into the air.

"Hi, Sis," her own voice came back to her. "Feeling any better?"

"Much better. Not only that, but we found out Dr. Victor was being blackmailed. The bad guys had his twin sister and were threatening all kinds of horrible stuff to her —AND him."

"Wow," Chadwick said, stunned.

"And what is that status?" Holmes asked.

"Good," Skye grinned. "Sherlock located the sister and he and 'our' MI-5 team extracted her. She and Dr. Victor were whisked into hiding, and Sherlock's gone to try to find some clues as to where our murderers have holed up in the meantime."

"Capital," Holmes replied. "I am glad to see Brother Other Me is quite on top of things."

"Absolutely," Skye averred firmly. "The two of you aren't at all different in that respect."

"Indeed, it would appear so," Holmes said thoughtfully.

"Meanwhile," Chadwick remarked, "does my Sis feel up to seeing what I've done in the interim?"

"I sure do," Skye said cheerfully. "I have orders from Watson to take my medicines, and to rest if I get tired, but right now I feel pretty darned good. So let's go."

"Wa-Watson?!" Holmes exclaimed, badly startled.

"Yeah," Skye grinned in the direction of the voice. "If you ever make it over to Great Britain, or rather WHEN you make it over, be sure to check out retired Dr. John H. Watson, M.D., now of Number 10, Willow Tree Close, Wickham Market."

"Dear God," Holmes said blankly. Skye heard a slight thud, and thought it sounded rather like the former detective had sat down suddenly.

"He nursed me through the flu, while Sherlock went off to find the Victor woman," Skye explained softly. "My Sherlock was as glad to find Watson as you are to hear about him. And I think it's why I'm feeling so much better. He judiciously adds old-fashioned remedies to the modern medicines, and the results are better than either one alone. He's a good doctor."

"He always was," Holmes murmured quietly.

"Wonderful!" Chadwick exclaimed happily. "Holmes, once we get this mess straightened out, we'll look him up."

"Indeed," Holmes agreed, voice slightly hoarse.

"So. Let's get to mess-straightening, guys," Chadwick noted. "Sis, here comes the notebook..."

The spiral bound pad appeared through a wall, hurtling at Skye, and she snagged it out of the air.

"Down to work," Skye said, opening the pad. "Whatcha got?"

"Turn to page 145," Chadwick said, "and I'll fill you in..."

———

Thus ensued a period of give and take between the three, Skye asking about the rationale for certain directions the work had taken, and the other couple explaining the differences between their tesseract design and hers. They iterated back and forth a few times, with Skye suggesting alternative approaches and catching one or two arithmetic errors, but by and large the three followed the calculations contained in the notebook.

They had been at work for a couple of hours when Holmes remarked, "Ladies, if you will excuse me, I must take a brief break."

"Of course," Skye murmured politely, continuing to concentrate on the calculations her doppelganger had made.

"Sure, Holmes, go ahead," Chadwick agreed. "You had that big cup of coffee before we came downstairs."

"Precisely," Holmes muttered, the barest hint of what might have been embarrassment in his tone. "I also find myself in need of sustenance, as I had little breakfast this morning; I shall return shortly."

"Oh, hey, if you feel like it, bring a snackie my way when you come back," Chadwick suggested. "I wouldn't mind something to nibble on, myself."

"Very well," Holmes said amiably.

There was the sound of a chair scraping back, then footsteps retreating. A door closed, and all was silent.

"This looks good, Sis," Skye decided after a few moments, looking up. "I think we're getting really close."

"Okay, flip to page 208 and look at the observational data," Chadwick suggested.

Skye did so, and scanned through the table there. "Oh, that's bang on," she said after only a few seconds.

"I thought so," Chadwick agreed. "But take a look at row twelve, column four. Does that data point look off to you?"

"Mmm..." Skye considered. "No, not too badly. Lemme see..." She turned to the desk and scrabbled in a drawer, extracting a calculator. Fingers tapping like a machine gun, she entered data points rapidly, then calculated the mean and standard deviation. "No, it's within the standard deviation, Hon, by a good twenty percent."

"Good," Chadwick said. "I hadn't had time to work the statistics on it yet. I was considering throwing out that point."

"No, it looks like you've got good data, all the way through," Skye said. "But we can go through it point by point, if you want to."

"I think I do," Chadwick said.

"Okay," Skye agreed. "You got a copy?"

"Yep."

"Okay. Point one: three point oh four five, ten fifty-six point three seven."

"What was the standard deviation again?"

"Oh, it was...lemme see..."

———

While Holmes was gone, the two women looked over the experimental results once more.

"Looks good to me," Skye finally decided, mildly nasal; it was nearing time for her medications. "I think we've got our confirmation, in spades."

"I'd say so," Chadwick agreed. "When Holmes comes back, we'll get started."

"Okay."

———

"Um, Skye, changing the subject a minute—can I ask a question?" Chadwick wondered hesitantly, her mind temporarily slipping away from the tesseract and its readings. "Something kinda personal?"

"Uh, I guess so," Skye agreed uncertainly. "I may not answer, if it's too personal, but you can ask."

"Fair enough," Chadwick said. "I don't think it'll be anything really bad. I was just wondering...does your Holmes...love you?"

"Oh yeah, no question," Skye informed her other self with a grin. "He loves me."

———

Sherlock came in through the door to the garage, doffing his coat and hat as he did. He heard the soft back and forth sounds of a conversation, exclusively in his wife's tones, and knew the tesseract was active. He nodded to himself, his lips compressing slightly, and headed for the study.

But as he approached the door of that room, he began to piece together the topic of discussion.

This is not a tesseract brainstorm session. They are conversing about me, and about our marriage, he realized in some disquiet. *Surely Skye would not disclose any... personal...private...information...*

He stopped in the hall, listening, perturbed and mildly bewildered.

———

"But...how do you KNOW he loves you?" Chadwick wondered.

"He tells me," Skye said simply.

"TELLS you?" Chadwick nearly blurted in her amazement. "You mean he actually SAYS, 'I love you, Skye'?"

"Sometimes, but not very often." Skye laughed. "He'll talk all the way around it, though. Like maybe I say, 'I love you, Sherlock,' and he answers, 'And I, you, my dear.'"

"Hah!" Chadwick exclaimed. "Everything BUT the L word."

"Right. See, Sherlock..." she paused, trying to figure out how to explain while keeping faith with her husband's privacy. "Sis, have you ever heard the expression, 'Still waters run deep'?"

"Yeah," Chadwick said succinctly.

"Well, that's Sherlock," Skye noted. "Mine and yours both. The things that mean the most to him, the emotions that run the deepest, are the hardest for him to say. So— this might sound odd—the fact that he's only able to say those words to me once in a while is one of the surest proofs I've got that he really does love me."

"Oh," Chadwick murmured thoughtfully.

———

Hidden in the hallway, Sherlock stood listening. It had not yet reached his consciousness that what he was doing might be construed as eavesdropping, and as a detective, such things mattered little to him anyway. He now knew his wife would not say anything behind his back to which he would object, and he was fascinated by this conversation.

I have long known she understands me better than any other, he thought, *but really! I had no idea her comprehension of my being was this...complete.* He pondered for a moment. *I am glad she...knows...*

He eased silently toward the door, intent on watching his wife as she discussed their relationship.

———

"But that's not the only way I know," Skye continued. "I realized pretty quickly that he had ways of telling me how he felt without ever saying a word."

"What do you mean?" Chadwick asked, curious.

"Oh," Skye shrugged, just as Sherlock peered surreptitiously around the doorframe. "There's a way he can look at me, for instance; it's his way of telling me he thinks I look nice, he likes my outfit and stuff, without saying anything. You might have seen it once or twice—his eyes start at my head and go all the way to my feet, then he reverses it and moves back up to my face. He meets my eyes, and then his own eyes crinkle like he's going to smile, only he doesn't, quite."

———

In the Chamber, Chadwick sat at the console, stunned.

"Y-yes," she stammered slightly, "yes, I think I've seen that."

HELL yes, I've seen that, the scientist thought, startled. *I've seen that in "my own" Holmes, just last week—though I don't guess I really have the right to call him mine. I've often wondered what he was thinking, when he did that.*

Not, I suppose, that it matters, or really means anything. Other than, "I like what you're wearing," I guess.

She sighed and turned her attention back to her counterpart in the other continuum.

———

"And there are other ways he 'tells' me," Skye went on. "Once in a while I'll find a flower left somewhere for me, usually a lupine."

"My—your—our favorite flower," Chadwick noted, stumbling over which possessive pronoun to use.

"Exactly," Skye smiled. "Last September, he found out I loved a particular Celtic singer. So imagine the monumental coincidence when a CD of that singer's latest album showed up on the kitchen table one morning about a week later."

"Aww!" Chadwick chortled, delighted. "That was sweet."

Sherlock flushed in embarrassment, still peeping around the doorframe, undetected.

"And there are other, day to day things," Skye added. "Like the way he'll say my name, or the way he touches me. And I almost never have to tell him I'm hungry anymore—one glance at me, and he's suddenly declaring it's time to eat. I swear, lately he knows I'm hungry way before I know myself."

Chadwick chuckled, then sobered. "You know, Holmes does that a lot, too," she murmured thoughtfully. "'Mine,' I mean."

"We're all so darned obsessed with our work," Skye pointed out, "we have to look after each other, I guess."

"I guess," Chadwick agreed.

———

The door of the Chamber opened quietly, and Holmes put his head through, intent on asking Chadwick what she wanted to eat. A quick glance took in the posture of both "his" Chadwick and Dr. Chadwick-Holmes, and he instantly realized that the two women were deep in a discussion of their respective companions. His own surname on Chadwick's lips provided confirmation of his deduction.

He paused, uncertain, in the doorway. *Do I really want to hear this?* he wondered, brow creasing in sadness.

Holmes stood there for only a couple of seconds before silently withdrawing.

———

"So do you love him?" Chadwick asked. "I mean, it sure looks like you're nuts about him."

"Oh, I am," Skye grinned. "I'm crazy about him. I'm surprised you even had to ask, after the beta burn scare."

Warmth flooded the detective who stood just outside the study door.

"Why?" Chadwick wondered. "I mean, what is it about him you find so appealing? He can be so…"

"Sharp?" Skye grinned. "Distant? He can, but it's important to remember he never means it personally, Sis. There's a caring heart underneath his reserve. And that's one of the things I love about him. Not to mention, he's handsome! I don't think a day has gone by since he arrived in this continuum that I haven't made a mental note of just how good-looking he is!"

"Well, he is, that," Chadwick agreed with a smirk.

The two women giggled, and Sherlock flushed again. *I did not know she thought that,* he considered. *I knew she found me appealing, but handsome? After the likes of "our dear Lily" and similar, I had long since assumed such matters of appearance were beyond my purview.*

"And there's his intelligence—the man's a positive

genius, but I don't have to tell you that," Skye noted. "And he has so many talents! His makeup, and acting, and the violin, and—has he ever drawn anything for you?"

"He's done one or two design sketches for the tesser- act," Chadwick admitted. "They were really good, very precise and detailed."

"Get him to sit down and just draw something for you, something out of his own head," Skye suggested. "He's really amazing."

"I'll do that," Chadwick decided.

"And his sense of humor," Skye continued, face breaking into a broad, affectionate smile. "I never realized, from reading the stories, just what a devilish mischief he can be."

"But there are hints in the stories, even so," Chadwick grinned. "I know exactly what you mean there...although Holmes doesn't laugh much anymore. Neither of us does, I guess. We've been in too serious a situation for too long. I sometimes think it's a wonder he and I are still speaking to each other."

———

"Well, that's where the caring comes in, I'd say," Skye said shrewdly. "No matter what happened between you, and I'm not gonna ask, but I know you'd stick by him regard- less, because it's what I'd do. And I know he has to under- stand you're fighting with everything you've got, and you're under a lot of stress, and he'll make allowances. He may not always understand precisely why you react the way you do," she added, recalling Holmes' puzzlement in more than one recent incident, "but he understands the root cause, I think. He cares, Skye, I'm sure of it. He just doesn't know how to show it...and he may not even quite realize it."

Chadwick sighed. "Well, we'd better get back to work, or the whole thing is gonna be moot," she pointed out. "There's no relationship here or there, if the continuums collapse."

"True," Skye murmured, sobering. "Let me see those results again..."

———

A deeply gratified Sherlock slipped silently back to the mudroom, where he opened the garage door and closed it firmly. "Skye?" he called, fiddling with the coat and hat hanging on the rack, and making a considerable rustling noise in the doing.

"In the study, Sherlock. The Other Me and I are in here working. C'mon in. She'll defocus for you."

"Very well," he called back, then recalled some important issues raised in her recent discussion. "Have you eaten lately?"

"No, I was waiting for you."

"Very well, I shall pop by the kitchen and put together some sandwiches, and be right in," Sherlock offered.

"Actually, there's already some made in the fridge," Skye informed him. "Just grab 'em, slap 'em on the tray I left on the table, pour some tea, and bring it all in."

"And here comes Holmes, with a tray for us, too," Chadwick's voice added. "Thanks, Hon."

Within five minutes, both couples were eating lunch, while discussing the experimental results, and their likely significance, across the wormhole.

———

Right after lunch, the phone call came in. Sherlock took it, as the other him, and the two Skyes, resumed work.

"Mm," he murmured, sounding thoughtful and mildly displeased. Skye looked up.

"What is it, Honey?"

Sherlock held up one finger, listening intently, and the others silenced.

After several more moments, he replied, "Very well; thank you, Beasley. I shall notify Ryker directly." The detective hung up the phone and turned to his wife and their doubles. "Fereaud and Cunningham came by the cottage in Melton, stayed a scant three minutes, and left as if the place were on fire. MI-5 surveillance tried to track them this time, but still lost them on the A12 in the after-lunch rush."

"Damnation," Holmes muttered.

"Precisely," Sherlock agreed sharply, annoyed by the fact. "I intend to run over to the McFarlane farm to inform Ryker directly, and see how the cave closure efforts are proceeding. It is entirely likely that they are headed there, deciding to rush their plans to conclusion."

"All right, Honey," Skye said, standing and giving him a light peck on the cheek. "I'd tell you to be careful, but I know you always are."

"I shall return as soon as may be," Sherlock noted, accepting the chaste kiss and returning it in like manner.

"Okay. I'm here working," Skye agreed.

The three returned to their data as Sherlock left the house at speed.

———

The trio continued to work intently, trying to coordinate

their efforts, for over an hour, when Holmes glanced at his instrumentation.

"Ladies," he interjected into their soft give and take conversation, "I am seeing a particular pattern developing on my instruments."

"Whatcha got?" Chadwick wondered.

"It is the same sequence of readouts I have seen before, shortly before an instability wave comes through," Holmes noted.

"Shit. You sure?" Chadwick verified.

"Very," Holmes confirmed. "I strongly recommend defocusing in order to protect Brother Other Me's wife. We can, hopefully, focus back in when it has passed."

"Do it," Chadwick ordered. "Catch you in a bit, Sis, if all goes well."

"It will," Skye encouraged. "Hang in there. I'll be here."

"Gone," Holmes declared.

There was a soft pop, and a sense of aloneness in the house. Skye nodded to herself, and bent back over the notebook, intent on making the last of the adjustments to the calculations, while some part of her mind wondered when Sherlock would get back, and if he would be in any sort of mood for dinner.

————

Outside Gibson House, near the kitchen garden door, two men crouched in the winter shrubbery. They glanced at each other; the taller one nodded and jerked his head at the door. The shorter of the two produced a lock-pick kit and moved to the door to begin work.

————

In the other continuum, Chadwick and Holmes watched the readouts on Holmes' instrumentation, trying to ascertain a method of predicting the instability waves. In the tesseract core, Skye could still be seen, bent over the desk, scanning through the notebook and occasionally annotating what was there. But there was no longer a direct connection with her continuum.

"Rest energy of closed-loop strings beginning to peak," Holmes noted, pointing at the computer screen graphic. "When the readings reach..." he put his finger at a point on the vertical axis, "here...we should experience a tremor."

The pair watched the graph climb inexorably toward Holmes' finger. Just then, they heard Skye scream.

Blonde head and black shot up to look over the console at the core.

"Damnation!" Holmes cried, leaping to his feet.

"Oh, SHIT!" Chadwick exclaimed simultaneously.

For the core depicted Skye, in her study, attempting to fight off two men. One was tall, with brown hair and blue eyes; the other possessed Gallic features and a dark complexion.

Just then, the graph hit the critical mark. And abruptly jumped past it.

"Hang on!" Chadwick cried, grabbing Holmes and yanking him back into his seat.

The Chamber felt as if a meteor had hit it.

———

"Let...me...GO!" Skye cried, struggling against the two men as they manhandled her, attempting to get a solid grip on her. Papers slid off the desk onto the floor. "What do you think you're doing?!"

"Getting ourselves a little insurance," the tall man said in a patently northeastern American accent—Brooklyn in Skye's estimation—as he batted away her fist. He kicked the desk chair out of the way, and it overturned. "That husband of yours won't be so damn hot to get in our way if we've got his pretty little wife, now, will he?"

"You have no idea," Skye ground out through gritted teeth, clawing and slapping and punching and kicking at the men. The short man drew back and swung at her, but Skye ducked, and he struck the side of the computer monitor instead, overturning it. "Get away from me!" Snatching up a handy paperweight, she flung it at the short man, who also ducked.

But her energy was still low from her illness, and within moments, Skye's wrists were pinned behind her back by Fereaud, while Cunningham tied them together. They gagged and blindfolded her; then the heavily muscled Fereaud casually threw her across his shoulder and carried her out the back door. They made their way through the kitchen garden, scrambled over the low stone wall, and down a hedge-lined alley to their waiting vehicle.

Fereaud callously dumped Skye into the back seat. Then he and Cunningham climbed into the front, and they drove off.

————

A horrified Holmes and Chadwick watched helplessly as they held onto the consoles for dear life. The tremor was a particularly bad, sustained one, and they could do nothing save watch as Chadwick's alternate self was kidnapped.

One of the control monitors vibrated toward the edge of the console, and Chadwick shouted, "NO!" She snatched at it, managing to knock it back enough to prevent its crashing to the floor. She braced her feet and leaned forward, attempting to stabilize it.

"Holmes! Help me! If we lose any of the equipment, we'll have to replace it, and we'll lose track of Sis! And if we lose her—"

"We lose everything," Holmes finished for her, lunging forward and spinning around, placing himself at the edge of the console and leaning backward into the bouncing equipment, long arms outstretched to hold it all on the desktop. Chadwick redoubled her efforts to help stabilize the monitors and keyboards, spreading her arms below Holmes' as they attempted to create a human fence to corral the precious electronics until the temblor ceased.

Which it eventually did, a seeming eternity later. Within seconds the pair had checked connections and ports, ensuring everything was still properly hooked together, then they picked up their overturned chairs and sat down.

"Expanding field of view," Holmes noted, keying in parameters, "adjusting locus to ground level plus twenty metres."

"Good," Chadwick agreed. "They turned left out of the study, so they either took the front door..."

"Unlikely, as the risk of being seen from the lane is too great," Holmes remarked.

"...Or the kitchen door," Chadwick finished. "So let's look along the back of the property."

"On it," Holmes nodded. He began executing a grid sweep search, beginning at the rear property line and extending outward, as the pair watched the bottom of the core intently.

"There!" he exclaimed, pointing. "Did you see the blonde head in the rear window of that dark blue automobile? The one with the long scratch upon the side?"

"Bingo," Chadwick said grimly. "As they say in the old movies, 'Follow that car!'"

"You have but to ask, my dear Chadwick," Holmes said, equally grimly.

———

Sherlock arrived at the McFarlane farm, parked the car out of sight, then made straight for the cave entrance, first ensuring there were no observers about. There he found Ryker and several of his—and the other unit's—personnel, just inside the entrance, where they would not be readily visible.

"How is the closure progressing?" Sherlock asked without preamble.

"Oh! Holmes," Ryker said, glancing up from the preliminary sarcophagus plans. "We've about got the wall in place. What are you doing here?"

"I should rather ask why I was so readily allowed in, and why you are surprised by my presence, before answering," Sherlock remarked in a biting tone.

"Because we have dossiers on you and Dr. Chadwick-Holmes," one of the unknown operatives noted, "and I got a call you were coming, when you were still over at the McFarlane croft. I'm Unit Leader Gregory, by the way." He held out a hand.

"Capital," Sherlock said in satisfaction, shaking the proffered hand. "Yes, Ryker here says you and your men are excellent. Keep on your toes, however. Cunningham and Fereaud know the bird has flown the coop, as the saying is, and will likely be on their way here, if, as I suspect, they have accelerated their plans because of it."

"All over it," Ryker said, immediately picking up his radio. "All teams, attention. We are now under Alert Level

One. Repeat, we are now under Alert Level One. Report."

"Team Red copies," came back the first response. "All clear."

"Team Orange copies; clear here."

"Team Yellow copies; compound clear."

"Team Green copies; nothing here."

"Team Blue copies; restraint nearly complete."

"Team Purple copies; we're clean."

Ryker looked expectantly at Sherlock, who nodded.

"Excellent," the detective noted.

"Want to take a look at the lockdown?" Ryker asked the detective.

"I should like that. Do we need MOPP gear?"

"Not at this point, no. The barricade and door are being installed far enough out from the...material...that we don't have to worry about contamination. Besides, it's lead, covered with polyvinyl chloride, to protect it from the elements—it was heavy and awkward as hell to get in there, especially without damaging the PVC, but we did it —and it's already up. They're just anchouring it into the rock and sealing off the edges."

"Then let us go."

The two men walked into the depths of the cave. Just outside the bend leading to the floor collapse, they found the wall. Half of Team Blue was busily setting and acti- vating the last of the pyrotechnic bolts anchoring it into the rock walls of the cavern; the other half was following behind, applying special concrete to seal the edges. In the center of the plastic-coated wall was a big door, nearly the size of the garage door at Gibson House. Beside the door was a card-swipe lock powered by a battery system bolted onto the wall near the base.

"I assume this is the lead-doped concrete?" Sherlock queried, pointing.

"It is. We have to mix it using filter masks and stuff, but it works."

"What about the door? Why is it so large? To allow entry of the sarcophagus construction materials?"

"Bingo," Ryker grinned.

"Do you intend to change out the battery on a regular basis?"

"No," Ryker shook his head. "That battery pack will last until we can get the sarcophagus rebuilt. Once the battery dies, the door becomes permanently locked. Before that happens, the front of the cave is going to be sealed with a stick of dynamite and covered over with regular concrete. We decided to play off the Nazi smuggling idea and put out the story that a Nazi spy, who was prepping for an invasion of Great Britain, stockpiled chemical weapons in here, specifically phenyl dick..."

"What in heaven's name is that?" Sherlock interrupted.

"Oh. It's phenyldichloroarsine," Ryker explained. "It's a vomiting and blister agent, which would explain McFarlane's symptoms, but it's not under the Chemical Weapons Convention ban, so we don't have to report it or have it investigated, and thus raise Bedlam we don't want raised."

"Ah, excellent."

———

"So by the time the phenyl dick was recently discovered, it was unstable and needed to be sealed off, rather than carted off and destroyed."

"Wiggins has given this considerable thought." Sherlock nodded, impressed.

"He has," Ryker grinned. "He has a good teacher. Did he do well?"

"He did excellently, insofar that I can see," Sherlock said, meeting Ryker's eyes.

———

Ryker saw the barest hint of pride in the grey gaze, and his cheeks colored. "Good," he murmured, slightly embarrassed. "He tried hard."

"In that case, I shall leave the matter in Wiggins' most capable hands, and betake myself back to my wife," Sherlock said affably. "I trust you will keep me posted, as I shall, you."

"Of course," Ryker beamed, as he escorted Sherlock out of the cave. Soon Sherlock was en route back to Gibson House.

———

All appeared normal as Sherlock pulled into the drive. He hit the remote control for the garage, mentally shaking his head as he often did at how very much such things had changed since his original day, let alone how rapidly he had adapted to said changes, then parked the car in the garage. He closed the garage door, unlocked the door into the house proper, and stepped into the mudroom to remove his coat and hat.

"Skye!" he called into the house. "I have returned."

No answer.

The sleuth paused briefly, extending his senses as much as humanly possible. *No sound,* he realized. *No conversation, no scrape of chair on floor, no ruffle of pages turning, not so much as the scratch of pencil on paper. Something is not right here.*

Immediately he headed for the study. There, a shocking sight met the detective's eyes: the study was a disaster. Papers were scattered everywhere. The precious notebook of calculations lay splayed open on the floor, its pages crumpled. A marble paperweight had found its way across the room with enough force to produce a dent in the sheet rock, and lay on the floor near the far wall. The desk chair was completely overturned in one corner; the flat-screen computer monitor lay on its face.

Sherlock stood in the middle of the disarranged study, horrified. *Skye is gone,* he realized, *with every sign of having been taken in the midst of a struggle. So it was not the dissolution of the other continuum while the tesseract was active, but another, very human agency. But where has she been taken? I must search the clues, and then I must use my deductive skills to their utmost, or I shall lose the one being I could not bear to lose.*

"Holmes? Holmes, where are you?" he suddenly heard her voice call, and his heart leaped before he recognized that the mode of address was incorrect. Pain shot through him, and he bit his lip momentarily, eyes closed, steeling himself into cool impassivity before answering.

"In the study, Dr. Chadwick," he replied calmly. "Skye —my wife, Skye—has been kidnapped."

"We know," his own voice responded. "We saw it happen, and could do nothing save observe, because we had defocused to allow an instability wave to come through without affecting your continuum. But afterward, we could follow without their awareness—so we did. We have only just returned here from watching."

"Then for God's sake, man, tell me!" Sherlock exclaimed, spinning toward the voices. "Who was it, and where was she taken?"

"It was the two men Dr. Victor was afraid of," Chadwick noted grimly. "The ones who faked the will. They took her to an old abandoned house outside Shottisham. We can show you."

"I'll bring the car around; you follow me, and give directions," Sherlock ordered.

"Of course, old man," Holmes replied. "And we will notify Ryker while you get the auto."

"Capital," Sherlock agreed. "He is at the McFarlane farm, at the cave."

"On it," Chadwick noted.

Sherlock heard the pop of the tesseract as he ran for the garage.

———

The drive from the cottage into Shottisham, with an active tesseract accompanying, was hairy for all concerned. Sherlock floored the accelerator, driving with every bit of FBI-trained skill he possessed, his alternate reality companions having informed him Ryker had cleared the way with local law enforcement.

While Sherlock drove, Chadwick and Holmes kept their hands on the tight tesseract focusing and their eyes on the road, so they could track Sherlock and instruct him en route while avoiding the inadvertent uptake of other vehicles or objects into the wormhole. All three were immensely relieved to arrive at their destination.

"Wait here," Holmes enjoined Sherlock, "while we go in and see what is happening; we will come back and tell you how to proceed."

"Very well," Sherlock replied impatiently. "But—"

"We'll be quick," Chadwick reassured him. "I know how to use this baby to be essentially in two places at once." The grin on her face was audible in her voice, and

Sherlock could not help but respond, mentally seeing the same comforting, if mischievous, grin on his wife's face.

"I know," he said. "Now go."

"Gone," Chadwick murmured. "Back," she added almost immediately.

"And?" Sherlock pressed acerbically.

"Is the cane you used after your fall still in the vehicle?" Holmes asked his alter ego.

"It is," Sherlock replied grimly. "Excellent thought. It is metallic, quite light, and will make a capital weapon."

"I'd prefer a gun," Chadwick said bluntly.

"I have that in my pocket, as well," Sherlock noted.

"Very good. Take both. Here is what you must do..." Holmes began.

6

Murphy's Law

"You're an idiot if you think that," Skye declared angrily, struggling against the rope binding her hands behind her back. "Going in that cave is certain death."

"So you say," Fereaud growled in a thick Gallic accent.

"Right," Cunningham sneered. "Like we're going to believe you. You're just a little housewife anyway. The detective's pretty young trophy wife."

"My name is Dr. Skye Chadwick-Holmes," she announced, incensed. "I'm a physicist. And I'm telling you, what's in that cave is lethally radioactive. I'm trying to save your life!"

"Yeah, sure," Cunningham said, turning away and going to study a map on the table nearby. "Last I checked, gold bullion wasn't lethal."

"Unless it falls on you," Fereaud chuckled, and Cunningham laughed.

"I'm serious!" Skye exclaimed. "You've gotta listen to me. Think about the sores on the cows, and the burns on Mr. McFarlane. Those were radiation burns. I don't care who you are, or what you've done, that's a horrible way to die!"

"Look, I've already told you, your pathetic little horror story isn't gonna work. Now be a good little girl and keep your mouth shut," Cunningham told her bluntly. "We only have you so we can force your husband's government masters to give us what we really want. Play nice, and do as you're told, and you won't get hurt."

"What're you gonna do? Kill me?" Skye scoffed.

"I'd rather not, but if necessary," Cunningham shrugged casually. "So I'd behave if I were you."

"Like that's gonna scare me." Skye sneered. "Dying's easy. You just let go."

———

"You sound as if you know." Cunningham raised an eyebrow, impressed for the first time.

"I do."

"So you don't care if you're killed."

"Nope." Skye's expression was calm and firm.

"But," Cunningham murmured, considering carefully as he observed Skye, "I bet that husband of yours would care."

Blue eyes faltered.

"Uh-huh," Cunningham grunted knowingly, watching her intently. "I thought so."

"Look, guys. What can I do, what can I say, to make you believe me?" Skye began, trying to reason. "Do you know what Cherenkov radiation is? Have you—"

Disgusted and out of patience, Cunningham spun on his heel, turning his back on the scientist. "Fereaud, shut her up."

Fereaud calmly backhanded Skye across the face with

STEPHANIE OSBORN

his fist. He was not gentle. The blow flung the scientist sideways, slamming her into the wall. She lost her footing and fell to the floor, stunned and barely conscious. Cunningham walked across the room, hauled her roughly to her feet and held her upright by the shoulders.

"Listen, I'll gag you if I have to. Now I'm going to tell you one more time. Shut up. Do as you're told, and you might walk away from this." Cunningham dug his fingers into her upper arms to emphasize his point.

"There is no 'might,'" a grim voice snapped behind them. "She will walk away, and you shall answer to me for daring to touch her."

And before either kidnapper could move, a furious avenging angel in detective form materialized in their midst, wielding his cane so swiftly it seemed almost to teleport from place to place.

———

Targeting the pressure points, the cane crashed down across Cunningham's wrists with such force even a dazed Skye heard the loud crack and wondered if the bones had broken. The grip on her arms instantly released. She crumpled to the floor, using her feet to shove herself into the nearby corner and out of the way, as she watched in dumbstruck awe while her husband effected her rescue.

Fereaud reached for his gun as Cunningham howled in pain and staggered back. But Sherlock was already there. The handle of the cane hooked Fereaud's wrist, jerking it away from the jacket pocket in which his pistol was secreted, as Sherlock's fist connected in a solid left cross to Fereaud's chin. The cane detached itself from Fereaud's arm and flipped around deftly, smacking down smartly on the crown of his head. Fereaud went down as if pole-axed.

Without pausing, Sherlock spun to find a fumbling Cunningham trying frantically to draw his own weapon and take aim at Skye. A snarl of raw fury emerged from the detective's throat, and he lunged forward, swinging the cane with all the force he possessed. The metal instrument became a silvery-grey blur, aimed directly at Cunningham's gun hand. There was a loud, nauseating snap as the abused wrist finally broke; the man screamed and dropped the gun from his now-useless hand. It clattered to the floor as Sherlock flung himself at the other man, cane now held in both hands.

He slammed Cunningham against the wall, metal cane pressed against Cunningham's throat, just as Ryker and four of his men burst into the room.

———

"You dared harm my wife," Sherlock growled. "The Evil One himself could not be lower in my eyes, or more deserving of retribution."

He shoved the cane harder against Cunningham's throat. Cunningham began to gasp and squirm desperately, struggling to retain a clear airway against the pressure on his trachea.

Fear filled his eyes as he realized that the detective likely intended to crush his windpipe.

———

Behind Holmes, Ryker's breath caught, as the Secret Service unit burst in, spread out and drew down on the scene.

"Holmes," Ryker murmured calmingly, "you've got

backup. The Boss is in the corner, and looks reasonably well. Everything's under control. Let us have him."

But Sherlock didn't move. He merely continued to stare into Cunningham's terrified blue eyes with a furious, merciless glare. His own grey gaze was dark, hard, and cold as ice.

―――――

Just then, a firm, calm voice from the corner spoke.

"Let him go, Sherlock. I'm okay. Don't do it. Please."

The detective blinked, then eased the pressure on Cunningham's windpipe without looking away from the man.

"You are certain, Skye?" he asked, daring the briefest glance at his wife from the corner of his eye.

"I'm a little bunged up, but I'll be all right," she said, averting her face to ensure he wouldn't see the bruising until after he'd released Cunningham. Holmes stepped back, letting the cane drop with one hand as it swung into its normal position.

"This vermin is yours, Ryker," he noted with distaste. "Please see that it is handled...appropriately."

―――――

Ryker gestured to two of his men, who instantly stepped in to take control of a badly shaken and decidedly injured Cunningham; an unconscious Fereaud was already hand-cuffed on the floor. The unit leader caught Holmes by the elbow while Murphy untied Skye's hands and gently helped her to her feet.

"C'mon," Ryker murmured, gently ushering them both

toward the door, "Enid—Dr. Wilder—is right outside, waiting to see about you. We'll take care of these two."

————

Outside, Holmes discovered his wife's true condition as Wilder examined her. She was badly bruised across most of the right side of her body where it had slammed into the wall. Her left cheek was puffy and lacerated from a ring Fereaud had been wearing; her left eye was blackened, and swollen nearly shut. Dr. Wilder delicately palpated Skye's cheek and eye orbital, checking for damage to the bone, before easing her patient's mouth open and inspecting her teeth, which were, for a wonder, all intact. Finally she nodded in satisfaction, and applied an antibiotic ointment to the lacerations.

"Nothing broken, just soft tissue trauma," Wilder said quietly, with an encouraging smile. "And it should all heal up with no scarring. As a precaution, we might take a few x-rays in a day or so, when the swelling has subsided, but I don't think you have anything to worry about. If the cheekbone or orbital were broken, you'd have howled like a banshee just now, when I palpated it. You'll be fine, Mrs. Holmes."

"She looks like she has been through hell," Holmes grumbled, pale with fury. "I arrived just in time to see the other man strike her—he knocked her halfway across the room."

"I'll be okay, Sherlock," Skye murmured through swollen lips. "Yeah, they were rough, but I'm all right."

"They did not...abuse...you in any other fashion, before I arrived, did they?" he queried intensely.

————

One look at his face told Skye he would not be put off, and even Dr. Wilder turned anxiously to watch her response.

"No," Skye said calmly. "They manhandled me when they first kidnapped me, 'cause I tried to fight back, but they only hit me the once, which you saw. And they didn't do...anything else." She added in discouragement, "I was still too weak to fight very well, I'm afraid."

Sherlock sighed in relief, and both he and Wilder relaxed.

———

"I think perhaps I shall teach you a few more hand-to-hand defensive measures. Something which will be effective regardless of your energy levels. Perhaps some Eastern martial arts will do." Sherlock sighed again, concerned at the degree of physical punishment his wife had taken in recent weeks.

Skye echoed his sigh, and looked up at her husband with a pleading expression that wrenched his heart.

"What do you want, my dear?" he murmured in response to that expression.

"Can we go home now?" she whispered. "I mean, back to Gibson House."

"Immediately, if not sooner," Holmes replied softly.

———

Back at the cottage, Skye went to the sofa in the sitting room and eased gingerly into a seated position. Sherlock brought an ice pack for her cheek, then watched from the kitchen door, eyes narrowed in pain.

This was all because of me, he decided gloomily, sinking deep into his own thoughts. *Because I violated my precepts*, *because I allowed her close. They targeted her to reach me. For the first time, I believe I may understand the other Sherlock's rationale in toto.*

"Quit that," Skye murmured, leaning her aching head back against the sofa and holding the tea-towel-wrapped ice pack against her face.

"Quit what?" he wondered, struggling to grasp her antecedent, his musings interrupted.

"Blaming yourself for this," she sighed, closing her eyes wearily. "I'm proud and happy to be your wife. I did try to tell them I wasn't the ignorant little drudge they thought, but it wasn't what they wanted to hear. That's why they hit me. Not because of you."

"But they kidnapped you because of me."

"And I'm no slouch at defending myself, despite the hand-to-hand thing." Skye shrugged. "If I'd been applying your principles, they'd never have gotten close, because I'd have seen them coming a mile away."

"No," Sherlock heard his own voice murmur regretfully, "instead, she was engrossed in her science, helping us."

"Yeah," Chadwick's voice sighed guiltily. "And her still weak from being sick."

"Yes, the science, AND what to make for dinner, AND when Sherlock was gonna get home, AND how the case was progressing, and running over the clues, AND, AND, AND, on and on," Skye protested.

"Still," Sherlock muttered, "if it were not for the fact we married..."

"No, no, Holmes," Chadwick corrected. "She's right. If we hadn't distracted her..."

Suddenly Skye snapped into an upright position, letting the ice pack fall to her lap. Her swollen face contorted into an angry scowl.

"SHUT UP AND CUT IT OUT! JUST SHUT UP!

ALL of you! It's nobody's fault except the two men who kidnapped me! I was busy, I had my mind on a dozen other things, and they snuck up on me! It's that simple! Now everybody, just...be..." Skye's face crumpled, and abruptly she was struggling to restrain tears, "quiet..."

Sherlock came to the sofa and knelt beside her.

"Skye, forgive me," he whispered, taking her delicately by the shoulders with a gentle hold, trying to avoid the bruises there. "I only...I do not like seeing you in pain."

———

"I know," she sighed, leaning into him and resting her good cheek on his shoulder. "I'm just...it scared me." She buried her face in his neck, ashamed at the confession.

"I bet I know why," Chadwick offered softly, through the wormhole. "Two reasons: You were afraid we wouldn't get the tesseract solution completed, and...you didn't want to leave Sherlock alone."

———

"Y-yes," Skye's muffled voice came from Sherlock's shoulder. "To both." The detective slid his arms around his wife, holding her comfortingly.

"Perhaps you would feel better if you ate a bit," he murmured. "I have it to understand you were captured before tea-time, and it is past dinner now."

"No, I'm just tired," Skye fretted. "And my head hurts from getting hit. I wasn't in their hands long; it's no big deal. I only want to go to bed."

"No, Sis, you need to eat, just a little," Chadwick scolded gently. "Let your hubby feed you a little something, then go to bed."

"And might I make a suggestion, Chadwick?" Holmes offered. "These two have done much for us. I think that perhaps it is more than past time for us to give something back. Perchance we can use the tesseract to stand guard over the house while she rests, that they may feel the safer?"

"Wonderful idea, Holmes!" Chadwick agreed immediately. "We can keep it a little out of focus to isolate any instability waves, and stay outside for privacy—maybe hovering above the house—and scan the area around the cottage so nobody can get in without warning."

"That would be greatly appreciated," Sherlock decided, seeing Skye was too emotional to answer. "Now, Skye, I know what it is to be struck in the face, so I will repair to the kitchen and prepare some soup while you rest here. Will that be acceptable? Do you think you can eat it?"

"I...I suppose so," she sniffled, pushing up. "But...um..."

"'Um' what?"

"Can I come along?" she whispered, unable to meet the grey eyes. "I...don't wanna be alone..."

"Of course, my dear," he murmured, eyes narrowing in pain.

"We shall remove to the outside of the cottage, my friends," Holmes noted softly. "The two of you need peace and quiet. We will keep close watch. Let yourselves rest well this night, for a change. Between Captain Ryker, and ourselves, no one shall reach you tonight. This I swear."

"WE swear," Chadwick added firmly.

"Thanks, guys," Skye murmured, as Sherlock helped her to her feet and led her toward the kitchen.

———

In the end, Skye was too drained to eat on her own. A certain detective put her to bed, brought in a tray, and helped her eat a large bowl of vegetable soup.

"You know, you once told me you weren't cut out to be a nursemaid," Skye sighed, as Sherlock fed her the last of the soup. "But lately you sure seem to be doing it a lot."

"I will not stand by and permit you to suffer, if there is anything I can do to prevent it." He shrugged. "I made vows to you, Skye, before God and every friend we had in this plane of existence. Even had I not meant them—and I certainly would never have made them had I not meant them—I would still feel bound by my word."

"Thank you, Sweetheart. You know," Skye said, recalling, "you were...that was..."

———

Her voice tapered off, and she blushed.

"That was what?" Sherlock wondered, not certain to what she was referring. He sat the bowl aside.

"I saw you fighting," she said shyly. "You're really amazing. I mean, I've seen you fight a couple times before—in your own continuum—and you're good. Really, really good. But before, you were always fighting for your life. This time, you put your own life in danger to fight for ME. My own knight, literally, coming to the rescue. It...you..." Skye lunged forward, wrapping her arms around him. "You're wonderful. I love you so much."

Sherlock felt his face flame before gathering his wife against his chest.

"Do you recall what I told you on my birthday, after we had gone to bed? When you were asking me about your importance in my life?"

"Yeah?"

"Do you recall my answer?"

"Yes..."

"How could I do any less?" Holmes shrugged.

Skye smiled as best she could, pushing back and looking up at him. Then she stretched up and brushed his lips with her own. Sherlock returned the gesture very tentatively, all too aware how bruised and swollen were the lips caressing his.

Then he gently put her away from him and reached for the bottle of naproxen Wilder had given them.

"Here," he murmured, extracting a dose, "take this, and try to relax, my dear girl. While you settle in, I shall prepare for bed, and we will make this an early evening." He turned and held out the medication in his cupped hand, all in one motion. To his horror, Skye flinched away.

"Skye?" he whispered, stunned. "What...?"

"I'm sorry, I'm sorry," Skye whimpered. She buried her battered face in her hands. "When you spun and put out your hand, for a split second, I saw...him...instead of you."

"Oh, my dear Skye," Sherlock breathed, gathering her into his arms. "You know I should never—"

"I know," she whispered, hiding her face in his chest. "That's why I said I was sorry! I know you wouldn't. But...you might have to move kinda slow around me for a couple days, until I get things under control."

"Of course," he murmured, stroking her hair. "Of course."

After several minutes, Skye eased away and reached for her glass on the bedside table. Sherlock gave her the tablets; she took them, and five minutes later they were both in bed.

———

Intimacy was eschewed that night in favor of rest. Sleep did not come easily for either of them, however. Skye's battered body refused to get comfortable, and Sherlock found himself focused on her attempts to find, if not a cozy position, at least one that did not cause pain.

"Perhaps if you rested against me more," he suggested, a full hour into her restless perambulations.

"No," she grumbled, shifting position yet again. "I can barely stand to have my bad cheek against the feather pillow. Your shoulder's a little too solid to rest it against."

"Hold still," he instructed, crawling out from under the covers.

"Sherlock? What are you—"

"I said hold still, my dear," he said amiably, clambering across the bed, directly across Skye, meticulously avoiding bumping her. Soon he was on her other side, flipping open the blankets and scooting beneath them. "There. We shall simply have to become used to sleeping on the 'wrong' side of the bed, until your face is well. I do hope your right side was not introduced to the wall sufficiently hard to prevent lying on it."

"It's kinda sore, but nothing like my face," Skye admitted, rolling gingerly onto her side and snuggling into Holmes with a relieved sigh. "Yeah, this is gonna work, I think."

Fifteen minutes later, both were at long last asleep.

———

They slept late the next morning, Skye needing the rest to heal and recover from her mental, emotional, and physical trauma. She awoke in pain, but Sherlock got some soft breakfast food into her, then gave her a prescription dose of naproxen for the pain. The detective was careful to move slowly and calmly around her, and in short order, she was feeling better.

"Okay," she murmured, "time to get back in the saddle. I'm almost done with the number crunching, and then I can hand it all over to the Other Me and the other you."

"But Wife," Sherlock protested, "should you not wait until after you are no longer on pain medication? How can you know you will be thinking clearly enough to 'crunch numbers' correctly, as you put it?"

"Oh, naproxen doesn't do that to me," Skye waved away his concern. "I'll admit, it used to make Caitlin pretty loopy, but I never had that problem. For me, it's just super-duper aspirin. I'll be fine."

"Very well. As my case appears to be complete, and Ryker's message this morning indicated that they have developed a method and logistical plan for permanently sealing the sarcophagus, I shall keep you company. If you have no objections to my pipe smoke."

"Nope," Skye grinned at him as best she could; her face was still swollen and she had a distinct black eye. "We're on the home stretch, and the end is in sight, Hon."

"It does appear so," Sherlock noted in relief. "But Skye?"

"Yeah?"

"You really did not need to compete with my record of black eyes to impress me, my dear."

They both began laughing.

————

Later that morning, an urgent call came in from Ryker. Skye, needing a momentary break from her numbers, answered it, careful to hold the receiver to the uninjured side of her face.

"Gibson House. Skye here. Hi there, Brae. Oh—oh no. No, no, no. Oh, shit! Do you know where?!" The scientist was obviously alarmed, and not a little afraid.

"What is wrong, Skye?" Sherlock rose from his seat in the wing chair and moved to stand close.

"Hang on, Brae, so I can fill in Sherlock." She glanced up at him. "Brae says Cunningham and Fereaud have escaped, and killed at least one policeman in the process. Two more are in hospital. It seems Brae's unit turned them over to the local authorities, on charges of kidnapping and murder. The police took them to the hospital to be treated —Fereaud had a concussion, and Cunningham's wrist had to be set and cast—and there was some sort of major snafu when they were released from the hospital. They're on the loose."

"Where are they?" Sherlock snarled, cold fury rising within.

———

"Did you hear that, Brae?" Skye asked the phone. She listened, then looked back at her husband. "Nobody knows yet. He wants us to be careful."

"Tell him we shall be. Exceedingly so."

"You hear, Brae? Okay. Um...keep us posted? Yeah. Yeah, it scares me, but I'd rather know. You need to go ahead and seal off that cave, Brae, as soon as possible. To hell with the sarcophagus for now. You can always go back in later and do that, then seal things off again. Listen, have you got a spare pistol? We've only got the one...oh. Yeah, I understand. Well, but I'm a representative of the Crown...yeah? Okay, good. Yeah, bring it by as soon as you get the chance." She hung up and looked at Sherlock. "He's gonna come by with another gun, so we can both be armed."

"As far as that is concerned, we can manage in the meanwhile." Sherlock disappeared down the hall, returning with the service pistol while casually swinging his cane. He handed the gun to his wife. "There. That is now accomplished."

"What is accomplished?" Sherlock's own voice echoed back. Skye jumped, badly startled, then shook a worried head.

"Fereaud and Cunningham got loose," she informed their doppelgangers, realizing the tesseract had just focused in and neither she nor Sherlock had registered the whiff of ozone, so intent on defensive preparations had they been.

"Oh, no," Chadwick could be heard to whisper.

"I'm expecting Captain Ryker in a few minutes, with a pistol for me—er, Sherlock," Skye noted, shoving the pistol her husband had just given her into the rear waistband of her jeans.

"We shall widen the focus to watch for him, and defocus to allow him entrance, when he arrives," Holmes conceded immediately.

"Thanks," Skye nodded gratefully.

"Hm," Sherlock muttered to himself. Then he raised his voice. "May I take it you can observe more than the interior of a room?"

"We can change the size of the field of view, yeah. We can take it down to almost the size of a car, which is what we did last night, or we can include the whole house," Chadwick confirmed. "We just haven't expanded it because of the danger of instability waves."

"'The best defense is a strong offense,' you are thinking, Brother Other Me?" Holmes queried.

"Indeed," Sherlock agreed. "If the two of you can stand guard over Skye—who is in no shape to pursue the game at the moment—I can join Ryker in tracking down the miscreants who harmed her and two policemen, and killed McFarlane and another police officer. They cannot be allowed to run free, especially with the sarcophagus undergoing repairs."

"What he said," Chadwick said. "We'll do it, Holmes. Um, MR. Holmes. You do what you need to do, and we'll notify you if anything suspicious arises."

"Ryker is on approach," Holmes observed.

"Excellent," Sherlock breathed. "Skye, are you all right with this plan?"

"Yeah, I think so. The naproxen helps, and I feel better than I did, but you're right, I don't feel at all up to going out hunting bad guys. I just wanna get these numbers run. And maybe take a nap when I'm finished. And having these guys," she jerked her thumb in the direction of their counterparts' voices, "around will keep me from being, or feeling, alone. It'll work."

"Very well. Do you sit back down and work on your calculations, while Ryker and I seek out these blackguards."

"Do not worry, Other Me," Holmes promised. "Chadwick and I shall keep a close watch, in addition to aiding your wife. If necessary, we can perform a lock-out with the tesseract, in the which case no miscreant shall be able to reach her, although it may give away the presence of the tesseract, which is admittedly not desirable; nevertheless. And we shall also endeavour to defocus swiftly if we feel a tremor coming upon us, and refocus as soon as may be."

"Capital," Sherlock replied, as a knock sounded upon the front door. He deposited a swift peck on Skye's good cheek, then headed for the door, grabbing coat and hat en route. "And my dear, I shall see YOU as soon as may be."

Then he was gone.

———

Outside, Ryker handed Sherlock the new weapon, and the sleuth tucked it into the concealed carry holster in his jeans, then shot a pointed look at the operative.

"The word is still unknown," Ryker informed him in response to that look.

"There are only two real options," Sherlock observed. "They are either headed out of the country, or they are headed back to the farm."

"True. We've got the borders on lockdown and an All Ports Warning issued on the two. I'll be notified immediately they're sighted, if they're trying to get out."

"Then let us to the McFarlane farm, and see what may be seen. But perhaps we should take both automobiles, in case we should need to split up."

"Okay. But should we leave the Boss alone?" Ryker wondered worriedly.

"She is not alone," Sherlock noted sanguinely. "She has the first pistol, and you know how well she handles those. Also, the Other Me and the other her are here, and keeping a close eye out."

"We are, indeed," Holmes' voice sounded softly. "Both inside and outside. All is well."

Ryker jumped slightly. "Hell's bells," he muttered, annoyed he had startled. "I canNOT get used to that. If I didn't know better, I'd think you were a ventriloquist, Holmes."

"I am," both Holmeses said simultaneously, with amusement.

STEPHANIE OSBORN

"Let's go." Ryker rolled his eyes.
They went.

———

One Holmes, one Chadwick-Holmes, and one Chadwick pushed hard to get the last of the scientific work completed to repair the tesseract. Aside from the obvious guard factor, and in despite of the instability danger, Skye was glad to have the wormhole including the entire house; it was quite convenient. It meant she could easily slip into the kitchen for a drink, or a snack, without needing to stop work or break off a brainstorming conversation. It also made her feel more secure, as she realized her compatriots could, if needed, "isolate the subject"—namely, her—and no one from outside could reach her.

So well did matters go that, in about an hour and a half, their work was complete. The details of what both Skyes mischievously referred to as "the brane drain" were thoroughly specified; the degree of variance from its rest energy was determined; and the method for fine tuning the string beam was developed. Even the way they intended to boost the brane had been thoroughly sketched out.

"By golly, I think that's got it," Skye said, elated.

"Thank God," Chadwick murmured fervently.

Holmes, who had been watching the instrumentation for some weeks, and was now becoming adept at predicting instability waves, announced, "It may be wise to reduce the size of focus, ladies. I do not like the readings I am seeing."

"Okay, yeah," Chadwick agreed after a moment. "I see what you're seeing. Take it down to just inside the room walls, and have your hands on the controls, ready to defocus. Sorry, Sis."

"No problem," Skye shrugged. "Better that than a big

mess. And I'm armed now."

"What you said," Chadwick averred. "Let's double-check the numbers, then we can go start work, and you can have a real break."

"Okay," Skye agreed. "We start off with the Berken-stein entropy of the string beam..."

———

Ryker and Holmes drove straight for the McFarlane farm, where they searched all the buildings, then moved through the fields. Ryker used his ciphered radio to check in with his men guarding the cave; they had seen nothing.

When every inch of the farm had been covered, Ryker shook his head.

"Maybe our APW will pick 'em up," he hoped. "I'm going back to local HQ and see if anything's come in."

"Very well. I believe I," Holmes decided, "shall pop by the Carvers and warn them to be on the lookout, then return to Gibson House."

"Stay in touch," Ryker said, and the two men parted.

———

Holmes popped by the Carver's dog breeding farm and informed them of the fugitives who might be in the vicin-ity. He dissembled only mildly in his explanation, noting that they falsely believed old Nazi gold to be hidden in the cave, and the men were more than willing to kidnap, injure, or kill to get it.

"And as you are adjacent to poor Mr. McFarlane's estate, it may be they will attempt hiding somewhere upon your property," Sherlock explained. "It is unlikely, given your most excellent dogs, who would, no doubt, raise a disturbance; but still, it is possible. Under no circumstances should you confront them, if you suspect them to be here. They are extremely dangerous, and will not hesitate to kill. Contact myself or my wife at once, then leave immediately if at all possible, and we will see that appropriate authorities are brought in to apprehend them."

"Gracious," Mrs. Carver murmured, paling. "The good Lord help us."

"Stay calm, Mrs. Carver," Sherlock soothed. "I think you are in little danger. Not only do you have the protection of your dogs, but also the fact your property is well frequented will serve as a deterrent. The men are far more likely to take refuge in the empty buildings of McFarlane's property. These, therefore, are being closely, if clandestinely, scrutinised. Nevertheless, I thought you deserved a warning, as a precaution. In any case, I'm sure the notable young Brendan and his littermates will put up a hue and cry, should anything untoward occur. I am seriously considering discussing the matter with my wife, and then purchasing the pup, when all this is over."

"Aw," Carver and his wife exchanged odd looks. "I sure wisht I'd'a known that afore now, Mr. Holmes. Y' see, Brendan, him's already been sold. Bought an' paid. I only got t' finish th' little feller's trainin', an' then he'll be sent off to 'is new owner."

"Blast," Sherlock said bitterly. "I should have acted sooner." He sighed. "Well, I shall definitely keep you in mind for the future, Mr. Carver. Your pups are excellent, and in my line of work, one may well come in handy."

"We'll be sure to keep an eye out f'r ya f'r another un like Brendan," Mrs. Carver agreed.

"Very well. Contact me should you see anything suspicious," Sherlock reminded, and departed for Gibson House.

———

"Guys?" Skye queried.

"Yeah, Sis?" Chadwick replied absently, studying her notations.

"Would you mind defocusing so I can...er, run down the hall for a minute?" Skye requested. "Only...don't go away. Stick around and keep an eye out, if you don't mind."

"You have but to wish it, milady," Holmes answered cheerfully and with more than a hint of humor. He defocused the tesseract, then watched as Skye exited the room. "She drinks as much coffee and tea as you do, Chadwick," he teased his companion gently.

"Yeah, too much," Chadwick admitted with a wry grimace, "but hey, it's caffeine. It keeps us going when the going gets tough. And long."

"True," Holmes agreed.

"Hey, where'd she leave the notebook?"

"Mm..." Holmes scanned the room inside the core of the tesseract with his sharp grey eyes. "Over there, on the corner of the desk."

"I need to take a quick look at something in it. 'Cause I'm not sure I copied it right. It won't take a second. Do you suppose we can readjust the focus and I can snag a peek...?"

"It should be simple enough, and will make use of the time Dr. Chadwick-Holmes is...ahem, relieving herself."

"Okay, let's do it," Chadwick grinned.

Swiftly the pair adjusted the centroid of the wormhole terminus, centering it upon the notebook on the desk, then focused in. Chadwick rose and moved to stand near one of the monoliths, craning her neck to look at the scribbles of her counterpart.

"Okay, good," she noted. "That's what I thou—"

A rumble began, swiftly increasing in intensity, as the entire Chamber began to shake violently about them.

"Chadwick!" Holmes shouted, alarmed, as the scientist lurched all too close to the edge of the tesseract. "I cannot control the locus, or the field of view! Grab for the monolith!"

Instead, Chadwick spun and dove for the back wall of the Chamber, yelling, "HOLMES! EMERGENCY SHUTDOWN!"

"Shutting down—NOW!" Holmes cried.

A blast wave erupted from the terminating wormhole, as the quake shook the entire continuum.

––––––

Sherlock was returning to Gibson House from the sortie with Ryker, leaving the MI-5 agent and his team to see to the McFarlane farm, just as the tremor hit. He didn't feel it until he stepped from the car, then abruptly realized the very ground beneath his feet was shaking, and it was growing stronger by the second. Within four to five seconds, the earthquake was too strong to stand upright, and he lunged away from the automobile parked in the drive, trying to get away from the potential danger it caused, as it shifted, lurched, and bounced about with the ground motion. Grasping a nearby tree trunk to stabilize himself momentarily, he flung himself into a clearing in the yard, away from anything that might fall upon him, then sprawled upon the ground to wait out the shock.

––––––

When the temblor subsided, Sherlock scrambled for the

front door of the cottage, sprinting for the library, where Skye had her desk and computer. An earthquake in this region of England could only mean one thing: The tesseract had been active when a gravity wave had come through it—a large one. *A very large one*, Sherlock decided with deep concern, fully grasping that it should not have been felt outside the tesseract core. *Possibly THE large one.*

He ran into the library of the cottage, where he found several overturned chairs, a few dozen books scattered helter-skelter across the floor, and the computer's flat screen upended again, but fortunately undamaged. He also found only half of the rickety old rocking chair, which had long since migrated from the sitting room, and a corner missing from a bookcase. Both were clean-edged, as if the other part had simply been sliced away.

What he did not find was his wife.

"Skye?" he called urgently. "Skye, my dear? Where are you?" There was no answer.

"SKYE!" he shouted into the depths of the cottage, at the top of his lungs. "SKYE HOLMES! ANSWER ME! *WHERE ARE YOU??*"

He got no reply.

He paused, and the grey eyes darkened, narrowing in pain.

"Skye?" he whispered, and the word was almost a plea, as agony shot through his being like a lance.

She is gone, some part of his mind whispered in despair. The straight shoulders slumped; the proud head bowed. *It is over*, that same part decided. *Not only my life, but perhaps all that is. It is only a matter of time now. A matter of waiting for the end.*

Sherlock turned and staggered blindly out of the room, aimlessly headed down the hall.

A light hand laid itself on his arm, and he spun instinctively, dropping into a slight crouch.

———

"Sherlock? Are you all right?" Skye asked worriedly, peering up at him. "You're white to the lips..."

Grey eyes blinked disbelievingly at her bruised face, as the despondent mind behind them struggled to comprehend.

"Skye?" he whispered, stunned. "Skye, is it you? Are you...here?"

"Yes, Sherlock, I'm here," she confirmed, understanding exactly what had happened to her husband and what was wrong. Concern etched itself into her face. "I was, erm, in the bathroom when the instability wave came through." She steered him through the adjacent door into the sitting room and eased him into a seated position on the sofa. "Chadwick and Holmes defocused the tesseract temporarily so I could take a little break. I guess they focused back in for some reason, so I felt the wave come through, and hunkered down on the bathroom floor until it was over. I suppose after that, they decided to shut down the tesseract rather than risk anything bad happening while waiting for me to come back; I heard the 'pop' it makes when it shuts down, but it was really loud, so I'm thinking they did an emergency deactivation. Then I heard you shouting, but the entire bathroom shelf rack, complete with all the towels and bath sheets and tissues and bottles and stuff, fell over on me during the quake, and I had to dig out before I could get to you. I tried yelling, but between being buried in terrycloth and the door being closed, I guess you couldn't hear me."

"Are you hurt?" Dilated grey eyes gazed up at her from the sofa.

"No, I'm okay. I didn't mean to scare you."

"I am quite all right." Sherlock waved away the remark.

"I know," Skye murmured, seeing past the attempt at nonchalance. "You always are. But I'm kinda shook," she admitted truthfully. "Would you mind stretching out with me on the sofa for a few minutes?"

"Of course, my dear," Sherlock responded immediately, moving over and holding out an arm. "Lie down and I shall hold you until you have settled."

———

The pair stretched out on the couch. Each wore a calm expression, but their pulse rates belied it, for their nerves were wound tight. In moments they were locked in a fierce, passionate kiss. The detective twisted, pinning his wife between his body and the back of the sofa, pressing close to let her feel his response.

"Skye," he breathed into her mouth, deft fingers tugging at her shirt.

———

"Not here. If they come back, they'll check to make sure I'm okay. This is the first place they'll look, after the study. There are only two rooms they won't risk intruding on…"

Suddenly she found herself scooped up, borne down the hall, and through the bedroom door. That same door was unceremoniously kicked closed behind them. Within moments naked limbs entangled in the middle of the bed, and seconds after, Skye's whole body was being adored, as firm lips deposited urgent kisses from crown to sole.

———

Somewhere in the midst of sensuality, Sherlock came to the realization that, since the tesseract was down, the cottage was completely without guard, and had been for at least an hour. He managed to locate his discarded trousers and fish the cell phone from them, while a distinctly amorous Skye attacked various areas of his skin with soft, moist lips.

"Ryker," he said into the phone, exerting great effort to concentrate on the conversation, "Holmes. Could you possibly send a guard t-to Gibson House? Well, it seems the tesseract experienced a s-severe instability. Sk-kye seems to think they performed an emergency de...activation, which means they w-will be some time recovering. Yes, precisely. Yes, that would be capital. No, just a light tap on the door will be sufficient. I have been inside tending to Skye—no, no, she was uninjured, merely...shaken. She is still jumpy, you know, and understandably so. Yes, a sweep of the perimeter is probably called for. Excellent."

Sherlock closed the phone and gave himself to Skye's attentions, managing to reserve a part of his mind for alert observation, in the event of an emergency.

Ten minutes later, a light tap came at the front door, and the detective turned his full consideration to his wife once more.

———

Several hours later, they still held each other tightly. The veil hiding a certain detective's sensitive heart had been temporarily ripped away by recent events, and as a result, that detective's wife had been given a sure and unequivocal knowledge of her place and importance in his life.

"Mmh...Skye," he murmured, pulling her close again.

"Shh, Sherlock, hush," she whispered, wrapping her arms around him and stroking the back of his neck with gentle fingers. "Everything is fine. I'm okay. And with any luck, the continuum will be stabilized soon."

"I know," he breathed into the golden hair. "I know everything you say is true. I fear I cannot explain the force of my reactions."

"I can. Months of dreams of losing me in spacetime, of being left alone in a world that's not your own, and then those dreams manifesting—after a fashion, anyway—in reality? The strain of a bizarre case, coupled with the knowledge that, at any moment, I could be jerked away, beyond all reach? That the membrane could collapse and destroy, not only their reality, but ours, too? Not to mention my getting kidnapped by crazy treasure seekers. That's a helluva lotta stress, Sweetheart."

"That is still little excuse. Good Lord, Skye, at this rate you will be unable to function properly tomorrow. At this rate, *I* will be unable to function properly tomorrow."

"So?" she giggled, catching him by the hipbones and tugging him closer. "We're newlyweds. And I've been either sick as a dog, or bent over a desk, for days and days."

Dark brows rose over silver eyes, and Sherlock sighed long-sufferingly.

"Very well, if you wish. But do not complain to me if you cannot walk correctly on the morrow."

Skye giggled again as Sherlock flipped the covers over their heads.

7

Considerations

Some time after, the pair awoke in the wee small hours before dawn, relaxed and content.

"Sherlock," Skye murmured, as her husband's sensitive fingers trailed over her skin, "I have a question."

"Indeed? What might it be?"

"It's really, really personal."

"And my fingers upon your breast are not?"

"Okay, you asked for it." A giggle floated through the darkness.

"I did."

"I don't understand how it is that you can spend pretty much all night making love to me, and yet when you were in your own continuum, you never even so much as looked at a woman. At least after the 'Lily' incident." She paused thoughtfully. "Our entire relationship as lovers has indicated you've got a strong libido. How on earth did you...?"

Sherlock felt his cheeks grow warm, thankful for the darkness.

"Yes. It seems I do. It is, I think, partially a function of my artistic heritage. I had been considering the matter earlier this evening, after you fell asleep. I had not planned for any other eyes save mine to see this, but...perhaps it is as well that I permit you to read this evening's journal entry. It is, quite likely, the...best...way of answering your question."

———

"Okay," Skye murmured into the darkness, well aware of her husband's reticence on the subject, "my eyes are covered. Hit the lamp."

Sherlock switched on the bedside lamp, then extracted his journal from the bedside table and turned to the last few pages while Skye uncovered her eyes and allowed them to adjust.

"Here," he said, very subdued. "It is...not something of which I am especially proud, but as my wife, you have the right to know." He placed the journal in her lap, then watched her face as she began to read.

———

February 24
3:32 A.M.

I have recently come to a startling conclusion. I believe narcotics no longer have a hold upon me, nor will they, ever again.

When I first started using cocaine and morphine, they were believed to be wonder drugs, with no thought of harm from them—the dangerous, addictive components of opium and coca were believed removed in the refining and purifying. My rationale for use was rather more cryptic than Watson gave me credit, however. The drugs—cocaine in particular, which was my preferred of the two, as its withdrawal effects were less...indisposing—indeed had stimulating effects upon the mind as he thought, and that is all I allowed Watson to believe, right to the end...though he may have suspected more. But it was not principally for its mental effects that I utilised the drug.

For...certain researchers...had discovered that cocaine in particular heightened the senses, sometimes to the point of ecstasy, and this could occur in a...shall we say, a VERY private fashion. Therefore, shortly after administering the dose, I usually retired to my room; there, Watson believed, to sleep off the effects. And this I did do, eventually. In point of fact, however, my reclusiveness at such times was to relieve said ecstasy in private; it was my relief from my imposed celibacy. And I only and ever used it between cases, never during.

For the effect upon my manhood and desires after the medication had worn off was precisely the opposite: All desires were then SUPPRESSED. Watson often noted my lack of appetite for food in the early days of our relationship, but did not equate it with the drug use. Nor did he recognise my lack of interest in women as partially enabled by the same. And this usage was deliberate. It helped ensure my head could not be turned while I was actively pursuing a case. Consequently it also enabled me to focus even more upon my observation and deduction.

But as time progressed, and Watson protested more and more at my use, research began to emerge proving the good doctor correct. Neither cocaine nor morphine was such as a man respecting his own intellect, let alone his body, should utilise for any reason, saving for the direst of pain or emergency. It was then I decided, what with my increasing age (being no longer a very young man in his prime, but nearing middle age) and habitual spurning of the opposite sex, that I could do without the artificial suppression. I therefore attempted to eliminate the use of both cocaine and morphine. This proved disastrous. I VERY shortly found that I had, to my horror, become addicted to the wretched stuff.

God bless Watson, for he had experience treating opium addicts, and he recognised delirium tremens when he saw it, no matter how adeptly I sought to conceal it. With a directness which did credit to his absorption of my techniques, he deduced my attempts and set out to help. After considerable research, he contacted some specialists on the continent—always from his consulting-rooms, and always with his patient anonymous. For, quite aside from the loss of confidence by prospective clients, it would not have done for my enemies, especially Moriarty, to have gotten wind of my condition; it would have meant a death sentence, possibly for both of us. And thus he eventually developed a technique to wean me from the insidious substances.

And so I became free of them, and so Watson allowed all references to them in his stories to fade away. Thus I believed myself also free of considerations of feminine attraction—until I met Skye. Initially I thought this as potentially disastrous as the narcotic addiction.

But here is the interesting fact: Skye is the only woman who garners my attentions in the least. Other females I may acknowledge as women, even attractive women, but only she is The Woman, My Wife. And SHE has become my "drug" of choice.

For I know she is always there when I should need or want her, and her response will be as fervent as my own. And it matters not any longer if I may need my "drug" during a case, for Skye most assuredly does not create in me the mental distortions of cocaine or morphine, and as soon as need is sated, my attention can fully focus upon the case once more. Indeed, sometimes she provides the divertissement my subconscious needs to work upon the problem, in precisely the same way as my violin, or a concert. Not to mention the fact that she is often beside me on said case, and even when not, is entirely capable of discussing it with me in minute detail, a thing which is a decided boon to the work. No drug can accomplish anything remotely akin to the many and varied abilities she brings me.

Moreover, the last thing I should wish is to do anything to harm that delightful conjugal relationship we share. This, cocaine would definitely do.

So it is that I conclude that narcotics no longer have a hold upon me— though I shall not tempt Providence by using them except in the direst of emergency injuries.

Rather, a certain scientist and detective holds me far more strongly than ever said narcotics did.

What a powerful thing is love.

———

Skye took her time, considering the entire matter carefully, and Sherlock realized from her expression that she was mentally placing herself in his position. When she got to the last page, she completed the entry, then sat staring at the page. Sherlock drew in a deep breath, trying to settle himself.

"Skye?" he queried hesitantly.

"I get it," she said, nodding. "It makes sense. It worked for you, at least for a while. And no one knew at the time that there were dangerous side effects."

"No."

———

"It's okay, Sherlock," she said softly, looking up at him and seeing a creased forehead and dark, solemn eyes. "Once you knew, you did the right thing. And your new 'drug of choice' is very happy about being chosen."

He drew a long breath, then nodded slowly.

"You are the answer to so many questions I did not even realise I had, Skye," he confessed. "So many needs, so many desires, none of which I knew were there. Until you filled them. In truth, I should wish to lose you no more than you do me."

"And that's as it should be." Skye smiled, reaching past him to place the journal on the nightstand and turn off the light. "And now your drug is after you again..."

"Heavens above," Sherlock's mock-appalled voice came through the darkness, "I never knew a drug could become addicted to its user."

A giggle was his only answer.

————

The next morning, they awoke very late, but together.

"Good morning, Wife," he murmured drowsily into her ear. "How do you feel today?"

"Uhn...that remains to be seen," she replied with a yawn, stretching gingerly in his arms, testing the bruising in her body and finding it acceptable. "I'm not awake enough yet to tell you."

————

"Take your time. I think we have little on the schedule for today. But I do have a question."

"What?" she wondered, rolling over to look at him. Her left eye was still blackened, but the swelling in her face had decreased to the point where it was almost non-existent.

"How do we know if our other selves have been successful or not?"

————

"Well, unless the absolute worst happened," Skye decided

after a moment's consideration, "they'll probably pop by—literally—at some point and tell us, one way or the other. After all, time goes by, both here and there, though the rates are different. There's only so much negation of time passage the tesseract will allow. It can," she explained, seeing confusion on Sherlock's face, "negate time passage here, for instance, but while time is passing over there, time is passing here, too, just at a different rate. So while they're working—and I expect they had to do some repairs and replacing of monitors after that tremor, let alone the emergency shutdown—we get to sit and wait."

"Ah, I see. And if the worst happened? For if the worst has happened, then they are dead and their continuum destroyed. There will be no one to tell us."

"I'd say if we don't hear from 'em in a couple days, think the worst. And we'll probably start seeing signs of instability in our own continuum by then."

Sherlock nodded silently. Automatically his arms tightened around her. They lay quietly for several minutes, pondering the matter.

"Skye?"

"Hm?"

"If...the worst should happen...is there anything you regret?"

"Other than not being able to tell the world that the real Sherlock Holmes loves me, I don't think so, no." She smiled up at him. The high cheekbones flushed, and the grey eyes glowed.

"If we determine the worst is happening, you might find the real Sherlock Holmes taking out a large advertisement in The Times of London to say so."

———

Skye's sapphire eyes grew huge, and she stared at him in shock.

"Sherlock...would you really...?"

"No," he said, allowing his silver eyes to twinkle mischievously. "But I was curious as to what your expression would be. It was quite amusing. I think I have never seen your jaw that slack before."

She smacked him on his bare shoulder. Hard.

"Rascal," she told him, and he laughed.

"With you? Indeed," he acknowledged. "But for a few moments, I shall be serious with you if you will, in turn, be serious with me."

"Of course," she said, sobering instantly. "What is it?"

Sherlock gathered her close and gazed into her azure eyes.

"If our world were to end soon, Skye, is there anything you have left undone you should have liked to do? Any dream unfinished, any fantasy unfulfilled?"

"Oh, I don't know, Sherlock," she murmured, overwhelmed by the thought. "It isn't important."

"Yes it is, my dear Skye, for if it is within my power, I shall see them accomplished before...it is too late. Now tell me."

"One of my biggest fantasies had to do with you." Her cheeks dimpled.

"Oh? Then it should be easy to grant. Tell me."

———

"I wanted to make you lose control," she told him with a smirk.

"I beg your pardon, my dear?" He stared at her in shocked puzzlement.

———

"You're always so in control," she said, a hint of her frustration in her tone. "Even in bed. I wanted to...to just drive you crazy. I wanted to see you banging around, shouting, even screaming my name," she admitted, grinning sheepishly, watching the color slowly creep up his face. "I wanted to know I could do that to you. But after last night..."

"Yes, well, after last night," the detective commented, flushing deeply, "I should think it a moot point. Are there any other such...matters...that come to mind?"

"Not really," she said, the smile fading from her features. "Nothing practical, anyway. I would've liked to have a family with you, Sherlock, our own little band of Irregulars, but..."

"Indeed. I doubt we should have nine days, let alone nine months."

"Exactly. So...what about you?"

"Me?"

"Yeah, you," Skye said pointedly. "Any dreams or fantasies I can manage for you?"

Sherlock considered briefly.

"As you say, nothing practical. And I could not go back to visit Watson in any event. We might, perhaps, go to visit Watson here, and have a few more conversations with him before...the end."

Skye swallowed, and she tried to keep the disappointment from her features as she added, "Nothing I can do for you personally? No fantasies of a wanton blonde hyperspatial physicist having her way with her husband?"

———

The detective gazed down into his wife's eyes, knowing what she had hoped to hear.

"I should have been curious about the children," he admitted. "Whether a daughter would present a kind of wormhole into your childhood; whether a son might show you myself as a boy." Then his mood brightened, and he smiled at her.

"As to...other fantasies," he acknowledged, "you must understand, Skye, even though we have been...together...in...that way, for over half a year now, I do not think of myself as a...as a lover. My dreams of you are simple, and they are fulfilled every day, when I awaken and see your face beside me on the pillow. Last night was..." he hesitated, flushing once more, "beyond dreams."

She blushed and smiled happily at him. "In that case, I—"

He froze.

"Hush," he breathed, raising his head and staring into space, concentrating intently. Skye silenced instantly, and she, too, raised her head.

"Voices. Someone's in the house." She stared at Sherlock. "Shit. Cunningham and Fereaud."

"And they are systematically searching," he observed, listening to the change in location. "Quickly, Wife, get up and—"

"They're here!" Skye hissed.

Sherlock flung himself bodily atop his wife in an attempt to shield her from the intruders, as she scrabbled the covers up around them both. He slid his hand between the mattress and the headboard, extracting the extra pistol Ryker had provided for his use. He brought the weapon up and aimed it at the closed door, still covering Skye with his body.

———

But instead of the bedroom door bursting open to frame the intruders, a soft call came from the hallway—in Skye's voice.

"Skye? Holmes? Are you there? It's us—the other you."

The couple in bed drew long, relieved breaths.

"Yeah, Sis, we're here," Skye answered. "We, um, we just woke up. Don't come in."

"Understood," Holmes' voice replied. "We shall not intrude. We merely wanted to let you know that extensive post-tremor repairs have been effected, the tesseract has been adjusted per the new parameters, and the deterioration appears to have halted." The familiar voice evinced even more familiar satisfaction and a distinct tinge of triumph.

"Wonderful!" Skye exclaimed enthusiastically as Sherlock replaced the pistol in its hiding place. "That gives everybody a chance to catch their breaths."

"Indeed," Sherlock muttered sotto voce, dropping his face into Skye's shoulder. "And about time."

"Exactly," Chadwick agreed, not having heard Sherlock's comment through the closed door, muffled by Skye's shoulder as it was. "But given the hard tremor that came through right as we were breaking connection, we wanted to make sure we let you know we were still here. Not to mention, checking on you to see if it caused any damage there."

"Thanks," Skye responded gratefully. "Everything's fine here. Well, a few things to pick up, I suppose, but nothing serious. You may have found half of a dilapidated old rocking chair and a bookshelf corner section, somewhere in the Chamber, Sherlock tells me, but that's about the extent of it. We'd just been discussing the matter, though. We hadn't heard from you. It was...concerning us."

"Mm-hm," Sherlock murmured into her neck. Skye grinned; it was becoming patently obvious to the scientist that, once having proof the other continuum still existed and no unwanted intruders were within the house, it no longer concerned the detective.

"Ah, so that is what produced the pile of kindling just outside the core," Holmes remarked with dry humor. "We wondered where on earth— well, where OFF earth— erhm, where off OUR earth—the wood splinters had come from."

"Yeah," Chadwick chuckled. "I'm afraid there's no point in sending it back across for repair. There aren't any pieces bigger than about ten inches, and a lot of it is just so much sawdust."

"Drat. I liked that rocking chair, too. Oh well. Never mind. So what are your plans next?" Skye queried.

————

One of Skye's hands left Sherlock's shoulder, vanishing under the bedclothes. Moments later, Sherlock raised his head, staring down into devilishly gleaming sapphire eyes.

"Imp," he breathed, just before his eyelids fluttered. He added fervently, "Dear God..."

————

"MY plans," Holmes' voice noted firmly, "are to see Chadwick, here, gets a decent sleep. No, my dear Chadwick, I know it is the middle of the afternoon here. But you—we —have been working without stop for days—weeks. And the tale of this little adventure is marked in years, years of hard, long work and anxieties. But now we have the system stabilised, and can afford to take our rest before we attempt strengthening the membrane. You, in particular, could do with it. You are as exhausted as your counterpart."

————

While his other self had been speaking, Sherlock tucked his head into Skye's shoulder with a sigh, more felt than heard. Now he lay, feeling his heart pound and his body flush as his spouse did amazing, and completely invisible, things to him.

"Minx," feathered into Skye's ear.

————

Skye bit her lip to stifle the giggle. "So you're going to take a break, then tackle boosting the rest energy of the brane tomorrow?" she addressed the other continuum.

"Yeah, probably," Chadwick agreed. "Or maybe a day or two after that, even. Or maybe not; I dunno. I gotta admit, Holmes is right. I'm dead on my feet. And he's not much better. It probably IS wiser for us to get some rest before tackling the brane. That's gonna be tricky enough as it is."

"Good plan," Skye concurred.

"A good plan," she heard a low voice pant in her ear, "would be to end this conversation quickly, Wife. Else it will shortly be interrupted by what is likely to be a very...loud...fantasy, fulfilled."

Skye bit her lip again, harder this time, as outright laughter threatened.

"Guys," she called softly, "Sherlock's fallen back asleep on my shoulder. Can we continue this later?"

"Sure thing, Skye," Chadwick agreed amiably. "Since you'd just woke up, it was bad timing on our part, anyway. Y'all take your time and we'll pop back later, probably in a day or so. I'd like to tag up with you once more before we boost the brane."

"Okay. Catch you later," Skye concurred.

An almost palpable silence emanated from the hall, and a sense of something missing—but no pop, hiss, or whiff of ozone was detectable.

Moments later, Skye's fantasy was enacted once more —most emphatically.

———

The pair sat quietly in their office upstairs, several levels above the Chamber. "If he was asleep, I'll eat my laptop," Chadwick snickered. "WITH its recharge cable."

"They certainly seem to...enjoy each other." Holmes chuckled wryly.

"They're married, Holmes." Chadwick barked out a short, bitter laugh. "Newlyweds, to boot. It's what newlyweds do. My parents 'enjoyed' each other right up until the end."

"They are in love."

"Very much so. Though, from what I've gathered, they —or at least he—doesn't verbalize it much."

"Then how does she know?"

"There are other ways of saying it, ya know, Holmes." Another barking laugh. "'Enjoyment' is one way."

"I find it intriguing," he admitted. He tipped his head and stared thoughtfully into space. "His heart is quite given over to her. Yet it does not seem to have affected his observation, nor his faculties of reason, in the slightest."

"No," Chadwick agreed. "You know, I asked her about

that the other day—I think you'd stepped out to the men's room for a minute."

"Oh?" Holmes wondered curiously, schooling his face into a bland expression. "And what did she say?"

"That he'd learned to integrate the two. And that in the process, he'd gradually realized something."

"What?"

"The fact that he cared for Skye—and Watson, as a dear friend—actually enhanced his deductive abilities," Chadwick shrugged.

"What?!"

"Yeah," Chadwick nodded. "Because he cared about them—and didn't want them hurt—it ramped up his skills and abilities. Probably an adrenaline rush or something. Think about when he rescued his wife the other day. He practically WAS a tesseract, he moved so fast."

———

The detective rose to his feet in astonishment, and now stood there, wide-eyed, as sudden comprehension dawned.

"Dear God," he breathed. "Of course. Of COURSE."

Chadwick watched him in bemusement, but his mind was distant, working on the ramifications of this revelation. Finally, abstractedly, he turned toward the door.

"I shall return shortly. I find I need a pipe to contemplate this," he murmured, and she stared.

"Pipe? But you haven't smoked in two years!" she protested. "You gave it up."

"I am afraid I require a bit of..." Holmes paused, seeking to explain. He sighed. "It is not tobacco, but a Native herbal blend I found at the trading post where you used to purchase my tobacco. It is actually healing to the system, I have it to understand, and there is some evidence that it may actually counter the effects of tobacco use upon the system. It is exceedingly rare for me to make use even of it these days; I think I have not used it in almost a year. Sometimes, however, when the mental need comes upon me, it is...beneficial. But I am thus able to still keep my promise to you."

"Okay," she agreed, understanding. "We have time. We got the deterioration halted, and we can actually manage to properly prepare, for a change, before we tackle bumping up the energy in the affected brane. I'll hit the couch in the corner and take a nap while you're gone, like you wanted."

"Capital."

———

At the door, he turned back. "Chadwick?"

"Yeah?"

"Before I go, I...there is something I need to know, a datum I require in order to factor into my contemplation. Perhaps two separate bits of data. But...they are very personal in nature."

"When did that ever stop you?" Chadwick shrugged again, wryly this time. "You may fire when ready, I guess."

"The first thing I should like to know is," Holmes internalized the wince, "in your estimation, how much is the other Chadwick like you? Psychologically, I mean."

"Mentally and emotionally?"

"Yes."

"Oh, quite a lot, I'd say," Chadwick decided after a moment's thought. "You've seen us finish each other's sentences a few times. And I know what she's gonna do about as soon as she does, because it's what I'd do."

"Like the fright over the beta burns?"

"Exactly."

Holmes' breath hitched, though he managed to avoid revealing the fact to his companion. *She would have dropped everything, come running, and examined me for injury,* he realized. *Even now, after...everything.* It led him to his other datum.

"And the other thing I should like to know," he began, then hesitated.

"Is what?" Chadwick pressed.

"Once, you...confessed...to a certain...fond regard, for me."

"I said I loved you, Holmes," she corrected quietly.

"Yes," he said, noting the past tense with some sadness, watching her with dark grey eyes as she watched him in turn, "you did. But...do you still love me, Chadwick?" he asked simply, watching her steadily, unaware his eyes were drawn and his forehead creased in pain. "Or have I completely destroyed that tender regard, in the intervening years?"

She averted her face suddenly and swallowed, as soft color suffused her cheeks.

"Do you remember what I told you at lunchtime, that day we...?" she began hoarsely. "That...last day...?"

"Yes," he recalled immediately, the memory of the dreadful day branded indelibly on his mind, in its every painful detail. "You said you had enough love for both of us, and you only requested time to...readjust your expectations."

"That's probably the best answer I know how to give you, right now." She nodded, continuing to avert her face. Holmes left the door and came to stand beside her chair.

"Still? After all this time?"

Chadwick shrugged, tossed a rueful, slightly wobbly smile over her shoulder, then sighed.

"One of your favorite words for me has always been

'loyal,' Sherlock," she dared to call him by his given name, just this once.

"It has," he admitted, instantly noting a mode of address he had not heard in several years, not since that decisive day, and realizing with a shock how much he had missed hearing it. "May I ask another question?"

"If I said no, would it matter?"

"Yes," he said, heart aching, and immediately silenced, turning to go.

"Go ahead and ask it," she sighed, and he stopped.

———

Then, to her chagrin, he came and stood directly in front of her face, then crouched down so he could look into her eyes.

"Why did you never grow angry?" he asked softly, holding her gaze with almost magnetic intensity. "Why are you still here at my side? I had thought—half-expected, even perhaps feared—you would turn from me..."

The scientist exhaled in pain, and tears filled the tired sapphire eyes, but as usual she did not let them overflow.

"Because I'm not suicidal," she told him bluntly, "and it would have killed me, as surely as a bullet to the heart. There wasn't anybody else left, not after Caitlin died in the tesseract accident. I knew I had your friendship, even if I couldn't have your love, and I was willing to take what I could get just to know you were here. It's pathetic, I know, but true."

They were silent for several moments, watching each other. Finally Holmes spoke once more.

"You have never grieved any of them. Not your parents, not Caitlin, nor any of the others who died in the sabotage attempt."

"No."

———

Then a blazing light went off in the detective's mind. "Great Scot, you lost me that particular day of which we speak, too, did you not?"

"In a way, yeah. I lost...what might have been."

And suddenly he knew what the difference was between his Chadwick and that of the other continuum. "You lost hope."

"I guess." She shrugged.

"And you have never grieved for any of it."

"I never had time. Too much has always rested on my shoulders. It's a luxury I couldn't afford."

"Why not?"

"For pity's sake, Sherlock!" she exclaimed in frustration. "You, of ALL people, should know THAT! If I let all that go, I'd come apart at the seams! I'd be worthless for days—weeks! Maybe permanently! I probably couldn't function, let alone think with anything like the clarity needed to solve the little problem we've had downstairs! So I took a page out of your book, and shoved 'the softer emotions' aside. In the end, I've gotten fairly good at it, I think."

Holmes sighed, deeply troubled.

"Over there," he waved a hand at the floor, indicating the Chamber below their feet, and thereby denoting the alternate continuum, "he learned from her—to integrate his emotions with his intellect. But here, you learned from me—to isolate them."

He looked deeply into his companion's eyes, seeing the dull, dispirited gaze, and contrasting it with the bright, vivacious glow he had always seen in the other Skye's eyes.

My Skye used to look like that, he remembered. *Before I turned my back on the priceless gift she gave me. Before our world began to fall apart—literally.*

"There's nothing wrong with that," she averred. "Maybe if you'd done the same thing he did, we wouldn't have been able to recognize what was happening to the continuum. Wouldn't have realized it was even destabilizing, let alone fought to stop it."

"I wonder," he murmured thoughtfully. Holmes rose to his feet, turning for the door. "All right, Skye, I am going to smoke my pipe now. I should not be gone long, and I will return straightaway I am finished."

"Okay. If I'm not here, I'll be downstairs puttering."

"No," he said firmly, "you will not. You shall remain here and rest."

"But I—"

"No, Chadwick," he said emphatically. "You need rest before we do another thing. You will run yourself into the ground otherwise. I will not have it."

"And what are you gonna do about it?" Chadwick's temper flared.

"Call Morris and Roberts and have you escorted from the premises, if necessary." Holmes folded his arms calmly. Then he returned to her side and laid a light hand on her shoulder. "I am not trying to be difficult, my dear. I am trying to care for both you, and the continuum. If you are insufficiently rested, and in your weariness you make a mistake..."

"All right. Point taken." Chadwick sighed, and subsided. "I'll be here on the couch, then. I may not be able to sleep, but I'll try to rest."

"Good girl. I shall return shortly."

Chadwick moved to the couch in the corner as Holmes left the office.

———

Sherlock left Skye napping on the sofa in the sitting room, put on his jacket and muffler, and stepped into the garden in the back of the cottage, where he sat quietly on the old stone wall. There was nothing in particular on his mind, though he lit his pipe and smoked it with some vigour. He was simply allowing his wife the opportunity to reclaim the sleep of which he'd deprived her the previous night, while he himself enjoyed the fresh air of a relatively mild winter's day. There was a peace within the detective this particular afternoon such as he'd not experienced in some time. *Perhaps since I arrived in this continuum,* he considered.

"Yes," he murmured aloud, "for if I correctly understood Skye, the danger is over."

"It is, we believe," he heard his own voice reply from somewhere nearby, and he raised an eyebrow.

No crackling, no champagne corks, and no whiff of ozone, he observed. *They have, indeed, fine-tuned the tesseract.*

"Good afternoon, Brother Me," Sherlock greeted his alter ego whimsically. "How are you and Dr. Chadwick, now the crisis has been averted?"

"Well, perhaps I should restate—the crisis is not wholly over," Holmes admitted. "We have stopped the ongoing deterioration, but have not yet reinforced the membrane. There is no longer immediate danger of spontaneous collapse, though there will be some risk when we fortify the brane. And Chadwick is resting upstairs in our office—as, I assume, she is within the house, as well."

"Indeed," Sherlock agreed. "Their labours have been great, and they have earned a respite. So you have come to speak with me in private."

"I have."

"I suppose it is necessary, though I cannot say I relish

it." Sherlock drew a deep breath, then let it out reluctantly. "Let us get it over with, then."

"Consider the matter as thinking aloud, rather than intimate discussion with another man," Holmes suggested. "That is, essentially, what you are doing, after all."

Sherlock pursed his lips, considering, then nodded. "Very well. It seems an acceptable stratagem. Pray proceed."

"Your Chadwick—your wife, now. You are in love with her."

"Well, I am."

"Why?"

"I have come to the conclusion that the whys and wherefores of love extend into matters metaphysical," Sherlock acknowledged, then chuckled ruefully. "They are only partly amenable to reason and rational explanation. Nevertheless, I suppose it might be said she is my complement, one of the few people—and the only woman—I have ever found who understands me in toto. She needs not to ask me a single question, Sherlock—nay, not so much as a single word, to know what I am thinking, what I am feeling, what I want, what I require. And I," he pondered, letting his gaze grow distant, "I can do the same for her. It is a singular relationship."

Puzzlement was evident in Holmes' tone when next he spoke. "Complement—she is your opposite, then? In other than gender?"

"No, no," Sherlock shook his head. "Oh, I suppose in the matter of certain skills, it might be said so. Betwixt us, we do have a deliciously broad range of knowledge, skills and talents. It proves quite useful at times. No, she is in fact, very much like me. In the early days of our friendship, for so it was initially, I used often to make the mistake of trying to compare her to Watson. There are some similarities there, I suppose, especially in the greatness of heart; but she is decidedly more like me than Watson. When once I consciously grasped that fact, it was the key to fully understanding her—at least, insofar as one human may understand another." He paused thoughtfully, then added, "Somewhere along the way I discovered..." he shrugged. "She is part of me, Sherlock, and I, her."

"You feel incomplete without her."

"You know better than that," Sherlock reproached. "I cannot, nor will not, speak for my wife, but I am far too independent to apply such a statement as that to myself. I am a complete being, in and of myself—as is she, I might add. One half must be added to one half to equal one, and neither of us is half a person."

"No, that is true," Holmes agreed. "My observations indicate each of you is a full, rich person."

"Precisely," Sherlock nodded. "No, I should say, not that she 'completes' me, but rather that I am more complete with her. The equation is not additive, or even multiplicative, but exponential."

"Ah," Holmes answered, understanding. "The whole greater than the sum of the parts."

"Exactly."

"And so how does this explain the depth to which you desire her?"

———

Sherlock settled back down on the stone wall, shoved his now-extinguished pipe between his lips, and said nothing. Insofar as an observer could have told, he did not hear the question.

"Remember, Sherlock, you are carrying on a conversation with yourself," Holmes reminded his doppelganger with amusement, then grew serious. "In truth, I am trying to understand how you came to be so...ARE you as happily married as you appear?"

An eyebrow rose; then grey eyes twinkled.

———

"Capital, Brother Other Me," Holmes' voice smiled. "I am...pleased for you."

"But you do not understand how the difference came about?" Sherlock confirmed, getting out his pipe tool and busying his hands with the process of re-igniting his pipe.

"The data is insufficient, you understand," Holmes answered.

"Of course. But if I may, what has triggered this sudden need to know?"

"Observation," Holmes sighed. "The similarities, and differences, between my Skye and yours. And the discovery that, after all this time...dear God, man, she still loves me."

———

"That does not surprise me," Sherlock nodded, gaze thoughtful. "She is faithful and constant, is Skye. Do you know, I very nearly broke her, when I..." He cut off what he had been about to say, and stared fixedly across the fields and hedgerows. A hint of pain glimmered deep in the grey eyes.

"I fear I did," came the low response.

"What is broken may be mended," Sherlock said calmly. "If mending is desired."

"I...do not know how," Holmes confessed softly. "Did you have a...misunderstanding, as well?"

"Though we did so term it at the time, and sometimes still do on the rare occasions when it is referenced, I do not think I should call it a true misunderstanding, looking back at it," Sherlock considered. "We understood each other perfectly. The problem was that for the first time I did not understand myself; and Skye, used to a confident, certain Sherlock, did not realise this. I have never felt more confused, or more wretched, in my life than that day..." His voice tapered off as he recalled the intense pain of their estrangement. A soft sigh was his only agreement.

"And yet," Holmes finally said, "the two of you moved past it."

"We did," Sherlock verified. "There were several things that wanted doing."

"And they were?"

"First, I had to admit to the truth," Sherlock confessed, waving his pipe in the air for emphasis. "Like it or not. Truth is truth, and there is no gainsaying it. And the truth was that I was tied to this woman, body and soul."

Silence came from the other side of the tesseract.

"Secondly, I had to decide what to do about it," he continued. "How was I going to act upon this knowledge? Had Skye not brought the word 'love' into play so quickly, I have sometimes wondered if we might have settled into a comfortable relationship allowing time for the thought to grow in me, of its own accord. But with that large heart of hers, Skye tends to emotional, though not intellectual, impulsiveness; it is one of the things I..." he paused, "love...about her."

"So you were forced to choose," Holmes agreed. "Accept, or reject."

"Precisely," Sherlock noted. "But the decision was not

all on my side. I fully expected to be told to pack my things and go. It would have been well within Skye's prerogative; by her lights, and with the information she had to hand, I had behaved the utter cad. She could not know the battle raging within, or how that battle centred upon the fact that I was fighting to keep her alive."

"Exactly!" Holmes exclaimed. "She was in danger, and the least distraction could have meant her death. My conscience...I could not have abided it, Sherlock."

Sherlock nodded, full understanding arriving in that moment.

"As Skye would say, hold onto that thought for an instant. I may take it that both Skyes informed us we would not be thrown out..."

"Correct," Holmes answered quietly.

"Which gave her initial decision," Sherlock pointed out. "It then came down to our making our own decisions, you and I. And I may assume that we made different decisions, but for essentially the same reason—her safety."

"It sounds so," Holmes admitted.

"And so the last thing to be done," Sherlock continued, "was to admit the truth, and my decision regarding it, to SKYE."

There was a long silence this time.

"You did not take that step, did you?" Sherlock pressed.

"...No. I did not."

"Perhaps it is not too late," he observed.

"Perhaps," Holmes agreed. "And yet...I am not, nor have I ever been, especially voluble in such matters..."

"We are much the same," Sherlock shrugged, before a recollection struck. "Do what I did," he suggested.

"Which was?"

"I wrote what Skye calls her 'love letter' from me," he confessed, heat suffusing the high cheekbones. "It was hardly the most eloquent thing I have ever set to paper...but The Woman—or perhaps I should say, The Women—in question are truly exceptional at understanding us, old chap."

There was a pause, and Sherlock could sense the consideration coming from the other continuum.

"Purely as a point of speculation, Sherlock..." the other detective murmured.

"Yes?"

"What would you have done if Skye had not been so forgiving?"

"If she had thrown me out, you mean?"

"No," Holmes said thoughtfully, "In all honesty, I simply cannot see Skye doing that. Vindictiveness is not in her nature. Rather, what if she had not...accepted your overtures...after that? Where would you be now?"

Sherlock pondered the question for a few moments. "Still by her side, I think, if not so close. I did, and do, value her friendship and advice too much to easily cast it aside."

"Yes," Holmes answered thoughtfully, "I believe we would have made the same choice there. And it likely will not surprise you to find that they feel the same."

"No."

There was a silence. Finally Holmes broke it.

"Thank you, Other Me. I know I asked much of y— of myself," he chuckled. "And I know how difficult it was to answer. All the more thanks, then."

"What do you intend to do with the information?" Sherlock probed.

"Think, for now," Holmes replied.

"Sherlock," Sherlock addressed his other self in all seriousness, "she is a treasure. More than you can imagine, more than my poor words can possibly express. I urge you, do not let this opportunity slip through your fingers. If you do, I fear you may not get another chance."

"I...understand," Holmes answered soberly. "I will be in touch."

"Very well."

There was a faint sigh, like the summer wind in the grass of a meadow. *Gone, for now,* Sherlock decided. *And the afternoon grows chill, for the sun is descending. Time to retire within, and see if my dear wife has yet awakened.*

He rose from his rustic seat on the low stone wall and moved to the back door of the cottage.

———

Inside, he removed his jacket, hung it on the kitchen coat rack, and draped his muffler over it. Then he slipped into the sitting room to check on his wife, anticipating a few happy, stolen moments of watching her sleep.

Skye still lay on the sofa, but to his surprise, her eyes were turned to the door in expectation of his entrance. A bright, knowing blue gaze met his own, and his brows creased in puzzlement. A movement out of the corner of his eye caught his attention, and he glanced aside.

The curtains were fluttering in a soft breeze from without.

The window was open, and she heard it, he realized in dismay. *She heard it all.* Blazing warmth rose in the high cheeks.

Skye got to her feet and came to him. Taking Sherlock by the hand, she led him to the sofa and seated him in its corner. Then, to his wonder, she crawled into his lap and curled up there, wrapping his arms about herself like a blanket before snuggling close.

She understands, he thought as he smiled to himself. *As usual, she understands.*

The detective's arms tightened about his wife, and as she pressed her face into his chest, Sherlock allowed his head to drop back until it rested on the sofa. He drew a deep breath and let it out in a contented sigh.

8

Mending Broken Things

Holmes left the Chamber thoughtfully. Making his way through the security airlocks, he ascended to the office level to check on Chadwick once more before going to the smoking area outside the building.

Inside their office, he found her lying on the sofa in the corner, soundly asleep. She was curled into a tight ball, face pillowed upon a cushion. He stood over her, looking down at her for several long minutes, studying her features pensively.

Her pale face was pinched and tired, even in sleep. The light tan she once sported had faded long since; the sunlit recreations they used to enjoy had been sacrificed years ago to too many hours in the Chamber with the tesseract. Her body was taut and seemed anxious despite her resting state, the cords of muscle in her forearms standing out plainly; her hands were balled into clenched fists and tucked protectively into her chin. There were lines on the forehead and at the corners of her eyes that were not there when he had arrived in this continuum. Briefly Holmes wondered what had put them there: The struggle against the continuum collapse, or the pain of a love rejected and a heart bereft and alone. *Both, perhaps,* he decided with a noiseless sigh.

Long, gentle fingers on a bare arm ascertained she was cold. Holmes turned aside, silently opening the supply cabinet in the opposite corner of the office and extracting a fluffy, knit woollen afghan in a peaceful shade of slate blue. He unfolded it and spread it over the sleeping form, tucking it protectively around the body that he suddenly recognized was far too thin. His breath caught in alarm at the realization.

She has not taken care of herself as she ought—which is typical, he comprehended. *And evidently I have not sufficiently done so for her. But had she not had the continuum destabilisation to contend with, to force her to keep going, in what condition would she now be? Hughes once said Skye was prone to withdrawing and simply...quitting...when in the midst of overwhelming grief and depression. And I saw that tendency firsthand after the tesseract accident. I had my hands full with her, then.*

He watched as Chadwick sighed under the warmth of the coverlet, and the tense huddle of her body relaxed, loosening into a comfortable sleep. Then another thought struck the detective turned hyperspatial scientist, and took his breath away with dread.

What will happen to her, once the continuum is stabilised? Once the threat to our world has been removed? She said she hadn't time to grieve before. What will happen when she is given that time? When she is given the opportunity to dwell on tragic events? Will she give up, and waste away? Has her body already been pushed past its point of resilience? What if she... He stared down at the frail, exhausted frame curled under the blanket, horror filling his being, *what if, even now, she has developed some dreadful disease, borne of too much stress, and too little hope...?*

Holmes' face contorted in anguish for a brief instant.

Finally, slowly, he turned away and moved soundlessly for the door.

Had Chadwick been awake to see, she would have observed in shock that Holmes was moving like a man of twice his years, and one in deep pain into the bargain.

———

Holmes was alone in the smoking area outside. He extracted his pipe, packed it with the kinnick-kinnick obtained at the trading post, tamped and lit it. He did not waste energy in unnecessary pacing; instead, he leaned against the nearby concrete column and stared past the dual perimeter fences, onto the sunlit open prairie. Uncharacteristically, he noticed neither the long shadow of the mountains beginning to encroach upon the view, nor the hint of autumnal gold starting to tinge the prairie grass. His dark grey eyes were drawn in pain, and lost in thought.

Gradually the aquiline face relaxed. The grey eyes warmed, turning a soft silver. The corners of his mouth quirked slightly. He nodded to himself, as if coming to some decision.

Finishing his pipe, he tapped the ash into a nearby receptacle, cleaned it with his pipe tool, and put it away.

Then he pulled out his cell phone and, with a mischievous half-smile, placed a call.

———

When Chadwick awoke, she did so slowly, with a reluctance to return to the waking world that had become commonplace to her in the last year or so. Her dreams were usually much more pleasant than her reality, especially given the unstable continuum, and her subconscious preferred to stay in a more agreeable place for as long as possible, on those rare occasions when it had the chance.

But as she awoke, her senses registered welcome, if unexpected, anomalies. For one thing, she was unaccountably warm and cozy. For another, there was a subtly sweet fragrance wafting into her nose—and something tickling the tip of said nose. Beyond the sweet fragrance was another scent, richer and more savory, which in turn blended with a slightly musky, familiar masculine smell. Her cheek, she gradually realized, no longer rested against a sofa cushion, but against something slightly rougher...and warmer.

With an effort Chadwick forced her eyes open, to find herself staring cross-eyed at a spray of lupine tucked into her hand, and whose blossoms tickled her nose. *So that's what smelled sweet,* she thought, her wits not fully awake as yet. *I wonder where it came from.* She stretched, then yawned.

"Ah, there you are," a deep voice, possessed of a distinct English cadence, noted quietly from somewhere above her.

Chadwick glanced up to see grey eyes smiling down at her. She blinked sleepily, trying to force her own eyes to completely focus. After a moment, she realized Holmes was not merely leaning over her; the warm pillow cradling her head was in fact his thigh, clad in wool trousers. And a scrutiny of his eyes revealed she had not been the only one who had taken a nap. Flushing at his proximity, Chadwick pushed away, trying to sit up.

"I-I'm sorry," she stammered softly, struggling to lever herself upright while not crushing her flowers. "I didn't mean to take up the whole couch. I—"

"Hush, my dear," Holmes murmured, his hands catching her shoulders and preventing her from rising.

"Not so fast. You have slept deeply for several hours, and I strongly urge you to take your time awakening. You are fine where you are."

"But I..."

"You are fine, Chadwick," Holmes reassured in a firm tone, smiling. "When I decided to join you in a nap, I placed you in a position I thought would be comfortable for us both. All is well, and we have both rested. And when once we are properly awake, a nice hot meal awaits us." Holmes pointed at the desk. "Courtesy of a certain hotel with British interests."

Chadwick twisted around to look, and saw the desktop filled with covered trays and platters; two china plates and two rolls of proper silverware in real linens lay stacked on the corner. A bud vase, containing merely water, sat in the center, awaiting only her spray of lupine to make the setting perfect.

"Oh, lovely," she breathed, delighted. "It'll be great to have something besides a sandwich and coffee wolfed down while sitting at console."

"Indeed. I thought it might do us both some good."

Chadwick let her head drop back to her companion's lap, where she lay for several minutes staring at the ceiling. Holmes, in turn, watched her without appearing to do so. After a moment, she brought the spray of lupine to her nose and inhaled the faint, delicate fragrance.

"Where did these come from?"

"From a greenhouse," Holmes replied, the barest hint of mischief in the grey eyes.

"I know that, silly," Chadwick retorted, "it's exactly the opposite time of year for the things. I meant..."

———

"You meant why," Holmes noted softly. He drew a deep breath; he had been pondering how to answer this question from the moment he had asked Billy Williams to obtain the blossoms. "For now, let us say that...a certain bosom companion desired you to know...you are appreciated."

"Gee, I wonder who that could be." Sarcasm tinged Chadwick's tone even as an impish grin lit her face—all too briefly, Holmes decided, before she sobered. "Well...for whatever it's worth, that 'bosom companion' probably kept me going, these last few years," she told him sincerely. "I don't think I'd have had the strength to keep on if he hadn't been here, especially after...after the sabotage, and losing half the team."

Then what I feared is likely true, Holmes thought, disquieted. *When once the brane has been repaired, I shall have to work hard to avoid losing her to her despair.*

What he said was, "Despite not having him as...close...as you would have wished?"

Chadwick shrugged and sat up slowly, having apparently grown stiff while asleep; Holmes' arm behind her back aided her in the movement.

"He stuck by me, and supported me. That's not about closeness. That's about trust. And he trusted me."

"And he will continue to do so," Holmes replied simply, then stood. "Now, let us see to supper. I have it to understand the hotel chef outdid himself." He offered Chadwick a courtly hand and pulled her to her feet.

———

After they ate, Holmes and Chadwick discussed their situation. With the cessation of tachyon condensation, the deterioration of the brane and resulting continuum destabilization had been halted. But there was still a small danger until the brane's rest energy could be boosted back to its nominal level—and that alone was dangerous: too much, or too little, and the current stability could be undone.

So Holmes pressed for a period of rest, with alert monitors on the tesseract, while they themselves took time to recover. After considerable discussion, Chadwick yielded to the idea, deciding Holmes had had a point all along: there was more peril in trying to adjust the brane with a weary mind than in letting it be until they were well rested. But she insisted on talking with her counterpart once more before taking a break, and Holmes agreed.

————

"...So I have to say, I'm in full agreement with Holmes," Skye declared.

The tesseract was inverted, and while she and Sherlock sat comfortably in their own sitting room in Gibson House near Bentwaters, the other pair was visible in the Chamber beneath Schriever, sitting in desk chairs across from them. The married couple noticed a certain relaxed behavior in the other Holmes; he sat casually slouched, legs crossed, body language more open than they had ever seen it, and directed toward his partner. Skye and Sherlock studiously avoided glancing at each other, but Skye felt the slight nudge her husband's elbow made in her ribs, and pressed back lightly before continuing her statement.

"It isn't like anyone's ever done this before, and the theory is still pretty rough around the edges," she noted. "You can calculate approximately what the rest energy should be, but you're gonna have to fine-tune it by the seat of your pants, watching the instrumentation, to get it exact."

"And I should think swift reaction times are needed," Sherlock chimed in. "Is not that correct, Wife?"

"Absolutely, Sherlock," Skye agreed. "So definitely go home and rest."

"But how long can we afford to put it off, do you think?" Chadwick wondered, worried.

"My preliminary calculations indicate we should have at least a week before matters begin to grow critical," Holmes noted confidently.

"I'd agree with that," Skye nodded, and the other three recognized the slightly unfocused look in the blue eyes, indicating she was running mental calculations. "Just remember that until the rest energy is back to normal, there's probably gonna be a slow bleed-off. But it's an exponential decay, which means it'll speed up with time. So I don't think I'd push it to two weeks. Ten days, max."

"Agreed," Holmes answered promptly, and Chadwick shot a glance at him.

"You've already looked at this? In that much detail?" she asked her companion.

"Indeed," Holmes confirmed. "I have been considering the matter off and on for several days, now. I could see the increasing weariness in both Skyes, and felt a brief holiday would be in order, once we reached this point."

———

"And you, Brother Me, could stand a respite, as well," Sherlock declared. "You and I have pushed ourselves to breaking before, but it will not do, now. Too much rests upon it. And I recognise the impending signs in your face, for I have seen them in my own."

"True enough, I suppose," Holmes agreed with only mildly acidic reluctance. Sherlock restrained an eyebrow; he had detected a certain hint of dissembling in the protesting nature of his doppelganger's tone, and suddenly realized it was being maintained for appearance's sake alone. So he delicately pressed ahead.

"In addition, it may give you opportunity to act upon some of those matters which we discussed," Sherlock added casually.

"I had planned upon it," Holmes answered unassumingly.

Chadwick shot the two men puzzled glances; Skye merely gazed into space, as if still performing calculations in her head.

"Capital," Sherlock murmured. "I can assure you, it will only aid you in your endeavours."

"Never fear," Holmes nodded.

———

"Good," Skye said, coming back to the conversation. "In that case, you two go get some rest, and Sherlock and I'll try to tie up the loose ends on our case, here."

"Okay, Sis," Chadwick finally relented, rising and moving to the control console. "We'll give the two of you the same number of days we take, before we come back to report in. Y'all need a break, too."

"Works for me," Skye agreed. "Take care, guys."

There was a soft sough like the wind, and the sitting room of the cottage returned, as Holmes and Chadwick disappeared.

———

Holmes and Chadwick left Schriever for the first time in several days, headed up Ute Pass in the pickup truck, with Holmes driving. When they arrived at the ranch in Florissant in the middling twilight, a younger couple emerged from the house to greet them, followed by a toddling girl of around three years of age.

"Hello Billy, Tina," Chadwick smiled to the MI-5 operatives, who now functioned ostensibly as the ranch foreman and cook, respectively; Violet Skye Ranch was now a successful, prosperous horse breeding and training facility, nearly four times the size it had been when Holmes had arrived in that continuum. But in point of fact, Billy and Tina Williams were the permanently assigned liaisons for Holmes and Chadwick, for both the British and American governments. "And how's our Martha?"

"Ooo!" the little one squealed, seeing both Chadwick and Holmes emerging from the vehicle. "Unca Sherwock an' Auntie Skye!" She promptly launched herself at Holmes, who smiled indulgently and scooped her up in his arms. "I habben't seed oo in so wong!"

"Hello there, little Martha. It is good to see you, too, child. And is Martha going to answer Auntie Skye?" he asked the child.

"Marfa's good," the little girl beamed, reaching out from the sanctuary of Holmes' arms to hug Chadwick's neck. "Mummy an' Da's good, too."

"Indeed we are," Williams noted with a fond smile, putting an arm around his wife. "So is the ranch—cat, horses, and bees; we're taking good care of things for you. But..." he hesitated, seeing the weariness in the pair who'd just arrived.

"How is the continuum?" a worried Tina pressed her husband's aborted question, as several of the MI-5 operatives-cum-ranch-hands emerged from the bunkhouse wing of the barn, anxious to hear the news. "We felt that big quake a couple of days ago..."

"The continuum is stabilized," Chadwick announced with a tired grin. "We decided to get some rest before tackling the membrane."

Soft exclamations of relief and triumph made their way around the assembled group. "You two are amazing," Tina murmured with a smile.

"Aw," Chadwick blushed. "We had help."

"Indeed," Holmes agreed. "And if the brain of one Skye Chadwick is formidable, how much the more, two?"

"Not to mention, two Holmeses," Chadwick retorted affectionately, elbowing her companion in the ribs. "Four of us made for a darned good team, I guess."

"Wow," Wang muttered, eyes wide. "Two of each of you. Cool."

"Now," Holmes interjected, before anyone else could speak, "the news has been duly delivered. Into the house with you, Chadwick. You are dead on your feet, and it is late."

"Have you eaten?" Tina wondered, taking Martha from Holmes and turning to lead the way into the house. A small feline awaited them in the partially open door, peering out eagerly. "Do I need to prepare a light supper?"

"No, dear," Billy noted to his wife. "Holmes called up earlier and had me contact the hotel. The restaurant kitchen sent a nice dinner to their office."

"Yes, and it was utterly and indescribably delicious," Chadwick smiled, scooping up Anna and petting the little cat affectionately. Anna purred loudly, rubbing ecstatically against Chadwick's cheek, then leaning out and head-butting Holmes' shoulder. "I don't think I could have faced another cold sandwich at console. Thanks so much."

"Inside, Chadwick," Holmes ordered amiably, briefly

scritching Anna's ear. "I shall not tolerate your diversions at this stage."

"Okay," Chadwick capitulated agreeably enough, allowing Holmes to herd her into the house with a rather familiar hand firmly on her back.

———

As the door closed behind the four adults and one child, the ranch hands glanced at each other, intrigued.

"Did they seem awfully...chummy...to you?" Wang asked Hargreave.

"Yeah," Hargreave agreed. "I've never seen 'em not snipping at each other before."

———

"Maybe it's because the stress is off?" Huggins wondered hopefully.

"Maybe," Wang grinned, "and maybe it's finally giving 'em a chance to realise what they've really got."

"Whaddaya mean?" Hargreave wondered.

"Well," Wang began, prudently lowering his voice, "they weren't always snippy. According to General Morris, originally they were the best of mates, and got along gang-busters from the very first."

"They did? They were?" Huggins muttered, surprised.

"They were," Wang confirmed. "Barely a cross word ever spoken between 'em. An' when I got here with Captain Ryker...well, let's just say Ryker an' I had a conver-sation or two. Looked to us like they were, uh, something more than best mates, if you get me. Nothing blatant, not outta those two. It was more...the way they looked at each other. You know what I mean?"

Neither said anything, but both Huggins and Hargreave had wide eyes.

"They haven't done much detective work in recent years; been way the blazes too busy with the tesseract mess. But if you'd ever seen 'em in action together, you'd almost think they were the same mind in two bodies." Wang shook his head in amazement. "Just mind-boggling. I swear, they were meant for each other." He sighed, and he grew glum, mentally reliving the sadness and stress of past events. He was silent for some time, remembering.

"Then, a couple days after we got here, they had some sort of row," Wang eventually added sadly. "We never found out what. There wasn't any shouting or such; that's not their way. But they were never the same after."

"Aw," Hargreave whispered, disappointed.

"If you had to say, based on what you saw," Huggins asked with interest, "what would you say happened?"

"If I had to say," Wang shook his head, "and I hate speculating about 'em, 'cause I've known 'em about as long as anybody alive now, an' I...I really care about 'em..." He hesitated, torn.

"C'mon, Wang," Huggins murmured encouragingly. "If we're gonna help 'em somehow, we gotta know. That flower Holmes ordered—it's gotta mean something. Didn't you see Chadwick holding it?"

"Yeah," Wang grinned weakly. "We can hope, I guess. Anyway, if I had to say, I think they musta got the shit scared out of 'em over something—it's why they called us in—and it made him revert back to his old Victorian patterns. You know, keeping EVERYone at a distance, and such like."

"Afraid he was gonna lose his objectivity, maybe?" Huggins suggested perceptively. "Be too preoccupied to notice clues? It would fit with what Watson wrote about him."

"Maybe," Wang nodded. "And if that HAD happened, his losing his objectivity and observational skills, it woulda been bad, really bad, given what was going on around 'em at the time. Like…'somebody not walkin' away from it' bad."

"Yeah," Hargreave agreed. "So they got snippy after that?"

"Yup," Wang verified. "And *I* think the snippiness is the sign of two broken hearts that never quite pulled away, and never quite mended."

"Two," Huggins murmured thoughtfully.

"Two," Wang declared, firm. "But you know, maybe…just maybe…now that the stress is off…"

"For the first time in years," Hargreave grumbled.

"Yeah, so maybe Holmes is starting to think about it again," Wang offered hopefully. "Maybe they both are."

"Now that," Hargreave decided, "would be really…good."

"Wouldn't it, though?" Wang agreed.

"Well, let's go, mates," Huggins offered. "We can think about it, and try to figure out how to help nudge 'em along. Meanwhile, it's time to drop feed for the horses, then loop the perimeter…"

———

That night, after Billy and Tina had taken little Martha off to their own house—a cozy, relatively new little cabin in a far corner of the ranch—Skye went into the study and sorted through the considerable stack of mail their liaisons had left. It was mostly periodicals and journals, as the Williams couple had handled matters like utility bills and such as they came up, leaving Holmes and Chadwick free to work on the tesseract. While she was thus occupied, Holmes took the opportunity to slip out of the room, unnoticed.

He moved quietly into Chadwick's bedroom. Having cared for her as she was recuperating from her gunshot wounds after the second sabotage attempt on the tesseract four years prior, he knew his way around intimately, even though he had been in the room little in recent years.

For that matter, I have been in my own room but little in recent years, he thought with a rueful chuckle. *No, both Chadwick—Skye,* he corrected himself, *and I have become thoroughly familiar with our desk chairs and the sofa in the office corner, instead. It will be nice to sleep in a proper bed for a change. My own bed, at that.*

He sighed, silently hoping that way of life might soon end, and applied himself to turning down the bedclothes and finding suitably comfortable sleepwear for the woman who, whether friend or lover, was still the centre of his existence. Quietly rummaging through the dresser in search of a pyjama top for Chadwick, he came across a flowing pile of pale blue satin instead, hidden at the bottom of the drawer, beneath a stack of folded sleep shirts and utilitarian flannel pyjamas. Pulling it out of the drawer, it spilled over his hands to the floor, the sleek feel of it deliciously sensual. His breath caught.

This is altogether lovely, he thought, surveying the satin and lace nightgown and picturing the physicist within it. *Her eyes would fairly glow, and her hair...* He swallowed hard, trying to put the appealing image from his mind, so he could focus on his intent. *I wonder when she obtained it...and why. I have certainly never seen her in it.*

Allowing the long-suppressed artist within to emerge, he yielded to the resultant impulsiveness and laid it on the bed, ready for Chadwick to wear when she retired. Then he slipped out of the bedroom and made his way to the kitchen.

———

A little while later, Chadwick felt a tap on her shoulder. "Here," a familiar English voice murmured over that same shoulder, "drink this, then go to bed, my dear." She turned to see Holmes standing there with a mug in hand.

"What is it?" she queried, accepting the mug as he proffered it.

"A milk punch. Similar to a hot toddy, but more soporific. You need to sleep, and sleep well, tonight. You have not had a proper rest in days, if not weeks."

"Aw," she murmured, touched by his consideration, dropping her gaze to stare into the cup lest he read too much in her eyes. "You're taking care of me?"

"Attempting to, at any rate. It came to my attention today while you slept that you are entirely too thin and tired, Skye. Expect to be plied with food and drink, and to be ushered into bed at a reasonable if not early hour, in the next few days."

"Deal, provided you'll do the same," she fired back, sipping the soothing hot drink. His use of her given name had not been lost on her either, and it pleased her. "You've dropped a little weight, too. Your jeans are hanging looser than they used to."

———

"Fair enough, I suppose," Holmes agreed. It suddenly dawned on him that in order for her to have noticed the fit of his jeans, she had to have studied his body in detail. The thought was disconcerting, but not displeasing. Before he could react, however, she spoke.

"This is good," Chadwick observed, staring into the mug. "Brandy?"

"Yes. With a bit of honey for sweetness, and milk as the base. I would recommend drinking it, then going to bed post-haste, else you may become too inebriated to manage. I made it rather strong."

"Okay," she agreed, putting aside the rest of the mail until the morning.

––––––

When a mildly woozy Chadwick entered the bedroom, she was startled to find the bed turned down. She was even more startled, and decidedly chagrined, to find her once-favorite nightgown laid out for her use. *I'd almost forgotten about that thing*, she thought in dismay. *I'd wanted...after Holmes and I...I'd hoped to wear it for him one day, but that day never came. I don't suppose it ever will.*

She sighed despondently, reaching for it and running her hand over its silken smoothness. *Tina must have found it, and thought I'd like to wear it tonight. But I think I'll just put it back in the dresser and get out a t-shirt. I don't think I...*

Then the envelope resting on the pillow caught her eye.

––––––

It was clearly and simply addressed: *Dr. Skye Chadwick.* The words were formed by a black cartridge fountain pen in a firm, precise, almost bold male handwriting. A familiar handwriting, Chadwick found, after so many years of working closely with its creator.

Chadwick bit her lip in embarrassment, wondering if

Tina had, after all, not been the one to see to matters of bedtime preparations, and opened the envelope, extracting the missive inside.

———

My dear Skye,

As you know, I am not especially glib with regard to my own internal discourse. Ofttimes I find the things that matter most are the things least easily spoken. I strongly suspect, after our long association, that you already know this about me. Still, it is essential you should understand this before I continue, and so I mention it now.

I likely should have explained this matter to you years ago; but it was that very reticence of which I speak that prevented me from doing so. I now realise you need to understand why I did not continue the relationship we had once begun. In one sense, it was a deliberate and considered decision. Yet in another sense, I had absolutely no choice in the matter.

It is really quite simple: You had been gravely injured, you were still too weak to defend yourself, and an attempt upon you was highly probable, indeed almost certain. Yet simultaneously, I faced the fact that I had come to care for you, far more than I ever anticipated, more than I thought possible. I had believed such matters laid firmly and irrevocably aside, years before. But the distraction of your charms proved...substantial. It was not until that last day, however, that I fully realised how substantial. For I no longer trusted my mind to override the demands of my body, or my heart, and focus unyieldingly upon the problem at hand—namely, recognising and countering possible threats to your safety.

Given those considerations, the potential failure of my deductive reasoning assumed immense, nigh monumental, proportions. For a failure of that ability would have meant the certain death of the one companion I had remaining to me. And that, I would not—no, Sher-

lock, be honest, with yourself and with Skye—I COULD not have abided.

Still, I perforce wondered if our budding affaire de coeur would automatically result in the dissolution of those mental faculties upon which your life depended, or if I might, as the saying goes, "have my cake, and eat it, too." Wondered if it were possible to integrate the two —heart and mind—smoothly, seamlessly. Wondered if I would be allowed the time to try.

I spent that entire dreadful day struggling with these thoughts, Skye. I knew I had wounded you gravely, and my regret for that was, is, and I suspect shall ever remain, deep. But in the end, I did the only thing I felt I could do, the only thing I was absolutely certain would best ensure your survival: I set aside matters of the heart in order to safeguard the one who had stirred it. I held you at arms' length because I cared, not despite, nor because such caring was lacking. I found I preferred to have you by my side, though more distant than ardour suffered, over spending a few nights in your arms, only to lose you forever. I hope you will understand my choice—if choice it may be called—as similar to the decision you yourself made; for I, too, am not suicidal.

I am uncertain if you have ever truly forgiven me, in spite of your protestations earlier today. In truth, I am uncertain if I have ever forgiven myself; I have often considered, had I been stronger, had I been wiser, I might not have ever acted upon those feelings which, in the end, only served to so deeply wound you. Watching our counter-parts in the other continuum has only managed to reinforce that discomfort, as I now perforce must wonder if my choices were correct. Ha! I suppose that thought must have a familiar ring to you. Suffice to say these days, I understand all too well how you sometimes feel about my arrival in this continuum.

At any rate, I decided it was high past time you understood the reasons for my behaviour those long years ago. If you can find it in your heart to forgive a stubborn, fearful ass, the fearful ass will be eternally grateful.

Always and ever yours,
W.S.S.H.

———

Chadwick finished reading the letter and stood staring at it in amazement.

"Ohmigosh," she murmured lamely after several moments. "He actually...explained."

She shook her head, then suddenly galvanized into action, all hints of alcohol-induced unsteadiness gone. Chadwick tucked the letter, now a precious communiqué, into its envelope and the envelope safely into the drawer of her nightstand. Then she prepared for bed, ending by slipping the gown over her head and letting it slide to the floor across bare skin. Momentarily she debated donning a robe, then daringly decided against it.

Chadwick slipped out of the bedroom and across the hall, where she tapped on the door of Holmes' bedroom. A faint light shone underneath.

"Holmes?" she called softly. "May I come in?"

"Of course, Chadwick," came the muffled reply. "You know I am always available to you, if to few others. I have already retired, but if you do not mind..."

"It isn't like I haven't nursed you through a case or two of the flu, so I don't think I'll mind." Chadwick turned the doorknob and entered with a smile.

Holmes put aside the book he was reading, sitting up in bed with dilated grey eyes as he took in the vision in blue satin standing before him. He scanned her from head to toe, then raised his gaze to meet hers, and his eyes crinkled.

He likes the nightgown, she thought, seeing his reaction and recalling her other self's explanation of it. *He thinks it's pretty. So he WAS the one who turned down the bed and put out the gown.* Her heart suddenly leaped with hope, and she fought it back down. *Don't be silly, Skye. Of course he cares, you've known that all along, but he never said he loved you. Don't read too much into that little letter, or you'll only get hurt again.*

She made her way to the bedside and sat, offering him another shy smile. He returned it, and asked, "To what do I owe the honour of this little tête-à-tête?"

"To the letter you left me," Chadwick replied, sapphire gaze soft. "I wanted to thank you for it. It...explains a lot. And that...helps."

Holmes nodded and dropped his gaze thoughtfully, saying nothing.

"And I also wanted to say, you really were forgiven, that very day. I didn't fully understand your reasons until tonight, but I had a...a feeling, I guess you could say. See, I knew, when you didn't leave, that you still wanted me for a...companion," Chadwick explained, searching for exactly the right words, desiring to express herself to him without causing either of them pain, if she could. "And I knew..." Her voice shook, and she cleared it, struggling to keep it steady. "You weren't a womanizer, so our...time together...hadn't been meaningless, for either of us."

———

Holmes' head shot up, and he stared at her, stunned at both her grasp of the situation and her complete acceptance.

"So," she continued, a hint of shy primness in her manner, "I kinda figured at the time that it was all more than you were willing to take. I just didn't quite know why. I thought maybe I'd somehow pushed you too far, too fast. Now it makes perfect sense." She ran a light fingertip tentatively over the back of his hand as it lay on the coverlet, and he had to repress a sudden, unexpected shiver of yearning. "Anyway, I wanted you to know that you don't have to worry. Let it go, if you can."

"Thank you, Skye," he murmured, staring at the blankets. "That is...good to know."

"Okay," she said cheerfully, with a gentle grin. Chadwick rose from the bedside and turned toward the door. "Good night."

"Good night, my dear." He reached out to retrieve his book, stifling a wistful sigh.

"Oh, one more thing." She paused at the door and half-turned.

"Yes?" Holmes stopped with the book in hand and looked up at her, his breath halting in expectation.

"NOBODY calls you an ass around ME. Not even you. Is that clear?"

Chadwick gave him a stern look, and her sapphire eyes glinted in something akin to anger.

"Perfectly." Holmes' lips twitched in amusement as he responded.

"Good." The blue gaze calmed, angry glint replaced by mischievous twinkle. "Remember that. 'Night."

"I shall. Good night, Skye."

The door closed behind her, and a certain detective sat staring at it with dreamy grey eyes for fully five minutes. Finally he discarded the unopened book on the nightstand and turned out the lamp.

———

When Chadwick woke the next morning, the small vase in which she'd placed her lupine the night before had found its way from an end table in the den to her nightstand. And a second spray of lupine rested in it beside the first. Her eyebrows rose in surprise. *What on earth has gotten into him?* she wondered, dumbfounded. *This isn't like Holmes.*

But by the time she meandered her way through her morning ablutions, dressed in jeans and a t-shirt—deeply thankful that urgency was not required in said ablutions—and ambled into the den, she found herself being met by that same Holmes. He promptly offered her a smile and a cup of coffee with plenty of cream, just as she liked it.

"Here you are, my dear Chadwick. I fear I cannot claim to have made it, only to have poured it for you. Tina is already in the kitchen preparing breakfast, and I have been duly chastised by young Martha for failing to be home more often."

"Dat's wight, Unca Sherwock," a high-pitched voice noted behind him. "Oo gots 'a bwing Auntie Skye home sometimes, oo know."

Holmes spun, grey eyes flickering in wry amusement, to face the child, who stood in the door of the south hallway with her little hands on her hips and a firm expression on her pixie face.

"Believe me, Martha, when I say I would if I could," he informed her with a grin, spreading his hands in tolerant deference. Chadwick sipped the coffee, smiling while she watched this interaction.

"Martha," she interjected, "it isn't Uncle Sherlock's fault we aren't home more often. It's Auntie Skye's."

"Auntie Skye done kep' Unca Sherwock away?" The child stared up at the two adults, confusion in the wide innocent blue eyes.

"No, honey," Chadwick explained, crouching down. The little girl came to her trustingly as Holmes reached down and silently freed Chadwick's hands of the coffee mug. "Auntie Skye's...machine...is all messed up, and I've been working hard to fix it, to keep it from harming Uncle

Sherlock, and you, and your mummy and da, and our friends, and everybody."

Behind her, Holmes' eyes widened at Chadwick's prioritized enumeration.

"You see," Chadwick went on, unaware that by this time Tina had also joined the audience, "before you were born, even before your mummy and da got married, a bad man tried to take away Auntie Skye's machine. And we only just found out he broke it when he did that, so it wasn't working right anymore."

"Oo! Da bad man!" An angry Martha stamped her little foot. "Him bwoke Auntie Skye's toy!"

"Right," Chadwick agreed, lips twitching as she attempted to stifle laughter at the child's simplistic, yet accurate, grasp of the situation. The slightest noise emerged from the man behind her, and she recognized a suppressed snort of mirth in the sound. "And Uncle Sherlock and I have been working hard to fix it, so it wouldn't hurt anybody."

"Is it shawp?" Martha asked, troubled and subdued. "Cut da baby?"

Chadwick looked blank at that one, not quite able to translate the toddler's terms into anything applicable to the tesseract, and cast her gaze back over her shoulder. Twinkling grey eyes met her glance, and of all people, Holmes came to her rescue.

"Yes, Martha, it is a big sharp thing," he informed the child, "and would cut the baby very badly. It would cut everyone, very badly. But Auntie Skye has almost gotten it repair—er, fixed."

"With tons of help from Uncle Sherlock," Chadwick added.

"Okay, dat's good," Martha declared. It seemed obvious to her that, if Auntie Skye and Uncle Sherlock said it was fixed, the matter was settled and there was nothing to worry about. No longer upset, the child toddled back toward the kitchen. "Wet's eat bweakfas' now. Marfa's hungwy."

———

Chadwick rose to her feet, and Holmes stepped forward, laying a light hand on the small of her back as he handed the coffee mug back to her. Chadwick took it, but remained staring at the floor, while Holmes watched her thoughtfully. Tina gazed at them soberly before asking, "The whole thing was Haines' fault?"

"It was," Holmes verified. "So all of Skye's self-recriminations have been misdirected. The maledictions should have been aimed squarely at Haines."

"I'm not surprised," Tina noted. "I didn't think Dr. Chadwick's calculations would have been that far off."

"Nor I," Holmes agreed quietly.

Sapphire blue eyes flickered in gratitude, and Chadwick cast appreciative looks at her companions.

"Well, let's get some breakfast," she decided.

"I hope you two don't mind eating with Martha," Tina offered apologetically as she turned and led the way into the kitchen. "The little moppet flatly refused to eat with Billy and me at our house. She insisted she wanted to have breakfast with her auntie and uncle."

Holmes and Chadwick both chuckled.

"You know it's not a problem, Tina," Chadwick declared. "Martha's a sweetheart, and we both enjoy being around her."

"But how are you going to eat, Martha?" Holmes only

half-teasingly asked the child, who stood patiently beside the kitchen table. "This is a big people's table, and you haven't your special chair."

———

The little girl eyed the table thoughtfully, then cast a considering gaze upon Holmes. She watched as he pulled out a chair for Chadwick and saw her seated before taking a seat himself, then she toddled over to his side.

"Gonna sit in Unca Sherwock's wap," she decreed, holding out her arms to be picked up.

———

"Oh, now this is gonna get interesting," Chadwick muttered in amusement. "I can't wait to see how you get out of—oh, Sherlock, you're not!" she exclaimed, as the detective picked up the little girl and settled her on one thigh. "How on earth are you ever gonna eat, yourself, like that?"

"I shall manage," Holmes shot her a brief grin. "Extra napkins may be in order, however."

"Done." Tina grinned widely, grabbing a handful of paper napkins from the cupboard and plopping them beside Holmes' elbow before turning back to serve their plates. "You know, Mr. Holmes, I never would have guessed, from Watson's stories, that you liked children so much."

Holmes shrugged.

"The clues were there, though subtle," he decided, feeding Martha a bit of scrambled egg before taking a bite of his omelet. "Mostly in the use of the Irregulars."

"Oo wikes kids?" Martha observed around chewing her egg.

"I do, Martha."

"Coo. When is oo an' Auntie Skye gonna make me a pwaymate?"

"Huh?" Chadwick looked up from her own omelet, startled and confused by the question. Holmes' expression indicated he, too, was somewhat startled, though rather less confused; his face flushed slightly.

"Hush, Martha," Tina scolded quickly, embarrassed. "I've already explained that to you. Friends, remember?"

"Oh," the child murmured in a subdued fashion. "I forgot."

"I don't understand," Chadwick said quietly.

"Martha thinks..." Tina began, turning beet red. "I'm sorry, Dr. Chadwick. Martha has it in her head that you and Mr. Holmes are...like her mum and da. A family. And that families are supposed to have children."

"Oh," Chadwick murmured, sounding much like Martha. "So you explained?"

"Tried to," Tina sighed. "I'll just keep repeating it until it takes."

"Okay," Chadwick replied softly, returning her attention to her omelet.

But Holmes noted she seemed to have lost her appetite. Grey eyes closed to hide the pain in them.

———

After breakfast, Chadwick disappeared into her room, and Holmes wandered down to the barn. He greeted Silver Blaze with an apple nipped from the kitchen and spent some time in general conversation with Williams and their staff before he wandered back to the house in Billy's company, thankful to have some leisure time.

Holmes found Chadwick on the deck in the lee of the house, clad in her old bubble-gum pink bikini, soaking up the autumnal sun like a cat.

"Chadwick," he reprimanded, taking a seat on a corner of her blanket, "you have put on your sunscreen, have you not?"

"Everywhere except my back," she replied lazily. "Oh, this feels so good." After another few seconds, she continued, "And don't worry. I was gonna call Tina to put it on my back when I was ready to roll over. She loaned me the kitchen timer." The egg timer Holmes had noted sitting nearby went off just then. "Oh, I guess it's time to roll over, or I'll be sunny side up," she noted whimsically, suiting actions to words. "Holmes, would you mind getting Tina for me?"

"No need," he decided, picking up the tube of sunscreen, which lay beside the egg timer. Before she could reply, nimble fingers had unhooked her bra top. "However, I should recommend you lie quite still while I do this. Several of the Aerotech Drive Irregulars have the buggy out, working on it in the barnyard, ensuring that it is in proper function in case you should wish to go for a drive. It would prove rather... revealing...should you move."

As he spoke, Williams emerged from the house, and Holmes watched absently as he sauntered across the back yard to chat with Wang, Huggins, and Hargreave as they overhauled the buggy. By this time Holmes already had a large blob of cream in his hand, and he spread it across Chadwick's back, using broad, unhurried strokes.

———

"Oh!" Chadwick exclaimed, surprised and mildly shocked at the feel of his fingers gliding over her skin. She struggled with the effort to avert responding to the unavoidable sensuality of the smooth touch, and wondered if she was only imagining a hint of possessiveness in it. "I—you don't have to do this, Holmes. I thought you'd rather..."

"Skye," he said quietly, continuing to work, "I should have thought by now you would understand that I will not let you come to harm if it is in my power to prevent it. Even in so simple a matter as sunburn."

––––––

In the barnyard, the four men huddled, murmuring together, and suddenly a wide-eyed Williams glanced over his shoulder, directly at the couple on the deck.

Holmes met Billy's startled gaze, then raised an eyebrow before deliberately directing his attention to the shapely back beneath his hands.

Williams' expression changed from surprise to smirking glee, and he turned back to his satisfied companions.

Holmes finished his work and capped the tube of lotion.

––––––

"I...I guess I didn't..." Chadwick glanced up at him uncertainly as he fastened her top once more, then she pushed up enough to reach for the nearby towel, handing it to him. "Here." She fished an ice cube out of her glass of water and gave it to him as well.

"Thank you." He allowed the ice cube to melt in his hand, then wiped off the residue of sunscreen, while she reset her egg timer and settled back down.

Then, to her surprise, he stretched out on the blanket, lying on his stomach, resting his chin on his folded hands, and staring her directly in the eyes.

"Skye, I know it is difficult, in the circumstances. But if you can, I should very much like it if you could try to relax around me. We have been together too long, and been through too much, to worry about giving offense, wouldn't you say?"

Chadwick blinked at the calm grey gaze. "I...I just thought..." she began, letting her voice fade away.

———

"I know," he answered gently. "And I appreciate your attempt at considering my feelings. But as you said yourself last night, I still wish you to remain my...companion. My closest companion, at that." He maintained her gaze, allowing his eyes to crinkle almost imperceptibly. "Had you considered it in that light? That you are my closest, most trusted ally? The best friend I have in this continuum, and on a par with Watson in my original spacetime?"

Chadwick stared at him thoughtfully.

"No, I haven't," she murmured, stunned at the honor being accorded. "I...thank you."

"And I thank you," Holmes responded softly. "Perhaps someday...I should like to see my two bosom companions meet..."

Chadwick offered him a shy smile, and he returned it. Then he closed his eyes with a sigh, content to absorb the warmth of the sunlight on his back.

———

Chadwick studied his face for several moments, then closed

her own eyes and tried to relax. She had almost managed it when he murmured, "Skye?"

"Yeah, Sherlock?" The name came unbidden to her lips, and she internalized the wince, refusing to open her eyes for several seconds lest he see it. So she missed the slight smile on his face at the sound of his given name.

"Have you ever been to London?" he asked laconically, appearing half-asleep. Noticing that fact, Skye closed her eyes again.

"No, I haven't. Why?"

"Have you ever given consideration to such a visit? Or even, to living elsewhere? London, or perhaps Paris, or maybe Washington?"

"Um," Chadwick pondered how to answer, her heart sinking. "I'd had it in mind to visit London with you some-time. But that was before the tesseract went to hell in a hand basket."

———

"What about living there?" he wondered, opening his eyes to gaze at her.

"I can't say I've thought about it," she replied flatly.

"Oh," was all Holmes said, disappointedly noting that her eyes were firmly closed.

———

"What brought on this subject?" Chadwick asked, hiding her reluctance to hear the answer, and discreetly peeping at him between veiled lashes.

"Nothing in particular." Holmes shrugged. "I have not been to the land of my birth since arriving in this continuum—as you say, with the tesseract in disrepair, there has been no time. However, my counterpart in the other continuum has not existed in that spacetime a full year as yet, but he is already visiting England..."

"Oh," Chadwick murmured, heart breaking anew. "Well, in a week or so, we'll be all done, and you can travel to your heart's content." She paused, thinking, then added, "I guess if you wanted to, you could go now. I'm sure Billy could have a flight set up for you in no time. You could probably fly out in a day or two."

———

Holmes blinked, heartache lancing through the grey eyes. "You...no longer wish me to...?"

But to his chagrin, he found Chadwick knew him far too well not to hear the pain in his voice, though he tried his utmost to disguise it. The blue eyes flew open, and she gazed into his face, her expression telling him that she could see the tautness in it that he struggled to hide.

"No, no," she protested instantly. "I do want you to. I just..." It was her turn to shrug. "What I don't want is for you to feel trapped. You can do whatever you want to do, Hon. If you want to go, then you can go. I'll...manage."

"Alone."

Holmes delivered the single word, then watched her closely, suddenly aware that this was her preliminary attempt at letting go. *Of everything, and everyone,* he realized. *When this is over, she believes she will have nothing left. Not even to live for. The only thing keeping her going now may very well be the knowledge that the lives of at least one universe, and likely more, depend upon her. She no longer cares for her own life.* Crushing pain seemed to grip the former detective, followed by determined resolve.

"If I have to. I've done it before." She shrugged again, dismissing his concern.

"No," Holmes shook his head firmly. "I shall not do that to you. I will not abandon you, certainly not now, at the moment of crisis. We can discuss the future once we have ascertained there is one."

Chadwick nodded dully. Just then, her egg timer went off.

"Time to go in," she observed, pushing up to her hands and knees.

"And just in time for luncheon," Holmes noted blithely. "Come, my dear. You need to eat."

————

That night the pair was informed that Williams had made reservations for them at his former workplace: the Cimarron Springs Hotel in Colorado Springs.

"It's time both of you had some nice leisure time, for a change," Billy told them in no uncertain terms. "Not to mention some good, fattening food! So you go get spiffed up and get down the mountain. No, no back-talk out of either of you! Your ranch foreman is giving the orders this time."

Holmes and Chadwick exchanged a bemused glance, shrugged, then turned for their bedrooms to get ready.

But Holmes cast a mischievous grin over his shoulder at Billy, who winked back.

————

So the week went. Each morning a new sprig of lupine appeared in the vase on Chadwick's nightstand, and each day the pair found some new leisure activity to occupy them, most apparently planned by their liaisons and the ranch help, though Holmes never seemed unduly surprised by anything.

Three days into their holiday, Tina presented them with a picnic basket and shooed them out the side door. Outside, they found Williams holding the reins of the buggy, with Buddy and Peggy Sue already in the traces. Huggins, in turn, stood by the gate, ready to let them out. Chadwick shook her head.

"I know what it is," she remarked whimsically, addressing Billy. "Y'all are used to us bein' gone, so you're tryin' to get rid of us. Are we in the way that bad?"

"Ah, you know better than that, Boss," Williams grinned. "Both of you have been down to the barn every day, messing with the horses. Now get in this buggy," he flipped the ends of the reins, "and go have some fun. We don't care where you go, just as long as you go, and have fun while you're about it."

Holmes handed Chadwick up into the buggy. She took the reins from Williams and held the team steady while Holmes climbed into the buggy, then to his surprise, passed the reins to him. At his querying glance, she shrugged.

"I feel like not having to think today. I've done way too much of that in the last year or so. Point 'em out the gate, and let's see where we end up."

"Attagirl!" Williams exclaimed, pleased. He exchanged grins with Holmes, and in seconds the buggy was off.

————

They eventually ended up near Dog-Leg Rock, a location where they'd picnicked before. Chadwick got the picnic basket from the boot of the buggy while Holmes took the horses out of harness and hobbled them so they could graze. Chadwick opened the basket and began extracting its contents.

Soon a delightful luncheon was spread before them on a blanket on the ground. This included china, silverware, and crystal, as well as a bottle of wine—a nice rich burgundy. The meal was composed of finger foods—julienned vegetables, cubes of cheese, sliced roast beef, fried chicken, freshly baked rolls, and strawberries and cream.

"Oh my," Chadwick murmured, looking over the fare. "This is lovely."

"It is," Holmes agreed, taking her hand to help her sit on the corner of the blanket before seating himself. "Quite a pleasant little repast."

"But I..." she began, then stopped.

"But what?" Holmes wondered, pouring two glasses of wine and handing one to her.

"It's a bit...much, don't you think?" Chadwick wondered, biting her lip. "I mean, you'd think we..." She paused, suddenly uncertain and horribly uncomfortable, as a thought struck. "You don't think they're trying to...match-make us, do you?"

"I think it is very nice," he decreed, surveying the meal spread before them as he sipped his burgundy. He completely ignored her last question. "A lovely day, a delightful meal, and an intimate friend. I cannot imagine a more relaxing, pleasant way to spend the day. It quite stirs the Vernet in my blood."

Chadwick's eyebrows shot up at that remark. She took refuge in her glass of wine, in order to think over the small details of recent events, before setting it down and beginning to fill the empty plate Holmes handed her.

"You know, speaking of which," she offered, "the...er, Other Me...indicated her Holmes was really talented in regard to sketching scenes, or something like that."

———

"Yes, Cha— Skye," Holmes answered her unspoken question, correcting himself in mid-name. He smiled around a mouthful of the roast beef sandwich he'd cobbled together from the sliced meat and a roll. "I can. In fact, I discovered a sketchpad and pencils in the boot a few minutes ago. Billy must have added them; I seem to recall mentioning a whim to return to it, a day or so ago."

"Ooo," Chadwick said, staring at him with wide eyes. "Do you think you could do something for me this afternoon, maybe? Or will that be enough time?"

"Oh, it is not as if I paint, my dear," Holmes replied, a cautionary tone in his voice, lest she expect too much. "I merely sketch. It does not take so very long to create an image in that fashion."

"Still, I'd love to see your work. I've seen your schematic drawings, and they're impressive. Very detailed."

"Then I shall see if I can produce something that will please milady," Holmes answered mildly, reaching for the strawberries.

———

After they ate, Holmes got out the sketchbook and sat back down facing Chadwick. He looked about, pretending to scout for a suitable subject, before cocking his head and surveying Chadwick with interest. Moments later, the pencil was dancing across the paper with a faint scratching sound as Holmes recorded the scene before him. Chadwick sat and watched him as he drew in silence.

"Um..." she began softly.

"'Um' what?"

"Holmes...uh, Sherlock...would you do me a favor?"

The dark head immediately looked up from its work, attention focusing on his subject. *I cannot recall the last time she asked a personal favour of me,* he thought in some startlement. *This is...excellent.*

"What do you need, Skye?"

"I don't want to bother you, but..." she began shyly, with a rueful grin. "It's too quiet. I...my mind keeps wandering back to the tesseract. And then I start worrying. Would you mind talking to me?"

"Of course, my dear," he said, expression softening as understanding dawned. "Do you have a preferred topic of conversation, or shall I simply start talking about whatever comes to mind?"

"Whatever comes to mind will do. Just keep my thoughts occupied and off a certain apparatus."

"Very well," he nodded, returning to his drawing pad. "I mentioned that I do not paint. For me, it seems to be a matter of developing appropriate brush strokes, and getting the colour transitions correct. As you did not even know I sketched, I suspect I have not told you about my experiments in painting, back in Baker Street."

"No, you haven't."

"One incident in particular comes immediately to mind. It really was one of my best attempts," he noted, reminiscing as his hands continued recording the scene before him. "It was a pastoral scene, a depiction of springtime in a field at the family estate when I was a child. I was very pleased at how it was coming along. But as you know, oil paints, which were essentially all I had to work with at the time, are very slow to dry. This has its advantages and disadvantages, of course. I personally found it advantageous to be able to come back to the thing the following morning, and pick up where I had left off. If, for instance, I did not like the way shadows were blending, I could stop and walk away, then return when my perspective was fresher."

"Makes sense," Chadwick decided. Holmes promptly recorded the contemplative countenance before him, then returned to his tale.

"However, as you also know, oil paints are decidedly aromatic, hence the decision to leave the easel in the sitting room, rather than keep it in my bedroom. I preferred to awaken fresh, rather than headachy from sleeping amidst the fumes of turpentine and the like—which is also why the chemical lab was in a corner of the sitting room."

"I can see that. I'd do the same thing."

"No doubt," Holmes agreed, setting to paper her quirk of eyebrow. "Unfortunately, it seems that Watson had wandered into the sitting room in the night, in search of something—I believe it was his book, though it may have been his pipe—and neglected to close the door into the hall," Holmes recalled. "Mrs. Hudson's cat, Marmalade, discovered this fact."

"The big orange longhair?" Chadwick verified.

"The same. Has it ever occurred to you what kind of brushstroke the agitated tail of a curious cat would make upon a canvas...?"

"Oh no!" Chadwick exclaimed, slapping her hand to her mouth. "She didn't!"

"I am afraid she did," Holmes grinned wryly, adding an amused twinkle to the eyes of the woman in his sketch. "Right across the center of the painting. This, after finding my fully-loaded palette and rolling in it. Then she proceeded to rub against the client's chair...and the sofa...and the chemical table...and my desk...and the door-frame...and right down the banister of the stairs. Making sure, I might add, to rub every single spindle in the railing."

"Oh my," Chadwick responded, stifling laughter with difficulty.

"Go ahead and laugh, my dear," Holmes offered, seeing her cheeks turning pink with the effort of restraining herself. "Even I laughed—eventually—as the full scope of Marmalade's perambulations revealed themselves."

"No, no, it's horrible that your painting was ruined," Chadwick protested, and Holmes saw the seriousness in her eyes—despite her contorted lips and red cheeks—as he continued his tale.

"Needless to say, the next morning, Watson was the only one of the household in good humour. The canvas was unsalvageable, Mrs. Hudson and I spent hours finding and removing wet artists' paint, the entire flat positively reeked of turpentine for days, and poor Marmalade had to have her fur trimmed of the greasy mess. Her tail, and much of her back, was decidedly bald in patches. I believe you would term it a 'Mohawk.'"

"Oh NO!" Chadwick gave up trying to hold in the laughter; she howled, doubling over. The happy sound echoed off mountains and outcrops near and far, until the air rang with her mirth. A grinning Holmes paused in his drawing, content for the moment to absorb the rare sound of his companion's merriment.

———

Upon their return, Holmes unveiled his work, showing it to Chadwick, the Williams family, and their "ranch hands." It was an impressive portrait of a pensive Chadwick, eyes twinkling in amusement at some thought, sitting on the corner of the picnic blanket amid the tall, sere grass of the high meadow, with Pikes Peak in the background.

"Oh, it's lovely!" Chadwick exclaimed softly.

"It really is, Holmes," Billy noted. "You captured her exactly."

"It's Auntie Skye!" little Martha cried excitedly. "Unca Sherwock, did oo do dat?"

"I did, Martha," Holmes confirmed unassumingly. "Do you like it?"

"It's boo'ful," Martha decreed. "Jus' wike Auntie Skye."

"Indeed," Holmes agreed, as Chadwick blushed. "Just like Auntie Skye."

As the scientist and the detective entered the house alone, their ranch help could just discern them in the hallway as Holmes deposited a light, affectionate kiss on the top of a blonde head.

Wang caught Huggins' eye and winked.

9

Putting Humpty-Dumpty Together

Over succeeding days, there were more buggy outings, several horseback rides, two movies viewed in the theater, and a couple of restaurant reservations, as well as considerable sleeping late and the occasional afternoon nap. Lupines regularly continued to appear mysteriously in Chadwick's bedside vase. The relationship between a certain scientist and a certain detective continued to remain warm and companionable.

But on the ninth day of the rest break, everyone—even the Irregulars—woke tense and anxious, well aware that the following day would determine whether their world would continue or cease to exist.

Chadwick, in particular, was restless and stressed. She ate little for breakfast, but by lunch was barely able to sit still, let alone eat.

"Chadwick—Skye—this will not do," Holmes decreed, deeply concerned. "You must relax."

"I know. Here I've gotten nice and rested, and I'm gonna wear myself out all over again before I ever get back down to Schriever. I didn't sleep hardly at all last night."

"Then she should take a nap," Tina urged. "Don't you think, Mr. Holmes?"

"I do," Holmes averred. "Go stretch out on the sofa, Skye, and let me prepare something to help you relax."

Chadwick did, and Holmes was as good as his word. Within five minutes he brought her a soothing hot drink. Twenty minutes after drinking it, she was asleep.

Tina gave the detective an approving nod, then she took Martha—who was herself fretful, apparently in response to the tension—and left, headed to the barn to inform the men to stay quiet, before going to her own home in the far corner of the ranch.

Holmes covered Chadwick with a knit afghan, then moved to the nearby armchair with a book.

———

Chadwick woke screaming and trying to fight. Her eyes opened, to find worried grey eyes gazing back, and firm hands gently gripping her shoulders.

"Calm down, my dear," Holmes soothed softly. "All is well. Calm down. There's a girl." He gave her a chance to catch her breath, then, still kneeling beside the couch, murmured, "The nightmare?"

"A nightmare," she panted, "but not THE nightmare."

"What, then?" he wondered.

———

"I dreamed I muffed the brane regeneration," she whispered, unable to meet his eyes. "I tried to go too fast, and overshot the rest energy. Everything was literally coming apart around us. I—I tried," she broke off suddenly, averting her face to hide the misery, humiliation, and pain,

"I was trying to send you back to your own continuum. I hoped maybe, just maybe, you'd be safe there. But I...I didn't make it. You didn't make it." Her voice broke, and she swallowed hard, struggling with all her might for control.

But in the next instant the battle was lost. Her tears overflowed, and utterly overwhelmed, she could only whimper, "I'm so sorry, Sherlock."

————

"For what?" he asked softly.

"Dragging you here...into the middle of this hell," she muttered despondently, her expression one of hopelessness and despair.

"I am alive, Skye," he murmured, gathering her into his arms to offer comfort. "That is more than could be said, had you not intervened at Reichenbach." Her terminology had not escaped his notice, and coming on the heels of her very specific nightmare, he grew concerned.

In her perception, she IS dwelling in a kind of hell, he realized. *A living nightmare from which she sees no awakening. And should we succeed in ending the fear, and the danger, what then? Will the nightmare end, or will it simply transmute?*

He noted, too, that the dream had revealed her subconscious' ultimate concern—his safety. With her own universe lost, she had sought only to place him beyond the reach of its destruction, even at the cost of her own life.

For certainly she would have had to stay behind, to operate the tesseract. I was right. Her own life is meaningless to her now. No, it will not do, he thought determinedly. *This cannot be allowed to continue.*

So he added, "And the continuum's deterioration has

been stopped as well, and I have every confidence we will be able to permanently stabilise it tomorrow."

"I wish I was so confident," she sighed miserably, burying her face in his shirt as she continued to cry quietly. "I've messed up everything I've ever done, I think. Sometimes I wish I was d..." She broke off. He felt her swallow hard again, and this time a shudder ran through her frame before she continued. "Sometimes I wish I'd never been born."

He pulled back, staring at her in shocked disbelief, seeing the agony of pain, misery, and uncertainty that was etched into her face. He had heard her completed statement, knew as well what statement she had aborted—he was too good a detective not to deduce so simple a thing, and knew her too well to think he had been mistaken. So horrified was he at the revelation of her thoughts, that he reacted in a way he had not done in several years—purely on instinct.

"No, my dear, never," he whispered, responding to her thought as much as to her statement. "Never let go. You swore to me you would not," he reminded her—just before he covered her lips with his own.

The kiss went on for nearly a minute, both reacting with equal intensity. When he finally broke it, it was only to tuck her head beneath his chin and cradle her for long moments. She nestled into his chest, seeming unsure what was happening, but welcoming the comfort and the caring, needing it badly. As she pressed close, Holmes breathed a single sentence into her ear, scarcely aware he said the words hammering in his mind.

"I love you," sighed past his lips.

But as soon as he'd said them, he caught himself. *Damnation,* he thought, shocked at what he'd done, *I had not meant to admit that to her as yet. I had intended to court her longer, convince her of my continued, and renewed, interest. This is far too soon. What if she does not believe it? What if she no longer wants it? I may have just ruined everything.*

Deeply worried, he raised his head and gazed down into the sapphire eyes. Tears no longer flowed from them, but he could discern no expression of emotion in them whatsoever, not even that of surprise.

Certainly, I deserved this, he thought sadly, waiting for a reaction, any reaction, and getting nothing. *She once declared her love, and I pushed her away. Now the situation has reversed, and she has her own back. Dear God, help me.*

"I...forgive me, Skye," he whispered, miserable and defeated, turning away and starting to stand, even as something within his chest threatened to shatter irreparably.

But small fingers caught at his hand—a meager yet powerful force, which prevented him from rising—just before lacing themselves with his own fingers. He glanced back at her, uncertain. She met his eyes with a slight, wistful smile.

"Don't go," she murmured softly.

He turned back toward her, hesitant and uncharacteristically unsure.

"What do you want of me?"

Chadwick lay back on the sofa, gave him a pleading look, and held out her arms to him.

Holmes immediately went into them.

———

He cooked dinner that night: Steak, with salad, baked potatoes, and steamed asparagus drizzled with balsamic vinegar, served with a delightful Australian shiraz, and a trifle for dessert. Unbeknownst to Chadwick until mealtime, he also fished out the good china, silver, and crystal, serving everything on a linen cloth spread on the kitchen table. Her grandmother's silver candlesticks finished off the presentation. The candles' flames danced in the dim light as Holmes led Chadwick to the table.

Their afternoon had made it plain that the candles were not the only fires in the room at that moment, and Chadwick allowed herself to be seated, then watched silently as her companion seated himself, not across, but alongside. Holmes acted the host, serving Chadwick solicitously as they ate their way through the delicious three-course meal.

Afterward, he led her into the den, where a fire was laid in the fireplace, for the autumnal evening was growing chilly. He set a match to the kindling, and soon the logs blazed, warming the room and its occupants. Little Anna wandered out from whatever hidey-hole she had occupied, to curl on the hearth as Holmes poured two glasses of brandy, then joined Chadwick on the sofa.

"Here you are, my dear," he murmured, handing her one of the glasses. Then he held up his glass and gazed directly into sapphire eyes. "To my bonny, brave comrade in arms, The Woman who saved my life and quite possibly my sanity, not to mention the universe as a whole."

Holmes started to clink his glass to Chadwick's, but she drew it back.

"And to my handsome, brilliant detective," she added, "who stuck by me and kept me going through the middle of my own personal nightmare, whose heart is far bigger than he knows."

His lips quirked slightly, pleased, and this time they did clink glasses and sip from them. Holmes kicked off his shoes and tucked his feet under himself, and they both settled into the couch, content to enjoy the fire and each other's company as twilight fell outside the windows.

Several of the erstwhile ranch hands were in the back yard, working on repairing the gate into the pasture; Silver Blaze, in his enthusiasm to greet his adored detective, had leaned on it too hard two days prior, and damaged one of the hinges. Huggins happened to glance up at the main house, and his eyes grew wide.

"Wang!" he hissed. "Quick! Look!" He nodded at the picture windows overlooking the deck and the ranch, and the others glanced in the direction he indicated.

Inside the house, silhouetted against the flickering orange light from the fire, could be seen two heads protruding above the sofa, one tall, one less so. The long, wiry arm of the taller person crept along the back of the sofa, past the other head, then disappeared downward. Shortly thereafter the heads drew closer together. The shorter one tilted, coming to rest partly hidden by the couch.

"Ooo," Hargreave grinned, "she's got her head on his shoulder."

"Bloody marvelous," Wang breathed, delighted. "Now c'mon, old chap...take the next step..."

As they watched, the other head turned until it was visible in profile, though still silhouetted. The first head fully reappeared and tilted up to meet the second, which bent and merged with the first.

"Woot!" Wang exclaimed softly. "Goal!"

"Oh my," Huggins murmured, watching. "They're disappearing behind the sofa..."

"Maybe we oughta leave now, boys," Hargreave muttered, face turning red. "This gate can wait 'til morning, don't 'cha think?"

"I do think," Wang agreed immediately, averting his

face. "Quiet and double time back to the barracks, lads. Quick march."

Within seconds, the back yard was empty.

———

The pair resumed their nuzzling and kissing from the afternoon, content to remain so as the evening wore on. Bedtime approached, and Holmes finally rose to stoke the fire against the night's chill.

"Come, Skye," he said softly, holding out a hand. "Tomorrow will be a busy day, and it is time you were in bed."

Chadwick stood and took his hand, walking with him down the hall into the northern wing of the house. There, she turned toward her bedroom door, pushing it open and walking through, all the while refusing to let go of his hand. Holmes' eyebrow rose, but he allowed himself to be led into her bedroom. She turned to him and smiled, still gripping his fingers securely.

"Did you like the blue nightgown?" she asked quietly.

"Yes," he whispered, meeting the sapphire eyes and reading her intent there. Chadwick nodded, her smile growing deeper.

"Okay," she said, finally releasing his hand and turning toward the dresser. "I'll get it out while you turn down the bed."

He simply stood there, looking at her, for several moments. Finally he observed, "My own accoutrements are across the hall..."

"Okay," she shrugged, coming up with the satin gown. She closed the drawer and shook out the fabric, smiling to herself.

"Perhaps I should go and..." Holmes gestured somewhat vaguely at the door.

Chadwick stopped, staring down at the silk and lace in her hands, as the smile on her lips faded. Abruptly her shoulders slumped.

———

"Oh. Okay," she murmured, her tone expressing her defeat. "I understand now. It's all right. You don't have to do anything you don't want to do." She glanced up long enough to shoot him a wobbly smile that tried to be reassuring and failed, then stared down at the top of the dresser, unseeing. "I know you're trying to take care of me, get me through this, but you didn't have to go that far with it. I kept going the first time; I'll manage this time, too. And after tomorrow, if...if you want to go to London, or Washington, or wherever you wanna go, don't worry. I'll be fine."

Holmes made no reply, and after several seconds Chadwick heard the bedroom door close softly. The silk nightgown slithered through her hands, unheeded, to the floor. She bit her lip hard to hold back the tears, and clutched the top of the dresser with fingers whose knuckles whitened under the force of the grip. She tried to laugh, a bitter sound, but it broke at the end, becoming a gasping sob instead. She drew back a fist to punch it blindly through the mirror, but it was caught firmly, as an arm wrapped around her from behind and pulled her back into a strong chest.

"Don't do that," a quiet, English-accented voice murmured into her ear. "It will send blood and glass everywhere. I should not like to have to dig glass slivers from your lacerated hand, or worse, rush you to hospital for stitches and a unit of blood."

"You don't have to keep up this little charade," Chadwick gasped and choked out, trying to be sharp, and failing. "I already told you, I'll be fine."

"I have been playing no charade. And this is only secondarily about 'getting you through.' I am here, Chadwick," he paused, corrected several years of habit, "I am here, Skye, and you will have to tell me to leave...if that is what you wish."

"Bu-but you," she stammered, struggling to hold back the tears, "you said you wanted...your things were across the hall..."

"Merely because it occurred to me that a fresh mouth and a close shave might be appreciated, given your apparent intent," came the mildly amused response. "My foresight was rather lacking in that regard, else I might have had grooming matters more readily in hand." He turned her to face him, tilting her head back to look into her eyes. "Besides, it is your decision, Skye. I meant what I said this afternoon, but I fully realise that, after all this time, you may no longer want it."

Chadwick searched his face intently, startled to see his expression was completely open and unreserved, nothing hidden from her scrutiny...including his uncertainty. She drew a deep, shuddering breath, then let it out slowly.

"Sherlock, do you remember—it's been years—not so long after you moved in here, we had a conversation about modern morals and relationships?"

"Ah, yes," Holmes teased, "the 'birds and the bees' lecture."

Chadwick shot him a glance that somehow managed to simultaneously convey mischief and reproof, then chuckled in a slightly wobbly fashion.

"Yeah, that one. So I take it, you do remember it?"

"I do."

"Do you remember asking me about my own stance on relationships?"

"Yes," he breathed. "You said you only intended to have one man, and marriage was to involve the husband, the wife, and their Creator."

"And a piece of paper, or the presence of clergy, didn't necessarily make a marriage."

"Yes, I remember," he said, grey eyes gazing steadfastly into blue.

"So maybe you'll understand when I tell you...you're that one man, and as far as I've been concerned, I've been tied to you from..." Chadwick paused, eyes going distant as she thought back, then shook her head. "I dunno, Sherlock. Maybe from the moment you set foot in this continuum. Or maybe from the instant I set foot in yours."

Holmes' breath caught, and he stared into her earnest face.

"You have loved me from the first?"

"I think...I did," she admitted hesitantly. "I just didn't know it initially. I know you didn't...might not feel...the same. But I...ever since...that night, you've been the man I think of as...as...my..."

Unable to continue, she dropped her head, and he pulled her into his chest, understanding that she couldn't meet his gaze in that moment of intimate confession. They were silent for a long moment.

"So," he suggested finally, allowing the faintest hint of whimsy to creep into his voice in an effort to lighten her intense mood, "this is less a 'starting over,' and more a reconciliation between spouses, would you say?"

"Maybe a little of both." Chadwick gave a watery laugh. "If...if it's what you want, too."

"Very well, then. But I do have one question."

"What?"

227

"Might I go across the hall and get my toothbrush and razor first?"

A peal of laughter burst from Chadwick's throat. Holmes pulled back, grinning, and gazed down into glowing sapphires. *THERE,* he thought in immense satisfaction. *There is my dear Skye, back once more. She has been gone for far too long.*

"Go," she ordered, still laughing. "But hurry up with it!"

"Heavens above," Holmes retorted, turning for the door. "Is that what I sounded like to poor Watson, in another place and time? Surely I was not so autocratic in my dealings!"

"GIT!" Chadwick exclaimed, lunging and swatting at his posterior, and only missing when Holmes executed a last-instant deft hip twist. "You've got five minutes!"

"I go, and stand not upon the order of my going!" Holmes shot back, headed through the door.

————

Some time later, the pair curled in bed together. The room was dark, save for the odd slice of moonlight filtering between the curtains at the windows. Chadwick had donned her blue satin nightgown, and Holmes wore the pyjama pants to which he had grown accustomed since coming to this continuum. He turned over in bed to face her, his concern expressing itself in the shadowed aquiline face.

"Skye, I know what you want tonight. But tomorrow is a momentous day, my dear, and rest, not intimacy, must be the priority. No, no," he soothed, seeing her face fall, "I swear to you, Skye, this is no charade. I do intend to hold you close tonight, and I have little doubt but that this will shortly prove to you my sincerity in the matter."

And he gathered his companion into his arms, cradling her against his body. Chadwick sighed in mingled capitulation and pleasure before snuggling into his side.

"You're warm," she murmured, taking comfort.

"Mm. As are you."

———

A few minutes later, Chadwick said reproachfully, "Aw, Sherlock."

"What?"

"You really were serious."

———

"Yes." He sighed into the darkness.

"That's gotta be torture. Are you gonna be able to relax and get any sleep?"

"That is not important." The arms around her shrugged. "Tomorrow, the spotlight belongs to you. I will assist, of course, but it is unlikely I shall be doing much more than what is required of a...I believe the term is, 'glorified go-fer.' You are the one for whom sleep is essential."

"Oh, no, no. That won't wash. You're much more than that in the Chamber, and you know it. You're my other set of eyes and ears, my extra brain, the one who double-checks my calculations and settings and does it as fast as I can."

"No matter. You know I am quite capable of high function, even without sleep."

"No, Sherlock, that won't do."

———

Suddenly she ducked under the covers.

"Skye, what— Oh." Holmes' grey eyes dilated as the room about him appeared to brighten, then they fluttered closed, and he settled into the mattress with a soft groan.

"Do you...like it?" Chadwick's uncertain voice was muffled under the blankets.

"Yes..."

"Good."

Holmes lay quietly, his respiration quickening until it came in sharp pants. He opened his eyes for a moment, staring dreamily into darkness, ecstasy filling him.

"Skye," he breathed, yearning. Once more, eyelids fluttered closed over silver orbs.

"Shh..." came her soothing response from beneath the covers. "Relax and enjoy."

———

He gasped, then suddenly cried out her name. His body stiffened, then arched, and only gradually subsided to the mattress. Unhurriedly, Chadwick's head emerged from beneath the blankets, and she gazed at his face. His eyes were still closed, but his lips curved in an almost other-worldly smile. She brushed a kiss against the corner of his mouth, breathing in his ear.

"I love you, Sherlock. I always have, and I always will. No matter what."

He never opened his eyes, but long arms wrapped around her, gathering her close.

"I believe I can sleep now, my dear spouse. Can you?"

"As long as you're here, yeah, I think so."

"And I am not going anywhere," he informed her,

opening shining silver eyes to her sight. "So lie back and take your rest, my dearest. I give you my most solemn word, I will be here when you awaken."

Chadwick drew a long breath. She tucked her face into Holmes' shoulder, and felt his cheek come to rest against her hair. She sighed contentedly, and heard its echo above her head.

Within a quarter of an hour, they were both asleep.

———

The next morning, they took their time arising, as much because Chadwick dreaded the day as because alarm clocks were, finally, properly and duly rung. Though this latter did not occur without intense consideration.

"Really, I should much prefer you did not risk exhausting yourself before today's important procedure, Skye."

"I understand everything you're saying, Sherlock," Chadwick replied, shaking her head, "and it makes perfect, logical sense, and in that respect, you're completely right. But this isn't my brain talking, Honey. It's my heart. I NEED you right now. I need the emotional connection, and I need the strength that comes with it. And most of all, if I mess this up, if we die today, I want us to have made love one last time."

———

Holmes capitulated then, pulling his mate close and kissing her deeply, allowing his hands to explore and caress, and secretly reveling in the sighs and mews that resulted.

Chadwick's own hands were busy as well, tracing the contours of her much-beloved detective's strong, wiry body. In short order, they could wait no longer, and the pair joined for the first time in over four years.

But although their foreplay was eager and swift, they took their time enjoying their lovemaking.

"For," Holmes pointed out, with a combination of determination and whimsy, "should this indeed be the last time, by Jove, it shall be done properly."

———

When they were finally sated, they lay contentedly in each other's arms for a long time, both reluctant to break the bond.

"Besides," Chadwick murmured, "once we get up, we start the downhill slide toward...whatever's gonna happen."

But in the end there was no help for it; the membrane's reboost to rest energy could not be put off any longer, or they risked undoing everything they'd worked so hard to achieve.

So at last they rose, showered and dressed, nibbled a little breakfast though neither was hungry, and headed out the side door.

Outside, their entire ranch staff awaited them. It caught the preoccupied pair off guard, and Holmes still had his arm around Chadwick in intimate encouragement when they first became aware they had an audience.

Chadwick immediately tried to pull away, in deference to Holmes' reticence; but he fisted his fingers in the back of her jacket, holding her in position. She glanced up at him anxiously, but grey eyes crinkled back.

"Relax," he breathed, his lips scarcely moving. "They shall have to be made aware of the new sleeping arrangements sometime."

With that, he subtly pulled her into position beside

him, allowing his hand to rest discreetly against the small of her back, and they looked up into a phalanx of smiling faces. Williams stepped forward.

————

"Good morning, Billy," Holmes greeted his liaison calmly. "To what do we owe this little gathering?"

"Good morning, Holmes, Boss," Williams smiled at the pair, nodding to each in turn. "I trust the two of you had a good night?"

"We did," Holmes replied blandly. Chadwick's blush told the tale, however, and their staff members' grins grew broader. "But surely such matters do not warrant a meeting at this hour of the morning?"

"No," Williams sobered. "We just wanted to...well, to show you our support. No matter what happens, we realise the two of you busted your bums to fix what Haines screwed up. We wanted you to know that; and to know...well..."

Billy's voice tapered off, too emotional to continue. So Tina Williams stepped forward, holding her daughter.

"We all want you to know that we trust you, we love you, and we're thinking of you and praying for you," she said staunchly, finishing for her husband. "And we're happy for you. No matter what comes."

Grey eyes and blue widened, then dropped to stare at the ground.

————

Chadwick felt the hand at her back clench, and Holmes swallowed several times, clearing his throat once. *He can't*

233

get the words out, she thought affectionately. So she spoke for them both.

"Thank you all, very much," she said in a low, husky tone. "We're doing our best. I won't lie and say I'm not scared, 'cause I am. If I could be one hundred percent sure this will work, I'd be as cool as Sherlock— as Holmes is," she corrected herself, and the delighted grins returned to her listeners. Chadwick straightened her shoulders, raising her head with newfound confidence. "But I'm pretty sure it's going to work, and with y'all's thoughts and prayers, and this guy here beside me," she nudged Holmes, "I think it's gonna be okay."

"Indeed," Holmes managed to get out. "I could not have said it better. And now," he said, stepping forward and allowing his hand to slide away from Chadwick, "we had best make our way down the mountain and get to work. Come, my dear." He held out his hand, palm up. Chadwick placed her hand in his and permitted him to help her down the steps.

Within minutes the little sports car was headed down Ute Pass.

————

While the other continuum was resting and preparing to boost the rest energy of the brane, Sherlock and Skye debated on what to do.

"You really should also use the time to rest, my dear," Sherlock pointed out. "Your endeavours have been quite strenuous in the last few weeks, not to mention you have sustained considerable physical abuse. You have at least a week, possibly more. That is a holiday in itself."

"I know, Sherlock. But frankly, I'm not going to be able to rest until one—the brane is completely re-stabilized, and two—we find Cunningham and Fereaud. I'm just NOT," she reiterated for emphasis.

Sherlock sighed, fully comprehending her point of view. *She is not going to feel safe until the two matters are completely resolved and finished once and for all,* he realized, *especially her kidnappers. As long as they are at large, she will not feel safe. And indeed, to some extent, no matter what I may do, she is not. Ryker and his people are already stretched thin, and I cannot stay awake continually.*

"Very well, Wife. I understand. In that case, it is time for a change of strategy in the game."

"So what do you recommend?"

"As has been noted in the past, the best defence is often a strong offence. And it is about time the miscreants in these parts discovered that there are two first-rate detectives dwelling here, not merely one."

"We go out looking?"

"We do." Sherlock's jaw was firm. "Had you prefer to remain a team, or do you feel comfortable separating for short periods?"

"Um, I'd rather stay a team, but we can, say, send one into a situation while the other waits for a signal or something," Skye decided.

"Then let us begin." Sherlock nodded. "Before we take you out, however, let me see about disguising your bruises. Especially that stubborn black eye."

"Good," Skye said, satisfied.

———

Soon Skye's appearance was near normal. In addition, Sherlock sat down with his art book and pencil, and produced two sketches of Fereaud and Cunningham, to aid in witness identification; and they ventured forth.

"The fact that we do not bother to disguise ourselves will be that much more disconcerting and disturbing to our quarry," Sherlock observed. "It is a strong offensive tactic, indicating neither of us is afraid of them."

Skye's chin rose, and her jaw grew firm.

"There's my girl. You are better than they, in every respect, and I believe you also have your concealed carry now, do you not?"

"I sure do," Skye said determinedly. "Not again. Not EVER again."

"Then let us see what the local ports may show. I think we may count on Ryker to tell us if anything happens at the cave." They got into the car and headed out.

———

Three-quarters of the way into Woodbridge, Ryker called, but only to inform them that reconstruction of the sarcophagus was well underway, as accelerated as they could manage.

It was concluded that the only real concern was the roof of the chamber; the cavern below was coated in concrete, then lead-lined, and appeared to be in reasonable shape, even despite the partial meltdown of the reactor core.

Therefore, remote-controlled, heavy-duty equipment was being used to carefully position thick lead sheets, wrapped in a heavy layer of PVC to protect against lead migration, across the opening in the cave floor. It was a tricky task, likely to be the slowest step of the containment, because of the need to anchour it on firm, solid rock; the last thing they needed was to increase the amount of cave collapse.

After that was completed, framed rebar panels, coated

with PVC over a thick layer of lead, would be lifted into place atop the lead sheeting, and a special lead-doped concrete poured into that. Essentially the entire floor of the cave would be covered with the concrete, all the way up to the cave walls. The last step would involve sealing the concrete with a classified polymer to protect it from water. Said polymer would literally seep into the pores of the concrete, all the way through, preventing any possibility of deterioration due to water, or leaching of the lead doping.

"Sounds well thought out," Skye decided, listening to Sherlock's cell phone in speaker mode as they drove. "That ought to take care of matters for a few centuries, at the very least."

"Right," Ryker agreed. "Nowhere near the half-lives of all that radioactive shite, but long enough, with proper record keeping, that they'll have developed something better to contain it by the time something else is needed."

"Yup," Skye confirmed.

"So," Ryker wondered, "what are you two up to?"

"We," Sherlock noted, "are in search of our two fugitives."

"Good on ya," Ryker replied. "Woodbridge first, I'd guess?"

"How many times must I tell you, Ryker?"

"Uh, that was an educated guess, Holmes. It's the closest thing approximating a port to this area. It's also the last place they were seen."

"That is much better," Sherlock said, satisfied. "And you are correct. And should we be unsuccessful there?"

"Um, Ipswich, then possibly—or maybe eventually is a better word—London," Ryker suggested.

"Very good, Ryker. Our Wiggins is getting better and better," Sherlock verified, a twinkle in the grey eyes as he glanced at Skye.

"Thanks," Ryker said, and they could hear the sheepish grin in his voice. "Let me know if you need backup."

"Wilco," Skye said. "Meantime, hurry up with that closure. I have a bad feeling about it."

"We're on it," Ryker said confidently. "Catch you later. Good hunting."

"Goodbye, Wiggins," Sherlock said mischievously, and Skye closed the phone.

———

Once in Woodbridge, Sherlock took Skye by the cottage where Mary Victor had been held prisoner, and together they went over the house once more. This time, however, they found a clue inadvertently left by the fugitives upon their last visit, after Sherlock's original thorough search: a matchbook from the Bishops Inn in Ipswich. They finished their search, but found nothing else.

They climbed into their vehicle and headed for Ipswich.

———

But they had no luck there. While the hotel staff was able to definitively identify Cunningham and Fereaud from Sherlock's sketches, as guests Harrison and Albe, respectively, the pair was no longer at the hotel.

"No, they checked out two days ago," the manager noted. "No forwarding contact information. I'm sorry, sir, madam."

A quick, spontaneous detour southeast to Harwich took them to the ferries across the Channel.

"They do not go to France directly," Sherlock

observed, "but even in my day, it would not have been difficult to get from Germany, Belgium or the Netherlands into France."

"True," Skye said, "and now with Eurail, it's even easier. And faster." So they checked all the ferries, showing the sketches. But they had no luck there, either.

"Should we really head for London, Sherlock? That's two needles in a really huge haystack. London's even bigger than it was in your day. But you've already seen that..."

"Call Ryker," was all he said.

————

Ryker confirmed that the Director had all regional airports, especially those in London, which were closest, crawling with MI-5 and -6, complete with mug shots of the fugitives. All ship ports were being scrutinized, as well. There was no point in the Holmeses going to London at this stage.

With a sigh, the married couple turned back. It was now late in the day, and they discussed the matter as they returned to Gibson House.

"Did anybody find anything at the place where they held me?" Skye wondered.

"Ah, an excellent idea, Wife. I did not myself go over it, as I was more concerned with removing you to a place of safety and rest, and have not had opportunity to search it since. I know Ryker kept it pristine, and it is likely still being treated as a crime scene, until this investigation concludes. Perhaps tomorrow we may go over it in detail."

"I dunno, Sherlock. We can, and probably should, I guess. But I think maybe," Skye decided, considering the various scenarios as her husband drove, "we should concentrate on the area around the cave. As determined and fixated as they were, I just don't see them fleeing the country without giving it one last shot."

"A 'gut feeling,' my dear?" Sherlock shot a sharp glance at his wife.

"Yeah."

"Then that is what we shall do."

———

Skye slept fitfully, despite the knowledge that Her Majesty's Secret Service were standing clandestine guard around the house. She woke bleary-eyed, but alert, especially after alarm clocks were rung. Then the pair rose and prepared for another day of searching.

It was difficult for Skye to enter the house where she had been held prisoner and mistreated, but she took several deep breaths and plunged ahead. Sherlock followed close behind, deliberately staying well within her personal space, a very tangible and comforting morale booster for his wife. Together the pair examined the abandoned, ramshackle old house. They found an old topographic map of the area, with the site of the cave marked, as well as over half a dozen different possible routes to the entrance.

"But Ryker has all these covered already," Sherlock decided, after studying it for a bit.

"They had several more maps," Skye observed, "and most of those were newer than this one."

"Which means this one may be a discard. Nevertheless, if you would extract a forensics bag, my dear, we can at least look for fingerprints upon the thing, to tie them definitively to the 'treasure hunt.'"

Latex-covered fingers delicately folded the map and

placed it into the plastic bag being held for it. Then the search was resumed.

"Here's where Cunningham smoked," Skye noted, bending over an ashtray on a table in one corner. "Easily six or eight cigarette butts right here."

"More evidence. Possibly DNA?"

"Yup," Skye said, getting an evidence bag out of their kit and upending the entire ashtray into it.

"And look there," Sherlock pointed to the area of the table revealed when Skye had lifted the ashtray. "Another matchbook from the Bishop Inn."

"And I got the evidence bag for it," Skye grinned, as Sherlock used forceps to pick up the item and transfer it to the poly bag.

———

Further search of the building turned up nothing. Sherlock decided to swing by the Carver residence in order to show them the sketches of their fugitives, so that the couple might at least know for whom to watch. Skye and the Carvers appeared, for all intents and purposes, to be complete strangers, though Sherlock wondered at the slightly odd expression on Jonathan Carver's face as he gazed at Skye.

"Is all well, Mr. Carver?" the detective wondered.

"Uh...uh, yeah, Mr. Holmes," Carver replied, shaking himself mentally. "D' ya see it, Hazel? It's th' eyes, Oy think."

"Yeah, Oy shore do see it, Jonny, luv. Oy cain't hardly miss it. Sorry, Mr. Holmes, Mrs. Holmes. It's jus'...Mrs. Holmes...she's got our daughter Jenny's eyes. It's..." The woman turned away for a moment. "She weren't but a wee babe, but it feels a'most like meetin' our daughter, all growed up."

"But we know Mrs. Holmes ain't th' right age, nohow," Carver said stoically, "it's jus'...odd."

"I'm so sorry," Skye murmured sympathetically, glancing at her husband. "Would you rather I waited in the car?"

"Not a-tall," Mrs. Carver said staunchly, regaining control of herself. "Th' both o' ye are comin' in here, sittin' down, an' havin' a cuppa wif us." She put away her old grief and bustled into the kitchen, gesturing the others along. "Now, what did ya be a-comin' over here for?"

"We wanted to show you some sketches Sherlock did of the men who killed Mr. McFarlane and kidnapped Dr. Victor's sister and me," Skye explained. "That way, you'll know who to watch out for."

"Now there's a fine idee," Carver said, as his wife poured tea for all of them and prepared it, accurately reading the wordless gestures of each to make it to their liking. "Lessee 'em."

"Have you seen these men?" Sherlock produced the sketches and held them up.

The Carvers studied the images.

"Oy think mebbe Oy did see this bloke," Jonathan Carver tapped Fereaud's image, "about a week afore James died. 'E was sightseein', 'e said. Wanted t' see th' forest."

"Was he on foot, or in an automobile?" Sherlock queried.

"Auto," Carver said. "Y' want a description?"

"It would be greatly appreciated."

"Yeah. The bastards—oh, excuse me," Skye blushed.

"No, no, luv! You jus' hush that apology, right this

instant," Mrs. Carver declared, a fierce light in her eyes. "Don't ya be layin' on no excuses f'r callin' a spade a spade, Mrs. Holmes. That's th' royght word as ever there was. Oy bin hearin' as how they beat ye, an' woulda killed ye, mos' loyke, if 'tweren't f'r yer brave husband, there, you bein' sick an' all. Only," her eyes twinkled, "don't be callin' 'em no sons o' bitches, now. Our bitches are right nice li'l dogs, thankee."

They all laughed.

"Now, as you wuz sayin', Mrs. Holmes?" Carver politely inquired.

"Yeah," Skye said, sobering, "they blindfolded me before they put me in their car, so I can't give a description of it."

"Oy can," Carver said solemnly. "'Twas a late model four-door sedan, only about two years old, Oy'd make it, navy blue, one 'a th' oriental makes...which one is it what's got the stars f'r the logo?"

"Ah, yes," Sherlock said, jotting down notes. "Any distinguishing features, or license plate number?"

"Didn' git th' license," Carver admitted, "but it had a long scratch down th' passenger side, a'most from the front wheel well all th' way t' th' back bumper. Kinda dented in, it was, too, like 'e'd got too close ta sumpin, an' dragged alongside it."

Sherlock nodded, recording the information. Only then did he pick up his tea. The others took their cue from him, and began sipping their own tea. Skye nodded her compliment to Mrs. Carver, who smiled.

"Oy hear tell you make a nice cuppa, too, Mrs. Holmes," she grinned.

Skye shot an amused glance at Mr. Carver, who smiled sheepishly.

"Thank you, Mrs. Carver," she replied with a smile. "I

do try."

"And now," Sherlock declared, "I should like, not only to introduce my wife to young Brendan, but to see the pup one more time before he departs for his new master."

"Oy kinda figgered ya t' be wantin' t' do that," Carver grinned. "Hazel, wouldja open th' back door an' call th' lit'le feller?"

Mrs. Carver rose and went to the back door. "Breeeeendan!" she called. There was an answering yap, and the little pup exploded through the door. Catching sight of Holmes, he let out a howl of delight, and ran directly to the detective, fawning all over him.

"Aw," Skye said, delighted by the scene, as her husband enthusiastically petted the small animal. "So he's already sold, you said?"

"I'm afear'd so," Carver said, straight-faced.

"What a shame. I'm sorry I didn't come over here with you sooner, Sherlock. The two of you are like bread and butter."

"Well, there it is," Sherlock sighed. "Here, Skye, meet the boy."

Skye held her hand down for Brendan to sniff, and the dog promptly began licking her hand, nuzzling in order to get the top of his head scruffed. Skye laughed and gave the puppy what it wanted.

The pair stayed for a good hour before departing.

———

As soon as they returned to Gibson House, Holmes phoned in a description of the car to Ryker, who passed it through the APW.

But nothing more was heard of the matter, saving one thing. A clandestine call to the hidden Victor twins revealed that the scratch on the car's side was produced during the kidnapping of Mary Victor, as they revved the car down the driveway, which was lined on one side by a stone wall.

A quick visit to the Victor residence turned up copious evidence, complete with paint markings and even tiny metal shards. Skye and Sherlock collected these into more poly bags, so the car could be positively matched to the kidnapping.

———

But the Holmeses could turn up no more clues.

"We have been searching diligently for five days already. Obviously they have gone to ground," Sherlock decided at lunch one day in Gibson House, "and have planned exceedingly well for it."

"Dammit," Skye muttered, patently uncomfortable with the notion that her kidnappers were still on the loose.

"We are safe here, Skye," Sherlock said, despite his own private misgivings. "It is only some two to five days before our counterparts return and begin brane regeneration, and you will be occupied again. In the meanwhile, sometimes, as you know, a good detective must be patient and wait for the clues to come to him—or her, as the case may be."

"I know. But I don't have to like it."

"Perhaps," Sherlock said, letting a twinkle appear in his grey eyes, "I can find a way to take your mind off of it."

"What, exactly, did you have in mind?" Skye raised an eyebrow.

"Oh," Sherlock said airily, "I am quite sure I can think of...something..."

He took her hand and led her, unresisting, back to the bedroom.

10

Weak Branes and Weak Brains

Five more days passed. The Holmeses stayed inside Gibson House, waiting on the other continuum and word regarding the case, generally pleasing each other. No news came in at all, save that the sarcophagus repair was taking longer than anticipated, due to the deterioration of the cave floor.

On the morning of the tenth day, they awoke together, almost as if the touch of minds brought them awake. They gazed at each other for long minutes, then by unspoken consent, pulled each other close and began the prelude to ringing alarm clocks. Afterward, they lay quietly, holding each other for some time, in silence.

After a while, again without a word, they rose together, showered and dressed, and moved into the kitchen, where they wordlessly prepared breakfast, in complete harmony and coordination. A large omelet was split between two plates, coffee was poured, and toast and jam rounded out the meal. Then they sat down to eat.

"It is day ten since they decided to rest," Sherlock

finally noted at the breakfast table. It was the first thing either had said since awaking.

"I know. They can't let it go much longer. The brane will start to deteriorate again if they do."

"We know," Chadwick's voice announced. "We're here. We wanted to let you know before we tried regenerating the brane's rest energy."

"Oh!" Skye exclaimed, putting her hand to her chest, startled. "Well, now I know what it feels like to be on the other end of the dratted thing, I guess."

"Sorry," Chadwick said sheepishly. "We literally just dialed in. You look a lot better, Sis."

"Thanks," Skye grinned ruefully. "The bruising is almost gone—finally."

"How are you both?" Sherlock asked quietly.

"Quite well," Holmes responded in an upbeat tone, "though Skye is anxious."

Both Sherlock and Skye noted the comfortable informality with which Holmes addressed his compatriot.

"Yeah, I have to admit, Sherlock's right on that," Chadwick added. "But we're both a lot more rested and...happier...than the last time you, er, heard us."

"Capital," Sherlock murmured, glancing across the table at his wife. "We are glad for you both."

"Oh, good grief," Chadwick grumbled, her embarrassment evident in her voice. "Is it THAT obvious?"

"Only because we know you like we know ourselves," Skye grinned, then sobered. "And because it was painful to us to see you together, and know what could have been."

"And now is," Sherlock added, heedless of grammatical conventions.

"True," Holmes agreed. "However, Skye—MY Skye— and I discussed the matter on the drive down the pass, and we have decided on a different choice from the one which you made."

"You decided to forego a formal ceremony, and file paperwork?" Sherlock verified.

"Someday maybe I'll get used to levels of deduction bordering on psychic," Chadwick complained. "Yeah, that's what we decided to do."

"I did offer to share my name," Holmes indicated, "but Skye noted, after all this time, she was happy merely having me by her side. And I am sufficiently Bohemian in outlook to allow matters to remain so, as she is content with it."

"I am," Chadwick declared. "Assuming we make it past today, we'll probably go get the forms tomorrow."

"And now we must see about matters of tomorrow," Holmes declared.

"How will we know if you succeeded or failed?" Skye asked.

There was a pause. Suddenly the kitchen around them began to fade, and Skye and Sherlock found themselves looking into the Chamber. Two figures rose from the control console, moving to stand just outside the core.

"We'll come back and tell you, one way or the other," Chadwick said solemnly. "We promise."

"Indeed," Holmes averred quietly. "And there is one other thing...just in case..."

Chadwick nodded, then choked out, "Thank you. Both of you. For everything."

The two at the breakfast table exchanged glances, then rose and moved to stand as close to the other couple as they dared.

"Thanks are not necessary," Sherlock noted softly. "Being who we are, we could do no less."

"He's right," Skye agreed. "We'd have done the same,

even if there was absolutely no risk to our own continuum."

"We know," Holmes nodded. "But thanks are given, nevertheless."

"Then we accept them," Sherlock nodded in a near mirror image of his counterpart. "And we will await your word."

"I'm sure everything will go fine," Skye soothed. "Deep breath and all that, girl."

"Don't I know it," Chadwick chuckled ruefully. "See you soon, Sis, for good or ill."

There was a soft hiss, and the cottage kitchen returned.

————

"All right, let's get to it," Chadwick said, drawing in a deep breath. "No sense in waiting any longer."

"Indeed," Holmes agreed. "Do you have the coordinates calculated?"

"Yep, here ya go," Chadwick passed a sheet of paper to her spouse.

"Hm..." Holmes scanned the numbers on it. "Those are...quite different from what I am used to seeing."

"Yeah," Chadwick confirmed. "Think of it as like the Cartesian coordinates: zero—infinity, I guess. We're going into the parent brane, so we're accessing one end of who knows how many universe strings."

"Ah, of course. This should be interesting."

"Yeah. I have no idea what the inside of the core will look like. I just hope it's not something that'll make us toss our cookies."

"Now that, I will agree with in toto. Before we actually begin, however, I should like to ask a question regarding the science. It may help me better anticipate matters, if I comprehend a few things first. I likely should have asked sooner, but I did not want to risk bringing worrisome matters to mind while you were resting."

"Shoot," Chadwick said.

"Why is it necessary for the brane to maintain a specific energy level?" Holmes wondered. "I comprehend well enough to calculate that level, and to determine bleed-off rates, but..." he waved his long, thin hands in the air. "I should have thought, once we got the brane stabilised, nothing more was needed."

"Well," Chadwick screwed up her face. "Sis and I don't have all the details pegged down yet, but our take on it was like this: You know Einstein's most famous equation."

"Yes," Holmes nodded. "$E = mc^2$, where matter and energy are shown to have equivalence."

"Right," Chadwick verified. "Specifically, MASS and energy are equivalent. Now, mass is a measure of inertia..."

"Yes."

———

"So what we're really working with here is the rest mass of the brane. A brane with several—an unknown number, at this point—strings attached."

"Read: other universes," Holmes translated.

"Yup. Now, each of those open strings has a particular vibrational energy state. And the brane is, for all intents and purposes, an anchor for the strings. It therefore has to have sufficient mass-equivalence to damp those vibrational energies, or the vibrations get passed to the other strings as instability waves."

"Ah!" Holmes exclaimed, suddenly grasping the entire concept. "And our brane is not currently 'heavy' enough to do so."

"Right, and that's why we're having tremors. Since our continuum—our string—is the source of the deterioration, it's the one initially most susceptible to feeling the vibrations being passed on. Sis and I haven't figured out quite why, yet, but we're working on it."

"And so even after stabilisation, the brane begins to lose energy again after a time, because of the vibrational energies flowing through it," Holmes mused. "I should think part of the energy of the brane is picked up occasionally by the vibrations..."

"Right. And transferred randomly to the various attached strings via instabilities."

"Excellent. I understand now. Thank you, Skye."

"No problem. Ready?"

"Insomuch as is possible, yes. I will handle the focusing, Skye, but you must handle the string beam."

"Can do. That's exactly what I'd planned. We're on the same page." She took a deep breath, then exhaled slowly. "Initiate focus."

Holmes dialed in the coordinates with care. Between the monoliths, a swirling, roiling, almost psychedelic neon maelstrom formed briefly, then faded into a homogeneous grey mist.

"Coordinates reached," he murmured, staring into the core curiously. "So that is what a brane looks like."

"In as much as we can perceive it, yeah, it seems so. Okay, how does the rest energy read?"

"Approximately ten percent low," Holmes read off his screen. "It appears to have recovered a bit on its own in the interim, since we stopped the tachyon condensation."

"Excellent," Chadwick said, surprised. "It rebounded by itself. Maybe we don't need to do anything. Maybe the vibrations had the opposite effect, and dumped some energy into the brane, instead of taking it away."

"No, rest energy just dropped two hundredths of a percent. The bleed-off has begun, just as the other Skye predicted. Three more hundredths down..."

"Damn. Okay, here goes, then," Chadwick drew another deep breath and began typing commands into her computer keyboard. "Higgs boson injection beginning..." she hit <enter>, "now. Commence read-off of rest energy and stabilization of brane."

Holmes nodded affirmation.

"Rest energy just rose to original reading," he observed. "Continuing to rise...slowly...very slowly..."

"How's this?" Chadwick tweaked the intensity of the string beam.

"Increase in rest energy to minus nine-point-three percent of calculated," Holmes read off slowly. "Nine point one...eight point eight..." Chadwick bumped the beam intensity another notch.

"Six point two! Five point seven! Five point oh!" Holmes exclaimed, the readings increasing swiftly now. "Four point three! Two point one! Reduce the beam, Skye, or we shall overshoot!"

Chadwick grabbed for the keyboard and entered commands as a tremor shook the Chamber.

———

No sooner had the other continuum broken contact than Ryker came by Gibson House in a decidedly agitated state.

"Come on, you two," he said, barely making it through the door before waving the Holmeses at the coat rack. "Get your things and come. Right now. We've had an...incident."

"What?" Sherlock barked as he and Skye shrugged into their coats.

"The guards on the cave," Ryker replied tersely. "One was assaulted while the others were patrolling the area. We can't tell for certain yet, but we think the entrance was accessed. The guards had electronic keys, in case of an emergency."

"Oooh, shit," Skye muttered as they followed Ryker outside. There, a Hummer awaited; Tin Can rode in the boot. The three piled into the military vehicle, with Ryker behind the wheel, and threw gravel as they headed for the McFarlane farm. "You think it was a disgruntled neighbor, determined to prove a government conspiracy, or...?"

"I'm banking on OR," Ryker replied shortly.

"And I agree," Sherlock vouched. "I assume Tin Can is along to verify what may or may not be inside?"

"It is," Ryker noted, taking the country lanes at the highest speed the wide vehicle could manage. "You were right, Boss, we should've finished sealing off the cave, right away."

"A big ol' wall in a hillside with a high-tech door in it ain't subtle," Skye shrugged. "Even if it is set back from the cave entrance. Not to mention all the materiel you must have going in and out."

Moments later they entered the McFarlane property and arrived at the cave opening. The rest of Ryker's unit was already there. Doctor Wilder was tending the injured guard, who had taken a nasty blow to the base of the head; Huggins had his control equipment set up and merely awaited the arrival of Tin Can to check the cavern's interior.

As soon as the Humvee pulled up, the unit sprang into action. Tin Can was extracted from the boot and activated, its sensors calibrated. Then the door was opened, and the little robot trundled in, while the decontamination team prepped for its eventual return. Sherlock, Skye, and Ryker bent over Huggins' monitor and watched the scene from Tin Can's infrared "eyes."

Nothing out of the ordinary was visible for a good fifteen minutes. Cherenkov radiation gradually came into view as Tin Can rounded the bend in the passage.

Huggins gasped. Ryker let out a long, low whistle. Sherlock said, "Ah," in an unsurprised but subdued tone. Skye simply stared, paling.

The bloated, burned, peeling bodies of Fereaud and Cunningham lay tangled in the rebar immediately beside the partly-covered opening in the floor of the cave. Pale blue light trickled through the cracks between the PVC coated flooring sheets, and a beam of Cherenkov radiation poured upward next to the bodies.

"They wouldn't listen," Skye whispered, before silence reigned.

———

"What do we do?" Skye finally asked after a time.

"You mean to recover the bodies, Wife?"

"Yeah."

"There's nothing we can do," Ryker replied with a shrug. "They're too close to the opening to send personnel in. Tin Can isn't powerful enough to get them out, and we don't dare bring any of the heavy equipment that close to the unreinforced part of the opening, or the whole mess could go crashing down with the weight."

Huggins looked up at his superior. "Finish the sarcophagus, and pour the concrete over 'em?" he suggested.

"Yes." Ryker shook his head grimly. "Follow today's plan to the letter. Unless you've got any better ideas."

Huggins thought for a moment, then shrugged. "We'll get on it."

"Get the last of the damn lead sheeting and rebar down, so we can start pouring concrete," Ryker ordered, bitterness in his tone. "I want the doped concrete going down by lunchtime at the latest."

"Righto." And Huggins headed off to help Team Blue wield the remote controllers for the heavy machinery.

"Dammit, we were almost done sealing it up, too. Twenty-four more hours and we'd have been clear. Well, at least this property is now owned by the government," Ryker murmured in disturbed annoyance. "We don't have that to worry about."

"The transaction went through?" Skye asked.

"Yeah," Ryker confirmed. "Ian McFarlane was glad to do it once he found out volatile Nazi chemical weapons were hidden in the cave." He offered the couple a weak grin.

"So you decided to go with that story," Sherlock noted.

"We did," Ryker said. "It's already being circulated that the cave had been used as a Nazi spy's base during the War, and he'd left a small chemical weapons cache there— nothing on the CWC list—which had become unstable over the years. His intent was to prepare for a Nazi invasion of Great Britain via U-boat, but it was thwarted. The cache was only recently discovered due to the efforts of a small terrorist group to recover the chemicals."

"And the UFO?" Skye wondered.

"Was a hoax perpetrated by the terrorists in their attempts to reach the chemicals. They were even willing to murder the landowner, under cover of the supposed UFO, to obtain free access to the cave." Ryker sighed. "Now I guess we'll have to add an addendum: the terrorists have been discovered dead inside the cave, killed by the very chemicals they were trying to recover."

"Because of their instability," Skye added with authority. "It was contact contamination, and no chemicals were released into the neighborhood."

"Ah," Ryker said, understanding the reason for her addendum. "Good point. We'll use that."

"It will do," Sherlock nodded approval. "It will work nicely. And provide any curious members of the general public with more than sufficient incentive to stay away."

"Exactly," Ryker agreed. "That was the intent."

The operative pulled out a palm computer and punched in the annotation, then emailed it. Just then, Ryker's radio went off. He pulled it off his belt and keyed it.

"Ryker."

"Captain, this is Team Yellow. We've got something here."

Ryker glanced at the Holmeses, who nodded as one. "Team Yellow, this is Wiggins. We're on the way."

———

Team Yellow was awaiting outside the equipment shed behind the barn.

"What is it?" Ryker demanded as the trio walked up.

"We think we've got the perpetrators' vehicle, sir," one remarked. "Indications are that they came in through a far back gate and along a farm track. Must've been one helluva ride; we never anticipated a vehicle could have made it along that route, and it's too many kilometres for a regular bloke to walk, or we'd have had a better eye on it. Have a look inside." He gestured toward the door of the shed.

Ryker entered carefully, closely followed by Sherlock and Skye. They meandered around a tractor and a hay baler, then stopped.

A late model navy car, of Oriental make, sat there, covered in road dust, with tufts of grass caught in its undercarriage, front bumper, and fenders, all of which showed signs of the rough passage. A long, dented scratch ran down the passenger side, from front tire well to rear fender. In addition, Sherlock noted, the tire tread pattern exactly matched what he'd sketched in the driveway of the cottage in Melton.

"Send it to Forensics," Sherlock declared. "I believe you will find it a perfect match to the metal and paint samples Skye and I took from the Victor residence, and the tread marks I obtained in Melton."

"It's a cinch those guys won't be needing it to haul off any Nazi gold," a wry Skye remarked.

"And that's the God's honest truth," Ryker agreed.

———

By near sunset, Fereaud's vehicle had been towed away; the doped concrete was poured and set, and Fereaud and Cunningham permanently entombed therein. "We'll let it cure overnight," Ryker noted. "The doping process affects the concrete, causing it to harden faster than regular concrete. By morning, we'll be ready to apply the water sealant. That'll take about two hours to soak in; it'll solidify on its own. By lunch, a couple of well-placed charges will bring the entrance down, and a cement truck will finish the job."

He turned toward the Humvee, gesturing to the Holmeses. "C'mon. I'll take you back to the house."

Sherlock offered Skye a hand in entering the vehicle, then climbed in beside her. Ryker took the driver's seat, switched on the ignition, and they were off.

————

Back at Gibson House, there was no evidence the other continuum had come back. Having missed lunch and tea, Sherlock and Skye sat down to a large dinner, whose preparation they shared; then they retired to the sitting room with two brandies.

And waited.

And waited.

Their counterparts did not appear.

Finally, near midnight, the married pair went to bed in some disquiet.

————

The next morning, they still had not heard from the other continuum. Ryker came by again, however.

"I thought you two might want to see the end of the thing," he said simply.

"Indeed," Sherlock agreed. "Skye, my dear, bundle well, and bring your medications. You sneezed three times this morning. I will not have you relapsing with that nasty 'bug.'"

"I'll stay well, Sherlock. But I want to do one thing first."

So she tore the covers off of a spare spiral notebook and used their insides to write large placards:

————

Gone to cave to watch final sealing
  Will be back tonight
  Please leave note
  -Skye

———

One placard went on the sofa in the sitting room, propped against its back; the other went on the desk in the study, leaning against the computer monitor.

"Okay," she said, gathering her medications and bundling up. "Now let's go."

———

The concrete sealant was already nearly applied when they arrived. Ryker brought the Holmeses over to the command unit, and they listened on the radio, as the last matters were coordinated.

Team Blue brought their remote equipment out through the electronic lead door, where a decontamination team was waiting to ensure the equipment was safe.

Once the "all clear" had been given, Ryker picked up the microphone and issued orders.

"Seal the interior door and lock it."

A dull clang echoed from the mouth of the cave. Within minutes all equipment and personnel had exited the cave.

"Pyro unit, commence," Ryker gave the command via radio.

A team unfamiliar to Sherlock and Skye moved forward, wearing explosives gear. They began delicately setting small explosives in strategic places around the cave mouth.

"Have you warned the Carvers to expect an explosion?" Sherlock wondered.

"We have," Ryker nodded. "And all the neighbours within a radius of some five kilometres. I might add there was a lot of relief to find that the 'nasty chemicals' were going to be sealed up 'proper-loyke.'"

"Very good," Sherlock said, and subsided, watching.

Half an hour later, preparations were complete, and a cement truck was trundling across the field.

"Take cover!" came the order from the pyro team.

All personnel took refuge behind prepared barricades.

"All clear!" the pyro team leader called.

The ignitions specialist executed a quarter turn to the right and shouted, "Fire in the hole!" Then he turned a quarter-circle to face the rear, calling, "Fire in the hole!" Another quarter turn to the right was followed by, "Fire in the hole!" A fourth quarter turn brought him full circle, facing the cave entrance once more. The pyro team leader began a countdown.

"In three...two...one...FIRE!"

A sustained detonation worked its way around the cave mouth's perimeter. The side of the hill slumped as a white cloud of chalk dust rose. As the sea breeze gently blew away the dust, everyone could see the cave entrance had disappeared, replaced by a pile of limestone and slate rubble.

The concrete truck lumbered its way across the field to the debris. Five minutes later, a concrete cap was taking shape over the cave's former entrance.

"And that's that," Ryker declared, somber.

———

Ryker took them back to Gibson House. Once inside, Skye immediately checked sitting room and study, to no avail.

"That's not good," she worried. "I would have thought we'd hear something by now."

"The other continuum?" Ryker asked.

"Yeah," Skye confirmed.

"And you have," Skye's voice suddenly announced. "It just took us a while to catch our breaths after."

"Oh, thank God," Skye muttered fervently under her own breath, putting her hand to her chest.

"I'm sorry, Sis. I didn't mean to scare you," Chadwick said contritely.

"It's okay," Skye said, smiling ruefully, watching in amusement as Ryker tried not to let his eyes pop from his head. "I take it, things got hairy?"

"You might say," Holmes' voice remarked dryly. "It was a near thing. We very nearly overshot the rest energy. The brane is decidedly touchy, it seems."

"NO SHIT," Chadwick added vehemently. "I've never entered commands that fast before."

"I think perhaps you may have done, over here," Sherlock noted with a slight smile. "Remember Haines' 'booby trap,' Skye?"

"Oh HELL yeah. I'll never forget it. Yeah, I think I know what you mean, Sis."

"But was it successful?" Sherlock asked, betraying considerable impatience and concern.

"It was," Chadwick said in triumph. "We had to kind of decompress for a while after, which is why we're only now getting around to contacting you. Sorry it worried you."

"Um, excuse me, Holmes, Holmes, Boss, and Boss," Ryker interjected lamely, "but not only is this bloody well creeping me out, I need to get back to my unit and make sure they get the heavy equipment loaded without any more 'incidents.' Is it safe for me to leave?"

"Just a moment, Ryker," Holmes' voice noted. There was a brief pause, followed by, "Now you may leave."

"See ya," Ryker said. "Call me when you're ready to head back to London, you two."

"That will likely be sometime tomorrow, by the sound, Wiggins. Perhaps even later tonight," Sherlock told him as he headed out the door with a wave.

After he had gone, Chadwick inverted the tesseract, and she and Holmes came to stand before Skye and Sherlock.

"I wish I could hug you both," Chadwick told them softly. "I can't begin to tell you..."

"You do not have to." Sherlock waved a dismissive hand. "As with your 'sister,' my wife, your eyes speak for you."

"Agreed, old chap," Holmes nodded, then hesitated a moment before continuing. "It is somewhat out of character for me, but there is one thing we CAN do, in a kind of surrogacy."

"And that would be?" Sherlock asked.

"This," he said.

Holmes turned toward Chadwick, taking her gently in his arms. Then he pulled Chadwick close and kissed her. Sherlock and Skye exchanged the barest of smiles. Then Sherlock opened his arms and Skye stepped into them.

"Capital idea, old man," Sherlock said, just before his own lips came down on his wife's.

———

After dinner, Skye and Sherlock began packing. By bedtime, everything except what they needed for the next day was packed, and the suitcases were sitting in the mudroom beside the garage door. A quick call to Ryker, and that worthy swung by to pick them up, promising that the bags would be in their rooms in London by that night.

As they climbed into bed, Skye noted, "As Brae would say, 'That's that.'"

"And as you would say," Sherlock added, "'Two up, and two down.'"

"And now we can finish our vacation—finally."

"What do you say we begin finishing it tonight?" Sherlock wondered, drawing her close before nuzzling her shoulder.

"I think you would say, 'Capital notion,'" Skye said with a grin, before turning off the light.

————

The next morning they were surprised to find Ryker waiting patiently outside the front door when they headed to the kitchen for breakfast. Skye let him in.

"What on earth are you doing out there? I know it's starting to warm up, but it's still awfully chilly out there, especially this time of morning. Have you had breakfast yet?"

"Waiting for you two, it's not too bad with my coat, and only a pastry," Ryker answered her rapid-fire questions in order, grinning.

"Then come into the house and let us prepare some proper breakfast for you as well, old chap," Sherlock offered. "At the very least, have a hot cup of tea or coffee."

"Well, that does sound nice. I'm here to formally drive the two of you back to London, by the way."

"That is not necessary," Holmes remarked, "but as you are likely under orders, we shall not protest."

"I am, and thanks," Ryker said, accepting the cup of coffee Skye gave him.

A quick, hot breakfast for three ensued, then they cleaned the pans and dishes and put them away. Ryker took out the trash, then stopped Skye as she lugged the bed and bath linens to the mudroom to launder them.

"That's not necessary. Leave them in the hamper there. Someone will be by tomorrow to clean house. It's standard after a safehouse use. I just didn't want the dirty dishes and garbage to get smelly."

So Skye dumped the laundry into the hamper as Ryker carried the last of their luggage to the car, then she and Sherlock scooped up their overnight kits, put on their coats, and bid goodbye to Gibson House.

———

Ryker drove them back to London. They were fully expecting to be taken to a hotel, either near their original, or perhaps close to Heathrow Airport. Instead, Ryker headed north, toward Regent's Park. He turned into Upper Baker Street and parked along the street, in front of the bank where Sherlock's old lodgings should have been, but weren't.

"Follow me," he said, getting out and heading for one of the side doors of the bank building. Skye and Sherlock, both mystified, got out of the rental car and followed their liaison.

Beside the substantial metal door was a security box. Ryker flipped up a metal cover, revealing a keypad; then murmured, "Watch, and memorise the code I punch in."

Puzzled, they watched as Ryker punched in a security code, memorizing it as he indicated, then followed their liaison into the building. Inside the door, they turned right, into a short hallway—which also teed off to the left, fading into the distance—before encountering another door—a door that looked suspiciously familiar to Holmes. To one side was a card reader and cipher lock, and a small brass plaque which read, very simply, "221B."

"Open it, Holmes," Ryker said softly. "It's already unlocked."

The detective shot the operative a meaningful glance, then put his hand on the doorknob and opened the door. At his shoulder, Skye gasped.

It was like stepping through the tesseract. The entrance to Holmes' old flat had been recreated with as much accuracy as Her Majesty's Secret Service could manage—which was substantial—using the information Holmes had provided in his sketches. Inside the foyer, the Queen and the Prince Consort themselves awaited, having painstakingly achieved a clandestine outing expressly for the purpose of welcoming them.

Ryker hustled the Holmeses through the door and closed it against any potential onlookers as a placid Sherlock bowed deeply and a chagrined Skye curtsied hastily. The Queen smiled and moved to them.

"Here you are," she said calmly, handing a card key to each of them. "Your flat is ready for you to take possession, Sir Sherlock, Lady Holmes. I think you will like what we've done with the place." She gestured them deeper into the apartment. "It is not often I have the opportunity to act as an agent of real estate. However, when Captain Ryker brought me copies of your artwork, and he, the Director of the Service, my husband, and I came to discuss the matter, there really was but one thing to be done. So," Her Majesty fairly grinned, "we did it. And the bank proved...most amenable. Welcome home."

"We did make a few changes, for the sake of logistics," Ryker admitted, as the stunned newlyweds moved past the royal couple to explore the flat. "The bedroom is bigger, for instance, with a king-sized bed, and the kitchen—which is upstairs now, across from the sitting room, where Watson's room would have been—has modern appliances."

"As we have yet to find you a Mrs. Hudson, and we are informed the Lady Holmes enjoys cooking in any event, we thought that might prove a most convenient and practical modification," the prince consort added.

"But even with all that, we tried to ensure everything fit with the overall 'look,' so you'd feel at home, Sir Sherlock," Ryker continued. "The downstairs, here, is a bit different. Rather than being Mrs. Hudson's rooms, it's mostly storage and a small modern forensics laboratory, though there is a full servant's quarters toward the rear, if you wish. Probably we'll install an operative there to at least function as caretaker when you're not here—you know, off on a case or the like. The main living area is upstairs on the first floor, and is as much like your old flat as we could make it, given logistics. A couple of spare bedrooms are on the second floor."

"For any clients, assistants, or...family additions...that may come along, in future," the Queen noted archly, eyes twinkling, and both Skye and Sherlock flushed despite themselves.

The group had been exploring the ground floor while the Holmeses listened to this explanation. In the very back was a substantial storage room; to the left of that, the servant's quarters, as yet unfurnished. To the right of the entry was the decidedly modern laboratory: It was well equipped with stereo microscope, computer, fax machine, cordless speakerphone, and several other electronic items, not to mention a compact but efficient forensics lab. So they turned to the next floor, moving up the staircase. Skye counted under her breath, much to the group's amusement, as they ascended; sure enough, the flight contained the correct number of steps. *Seventeen steps. They even remem-bered that little detail,* Sherlock thought, moved.

The first floor was just as Ryker had described. The sitting room was properly appointed, even to the wallpaper and upholstery, and looked out onto Baker Street through several windows, including a central bow window. A small chemical lab stood in its proper corner; a well-stocked tantalus stood opposite, just as it should. In still a third corner sat a small dining suite and sideboard. An old-fash-ioned desk occupied the fourth corner; in a niche of the desk a cordless telephone nestled discreetly. A warm, crack-ling fire already graced the exhaustless-gas fireplace. Ryker picked up an incongruous remote control from the tea-table and hit a button.

Panels in the back wall of the sitting room opened up, revealing an entertainment center, complete with stereo, VCR/DVD player, and wide-screen television. Skye laughed, and Sherlock chuckled.

The bedroom off the sitting room was identical to Holmes' old bedroom, saving that it presented the appear-ance of having been stretched: It did contain a king-sized bed, as well as a larger dresser and wardrobe than Holmes had possessed. To Skye's evident surprise, their luggage already awaited them there.

"Sneak," she told Ryker, who grinned.

"I've learned a trick or three, being around the pair of you," their liaison noted smugly.

Bath and kitchen were across the hall, the former conveniently opposite the bedroom, the latter over from the sitting room; a privacy door between divided the hall-way, effectively creating a master suite in the back of the floor, separate from sitting room and kitchen. A large shower was in the corner of the bathroom, in addition to a lovely claw-footed tub which notably resembled the one

Holmes recalled. *Though perhaps rather bigger,* he decided. *Maybe even big enough for...* He glanced at Skye with a thoughtful gaze, then shot a hard, inquisitive look at Ryker. The latter's unassuming expression told the tale, and the detective let his grey eyes crinkle in amusement.

The kitchen took Holmes back in memory to Mrs. Hudson's domain, despite the modern gas appliances and the microwave oven artfully tucked into a corner. The pantry was fully stocked, as was the refrigerator.

The second floor contained three moderately sized bedrooms and a bath, all of which had been themed on either Watson's bedroom, or Holmes' own.

"It's wonderful," Skye murmured, amazed. "I can't believe you did all this."

"We are well aware of what the two of you have just accomplished," the Queen noted softly. "To provide a special—and safe—home for you here is little enough recompense."

"There's security and to spare, around the entire flat," Ryker said quietly. "For obvious reasons. It'll even withstand a car bomb."

"The windows?" Skye's eyebrows rose.

"Bulletproof, one-way glass, and equipped with automated blast shutters," Ryker elaborated. "As soon as a sharp pressure gradient is detected, they snap closed."

———

Skye glanced at her husband, who as yet had said nothing. But the grey eyes sparkled, and his jaw was tight. The line of his shoulders, however, was relaxed. *He's deeply touched, and he loves it,* she realized. *And he feels right at home.* She smiled to herself sadly, making a decision. Drawing a deep breath, she turned to their companions.

"Braeden," the scientist asked, "do you think you could contact Billy and see about having our things packed and shipped over? The horses too, I suppose, and little Anna. Oh, and we'll need to find a place to board the horses, maybe outside the city..."

"Surely it would be more feasible to sell the horses," the Queen suggested. "I am quite certain that more than suitable mounts can be found for you here."

Skye bit her lip, as Holmes turned to stare at her.

"Yes, I'm sure you're right," she agreed, stifling a sigh at the thought of losing her beloved horses. "The ranch will have to go on the market, of course. Then there's the matter of my fitting in. I'll have to find a job—teaching, maybe."

"Possibly a baronetcy and a stipend can be found," the prince suggested. "That would cover the matter quite thoroughly, I'm certain. And certainly Sir Sherlock's ancestry is right in line with such a thing. 'Country squire' and all that."

Skye nodded, then continued, "And I don't have a clue about what it takes to become a citizen here..."

"Oh, I can help with that," Ryker interjected.

"Skye," grey eyes blinked in shock, "may I enquire what the devil you think you are doing, my dear?"

———

Holmes carefully hid the sudden strain in his voice behind a polite, vaguely bemused tone, for the sake of the royal couple. Skye turned to look up at him with a tired smile.

"It's perfect, Sherlock," she informed him. "You're home. 221B Baker Street exists here now, and at least on the inside, it's so much like it was in your own continuum, it's positively incredible."

"This is my continuum now, Wife," he pointed out, "and we already have a home. I certainly have no objections to this gratifyingly familiar additional domicile, but we really must discuss the details and options before making the sort of irrevocable changes you suggest. I see no particular reason to abandon the one in favour of the other, especially in our line of work." He turned to the royal couple. "The gift is most magnanimous, Your Majesty. I have no doubt we will make glad use of our new home, during our hopefully frequent stays in London."

———

"And that is all we could wish, Sir Sherlock," Her Highness noted, diplomatically hiding her understanding smile. "It is yours to do with as you wish. I believe Captain Ryker has the title to the flat?"

"No, Madam, the Director has it," Ryker said. "She thought it might be best kept in a special safe in Headquarters, given certain...circumstances. The Holmeses can have access to it any time they like, of course. Consider it the ultimate in safety deposit boxes. And," he added to the couple, "she suggests that, as newlyweds, you may not have considered the matter of wills as yet, but it should be your next priority, especially given your professions. She and FBI Agent Adrian Smith have already agreed to safeguard copies of that document, via the aforementioned 'ultimate safety deposit boxes;' you may, of course, choose your own executors."

"Hm. Excellent point," Sherlock murmured.

"Actually," Skye added, "I already worked one up, in case the tesseract work frazzed. It's in my luggage."

———

Sherlock fired a disturbed glance at his wife.

"I'll get it out tomorrow, and Sherlock and I can re-work it for both of us. We'll need witnesses, I guess, and maybe...do those things get notarized?"

"Not to worry," Ryker reassured them. "I'll witness it, and see to it everything is properly managed, both for British and American law."

"Excellent, then," the prince agreed. "Now, we know the newlyweds have had a busy time of it recently, and I see weariness in the Lady Holmes' face, Milady Wife, though I've little doubt she would deny it. May I respect-fully suggest of Her Majesty the Queen that we allow the pair some privacy to settle in?"

"A most thoughtful idea, sir," the Queen nodded. "Ryker, could you possibly spirit us out of here?"

"Right away, Your Majesty," Ryker smiled, turning briefly to the Holmeses. "I'll hold off calling Williams until the two of you decide what to do. My cell phone's on if you need anything."

"Gotcha," Skye nodded. "Thanks, Brae."

Holmes added, "And thank you, Your Majesties."

Within moments, Holmes was alone with his wife in his new, old flat.

———

The evening was quiet. Skye tried to convince her husband to relax in the sitting room while she prepared dinner, but Holmes would have none of it.

"I am no more blind than the Prince Consort, Wife. You ARE tired, weary beyond anything I have seen in you, after all you have been through; and the unexpected meeting with the Queen stressed you badly. The departure of adrenaline after so long living with it tends to leave one feeling decidedly wilted, as I have had occasion to know myself. I will not have you exhausting yourself further by waiting on me."

"But you're tired, too," Skye protested. "This case was stressful for both of us."

"All the more reason for the both of us to prepare dinner, and to make it a simple one."

In the end, Holmes had his way, and they ate hot sandwiches at the table in the sitting room, watched television over brandy, and went to bed early. Even so, Sherlock still poked curiously around the flat, especially interested in the forensics lab downstairs, before preparing for bed.

"Skye?" he eventually called into the air, as he crawled into the big bed alone.

"Yeah?" issued from another room; Holmes found himself uncertain as to which one.

"Where are you? You should be in bed, my dear."

"I'm coming," Skye called back from somewhere in the depths of the flat. "I got diverted by something I discovered in the apartment."

"A familiar complaint, I find. This flat is full of fascinating hidden surprises. And what might yours have been?"

"I found where the CD collection is hidden."

"Ah. Behind the painting of Lord Byron, I deduce?"

"Yup! And the movie collection is on the other side, behind Wordsworth. They're both nice compilations, too. I'm guessing Brae had Billy go through our collections in Florissant."

"Indeed," Holmes nodded with a smile, reaching for his journal where it lay on the nightstand. He stopped with it in hand, however, as it suddenly occurred to him that he had not unpacked it from the luggage. *Did Skye get it out for me...? Surely Ryker would not have so violated my privacy...* he wondered briefly, flipping quickly to the last page containing writing.

It was then he realized that the writing was not his own.

———

March 10
9:37 p.m.
Dear Sherlock,

First let me say that I didn't read anything in here. I don't even know what's in here other than what you yourself already showed me, those two times. You'll see I turned to a completely blank page to write this, to avoid invading your privacy. Please forgive me for even opening it, but you're entirely right about how tired I am. I think it's gonna be a while before I can close my eyes and see anything other than damn tensor analysis. But I think some time in London, just goofing around with you, will help a lot—I can decompress. If it's okay with you, I think I'd like to maybe see some plays over in the West End and do a bit of shopping, nothing fancy, but it'd be fun and get my mind off of wormholes for a change.

Drat! I AM tired! Here I am, rambling on in your journal, in ink no less, so I can't even erase it. I'm so sorry, Honey. Anyway, my whole purpose in writing in here was because I just wasn't up to a big discussion about where to live. So I figured I'd write my thoughts down here, and you could see and understand.

It's really simple, Sherlock. I don't have anything tying me to Colorado anymore. I don't even have anything tying me to the States anymore, when you get right down to it. So I don't want you to feel like you have to live there on account of me. Yes, I love the Rockies, but I love you more. And now there's a real 221B Baker Street, in THIS continuum. This is a beautiful flat. I like it a lot. But more importantly, I can tell you LOVE it, and you're comfortable here. So if you're happy here, then this is where we should live.

See, it's like this. Home, to me, isn't a place—it's a person. It's you. Wherever you are is home to me. "Intreat me not to leave thee, or to return from following after thee: for whither thou goest, I will go; and where thou lodgest, I will lodge: thy people shall be my people, and thy God, my God."

And that's it, in a nutshell, Honey. I love you.

Skye

———

Holmes sat there staring at the page for several long minutes, his vision misted. Finally he lifted his gaze to see Skye standing at the foot of the bed, wrapped in her robe and watching him silently. He drew a deep breath and waved her into bed beside him, holding the covers open as she discarded her robe on the bedpost opposite the one holding his dressing gown, then crawled into bed.

Once she was comfortably snuggled under the covers next to him, he uncapped his fountain pen, twisted to one side, dropped his shoulder so she could read over it, and began to write—right under her entry.

———

March 10
10:22 p.m.
My wife does me more honour than she realises.
Nevertheless, this is a marriage of equals. "Let me not to the marriage of true minds admit impediments." And impediment would it be, should one member dictate to the other. Skye's opinion is of great worth to me, as much in the matter of dwelling-places as in an inves-

tigative case. I should no more dismiss it than I should ignore my own reason.

And there is a thing which my dear Skye, in her weariness, may have failed to recollect, though I am certain she already knows. Watson would have the world—many worlds, evidently—believe that I am no more nor less than a thinking machine, and so I can be, when need demand; but I am a man, and one possessed of a decidedly Bohemian nature. And there is a certain log cabin to be found in the Rampart Range of the Rocky Mountains which holds many of my most intimate memories—not the least of which is my wedding. Both weddings, if we may so style the first, in the eyes of a righteous and merciful Providence. I find myself loath to allow the locus of those memories to pass into other hands.

Yes, this is London. But it is not MY London. In point of fact, it never was my London. Perhaps one day it shall become OUR London; I cannot say. Should that time come, we can reassess. But for now, as it is Skye's desire for us both to be happy, I put forward the concept that this may best be accomplished by keeping this flat in Baker Street, AND the ranch in Florissant. For I have it to understand that there are already cases awaiting us in Colorado, as there undoubtedly will be more cases here in England. A nearby "home base," if you will, is always wise to have.

———

Sherlock glanced up to ascertain that Skye was, indeed, reading over his shoulder. Glistening blue eyes met his grey gaze, and his own crinkled.

"So, is the matter settled, Wife?"

"The matter is settled, Husband," she answered with a smile. "Both, it is."

"Finally!" he sighed long-sufferingly.

Then he put away the journal and took his wife in his arms.

They spent two more weeks in London. These two weeks were, however, not spent quite so much as tourists; rather they settled into the Baker Street flat, making it thoroughly their own, and becoming nominal citizens of the city. To Skye's immense delight, Sherlock reverted to his old ways, the ones of which Watson had so often written: lounging about the flat in his dressing-gown, experimenting with his chemicals, organizing his notes.

At the Director General's urging, they constructed a will in two duplicate copies, had Ryker witness both, then placed them in his capable hands for appropriate care and handling. He assured them all legal formalities would be taken care of, and one copy should go into their British "ultra safety deposit box," while the other should travel by secure route to Agent Smith for similar safekeeping. Within two days, he informed them all was complete.

"After all, it's pretty simple," Skye pointed out. "If one of us goes, the other gets everything. If we both get taken out and we have children, everything goes into trust for them, unless they're of age, when they get it directly, even split. If we both get taken out, and we haven't had kids by then, the ranch in Florissant goes to the FBI for their undercover work, specification made that MI-5 gets to use it if necessary, as well; and the flat here goes to the Secret Service for use as a safehouse."

"Precisely," Sherlock agreed, hiding his personal discomfort regarding preparing for Skye's death; he was more sanguine about his own. "And regardless, my Stradivari goes back to the Crown, with some stipulations that it be assigned a certain sentimental value, and not merely historic worth."

"Works for me."

———

Dr. Watson visited for several days, enjoying the hospitality of one of their spare bedrooms, much to the pleasure of Sherlock and Skye. Each had come to love the old physician, and Sherlock was delighted to watch the interaction between the doctor and his wife, who often teased each other unmercifully, then laughed until they were breathless. The Holmeses were sorry to see him go back to his own home at the end of his visit.

"Don't worry," Watson told them with a twinkling smile as he departed. "You'll be back, and I'll be waiting. I may be a stodgy old sod, but I've got quite a few years left in me yet."

"And visits to America to make," Skye declared, to Sherlock's pleasure.

"Be careful what you offer," Watson fixed her with a twinkling, if stern, eye. "I'll take you up on it."

"See that you do," Sherlock shot back.

———

From time to time the couple rambled around the nearby park, or went shopping in the various London districts. Most of their evenings were spent attending concerts and plays in the West End. It was a relaxed and comfortable way to wind down their sojourn.

By the end of it, Skye was her usual vivacious, sunny self once more, relaxed, well-rested and healthy. Holmes was, however, becoming restless, his usual craving for a case setting upon him. Ryker and the Director General of the Secret Service tossed several intriguing little problems their way; Skye and Sherlock solved them with reasonable aplomb, one or two being worked out without ever needing to leave the confines of Baker Street.

———

On the evening before they were scheduled to leave for the States, a very special—and very classified—reception was held. Kensington Palace was the location of the reception honoring the Holmeses, and upon arriving they discovered not only were the Secret Service in attendance, but a substantial number of the Royal Family, as well as high RAF officials and certain top-ranking members of Parliament. Watson was even there, per special invitation.

Holmes was pleased to see his wife far more relaxed at this event, however: Ryker had given them advance notice of the function, and taken the time to help Skye learn proper protocol.

"So I finally know what to do, and I don't feel like I'm gonna cause a diplomatic incident if I blink," she told Holmes and Watson privately, with a smile.

"Excellent, my dear," Sherlock replied in a low voice, nodding and smiling at a duke across the room. "I am glad to hear it. Of course you were not reared with such considerations. But I find it helps to remember that, when all the titles and letters are pared away, all of the furs and jewels and baubles, they are people not unlike ourselves. They have hopes and dreams, and fears and foibles. There are angels and devils in their family trees, as there are in all families. Their ancestors were merely fortunate enough— or unfortunate enough, depending upon your point of view—to attract a considerable amount of attention and power."

"Listen to your husband; he's right," Watson nodded sagely.

"Well, I suppose that's true," Skye agreed consideringly.

"It is, indeed," a soft feminine voice spoke behind them. They turned to find the Duchess of Kensington standing there. "We have our joys and our heartbreaks, as much as any of the so-called 'commoners.' And a great deal of responsibility and expectation heaped upon our heads, into the bargain." She smiled at the couple and their friend. "Forgive me; I did not mean to eavesdrop. I merely came by to greet you properly, as my hostess duties have kept me uncommonly busy this evening, and I inadvertently overheard. I am quite certain none of us knew you were so afraid of us, Lady Holmes, or we should have taken measures to relieve you of your anxieties long since."

She gestured subtly, and across the room, the Queen took note. Several members of the Royal Family turned their way as Skye blushed.

"Oh, that's okay," Skye explained. "I didn't want to offend any of the Royal Family, but I didn't have the first clue what I was supposed to do around y'all. I was terrified I'd create some sort of diplomatic incident."

"Then it did not show, child," a smiling voice noted. Skye spun, but her husband hid a grin.

"Your Majesty," he greeted the queen before he'd even turned around. He and Watson bowed in respect.

"Thank you, Madam." Skye dropped a graceful curtsy, then smiled. "I was trying hard."

"And now you are more comfortable with us?" the Duchess asked gently.

"Oh, yes," Skye smiled wider. "Captain Ryker helped

me learn proper protocol, so now at least I KNOW if I mess up."

They all laughed, and the Prince of Wales signalled a passing waiter, who immediately detoured. The Prince gestured to the Holmeses as the waiter stopped at his elbow.

"Here you are, Milady Skye," he said graciously. "Have some champagne. You are, after all, the guests of honour."

Holmes nodded, taking two champagne flutes from the waiter's tray and handing one to his wife. Watson partook, as well. They lifted their glasses to the Queen, who nodded; then they all drank.

"Sir Sherlock was just telling his wife we are not so different from her," the Duchess of Kensington noted, "by way of calming her worries. And Dr. Watson and I agreed with him."

"Indeed," the Prince of Wales nodded. "And more so than, perhaps, the Lady Holmes realises."

"How so?" Skye's eyebrows shot upward.

The royals all looked expectantly at Holmes. His lips quirked in amusement, and he answered.

"I am certain you are aware of matters of propriety and suitability of marriage in titled persons in Great Britain, my dear," he began smoothly, and Skye nodded. "I have been aware that Ryker has been gleaning information about the two of us, off and on, for several weeks now, possibly months. As, I suppose, anyone who has ever read Watson's stories will know, I was descended of country squires myself, and might have aspired to a baronetcy had I so chosen, though it is more likely it should have gone to brother Mycroft. I am now a Knight of the Realm. And if you will recall, it was indicated to you that you were considered for the same."

"Mmm...yeah, I remember that," Skye nodded

thoughtfully again. "So...are you saying I was, um, 'vetted,' too?"

"You were," her husband chuckled. "And in the due course of things, a cousin of yours was discovered, here in this country."

"Oh!" Skye exclaimed, instantly interested. "Who? Can we meet them?"

"I fear the particular relation in question is now deceased, my dear, though I am certain his family would enjoy meeting you," the Duchess of Kensington remarked.

"But shall we say you come from a line of famous physicists?" Holmes added with a grin.

"Indeed," the Queen smiled. "Sir James Chadwick, Nobel Prize winner and discoverer of the neutron, is your cousin, a few times removed. Born the same year your husband departed his...original...continuum."

"Now there," Holmes decided, lifting his champagne glass, "is an interesting correspondence."

"Oh, wow," Skye murmured, wide-eyed. "James Chadwick was my cousin?"

"He was," the Prince of Wales nodded. "Had we anticipated your desire to meet his family, it could have been arranged for this evening. As it is, I am afraid it will have to await your next visit."

"Cool," Skye grinned enthusiastically. "We'll be back in a couple of months!" and everyone laughed.

"And now," the Prince noted, "I believe it is time for the Royal Proclamation."

"Is he here yet?" the Queen queried, signaling Director of the Secret Service, who hurried over. "Madam Director, has Captain Williams arrived?"

"Yes, Your Majesty," the Director informed the Queen, curtsying, "he is just now doffing his overcoat, and will be here in a moment. There was a slight weather delay."

"Very good," the Queen said, as Skye and Sherlock exchanged puzzled glances. "Sir Sherlock, Lady Holmes, Dr. Watson, do you join Captain Ryker and the Director. The others will be with you shortly. We have an announcement."

———

Puzzled, the trio followed the Director over to Ryker, and his unit, in formal dress, promptly ranked themselves. Moments later, Billy joined them, Tina on his arm. The Director placed the Holmeses beside herself, and Watson beside Sherlock, with Ryker and his unit on one side of the foursome, and Billy and Tina, evidently representing their American-based unit, on the other.

A bell was rung to attract the attention of all in attendance, and the Queen stepped forward, the members of the royal family meanwhile having arranged themselves in order of rank, as well.

"Let it be known to all present," the Queen announced in clear tones, "that Sir Sherlock and Lady Skye Holmes have performed admirably in support and defence of the Kingdom. They are therefore henceforward to be considered adjunct agents in Her Majesty's Secret Service, Lady Holmes' citizenship notwithstanding, and she shall be treated and regarded a citizen of the United Kingdom in despite; and a formal contract, in perpetuity, is being drawn up between said Service and The Holmes Agency."

Applause went around the room. An awed Skye decided, with hidden amusement, that her husband's expression resembled the cat that ate the canary.

"Let it also be known," the Queen continued, "that a new division is being formed within the Service. Its founding units consist of Unit 47, led by MAJOR Braeden

Ryker, and Unit 105, led by MAJOR Will Williams. They, and any other units which shall in future be designated as part of this division, shall serve as direct liaisons and assistants to The Holmes Agency...and any of their designated representatives." She gazed directly at Watson and smiled; Watson looked flustered. "This division shall be named The Irregulars. Unit 47 shall henceforward and forever be known as the Baker Street Irregulars. Unit 105 shall henceforward and forever be known as the Aerotech Drive Irregulars. Further units shall be named appropriately, as they are added to the division."

The applause became enthusiastic, as the members of Ryker's unit whooped with joy, and Ryker, Williams, and Tyler beamed.

"It seems," Sherlock murmured to his wife, "that my 'support group' is now formal and complete."

"It does look that way, Sweetheart," Skye agreed with a smile.

————

March 25

Once more across the ocean, from one home to another. How my life has changed in a year's time. For tomorrow shall mark one year since I arrived in this continuum.

My wife is resting on my shoulder, as before, but this time we are eagerly anticipating arrival at our principal residence. We have been assured all of the "critters," as Skye terms them, are safe and sound, and all is well. I must admit looking forward to seeing Anna, Blaze, the other horses, and my bees, not to mention sleeping in our own bed. Though the bed in Baker Street quickly became "ours" as well; it was quite comfortable, and the environment distinctly relaxing for me.

Still, this is one adventure I am glad to have ended. The sojourn in London was delightful; the McFarlane case a nice little puzzle. But the threat to the continuum, and to Skye—that, I am more than pleased to be putting behind us.

And in a few hours, we will have arrived at our first home. And —cases await there. My life here in this continuum is rapidly shaping into decided contentment and happiness.

11

Surprises

But when they arrived in New York to change to a domestic plane, a gentleman in a dark suit and sunglasses intercepted them.

"Mr. and Mrs. Holmes?" he murmured, falling in beside them in the international concourse. "I'm with the U.S. Government. I have a summons to Washington." He flashed identification, then handed a letter to Skye. It was addressed specifically to, "Dr. Skye Chadwick-Holmes," and simply stated that she was to accompany their liaison, one Agent Hugh Beaufort, to a waiting plane. Skye and Sherlock exchanged glances.

"We have only just returned from the United Kingdom, a decidedly difficult case, and a long flight," Sherlock noted smoothly. "Might this possibly wait until we have gotten home, unpacked, and rested for a few days?"

"You, Mr. Holmes, are not part of the summons," Beaufort observed, "and so you may certainly do as you wish. But Dr. Chadwick—excuse me, Dr. Chadwick-Holmes—must come with me."

"MUST?" Skye queried sharply. "As in, 'don't have a choice?'"

"Something like that," Beaufort remarked blandly.

"Then I most certainly am accompanying my wife," Sherlock said sternly.

"I'll see to it that all of your luggage is recovered and brought with us, then," Beaufort noted, pulling a palm computer and entering a quick text message. "Please come with me."

In moments they were in a small commuter jet headed for Washington, D.C.

———

They were taken directly to the Pentagon. Inside they were led through a maze of corridors and into a circular room. In the center of the floor was a large mosaic of the Emblem of the United States. On the far side of the room was a curved dais with a semicircular console. Behind the console sat the assembled Joint Chiefs of Staff; a stenographer sat at one end, at a computer. Behind the Joint Chiefs, a closed door led out of the room; it was obviously an attached deliberation chamber of some sort.

Beaufort led Skye into the center of the room and left her standing there, moving to the door and positioning himself before it as though guarding it. Sherlock slowly followed Skye into the center of the room, sizing up their environment.

"This appears to be a tribunal of sorts," he observed.

"As usual, Mr. Holmes, you are correct," General Charles Connelly, of the U.S. Army, and Chairman of the Joint Chiefs of Staff, noted. "We have convened to review the situation regarding Project: Tesseract and Dr. Skye

Chadwick's participation in the events that brought you to our continuum."

"I'm on trial," Skye said softly, in disbelief.

Several nods from the Joint Chiefs were her reply.

———

The tribunal swore in Skye, and Sherlock insisted upon being sworn in as well.

"This is not your concern, Mr. Holmes," General Connelly said smoothly. "You need not even be here. You are being accorded the privilege due to the fact that you are an ambassador, and highly regarded by this committee, not because of the relationship between the two of you."

"It certainly is my concern, General, for she is here because I am here," Sherlock retorted. "I have no plans to leave, and you may consider me a direct eyewitness to the events under question."

"Let it be so noted, then," Admiral James Hoffman, of the U.S. Marines, stated, nodding at the stenographer. "Let's get down to it."

———

In short order, Skye was being grilled about the details of Project: Tesseract and the arrival of Sherlock Holmes from his own continuum to theirs. Skye answered to the best of her ability, providing details as clearly as she recalled them, and referring them to the classified DVDs for more accurate information.

"And so Mr. Holmes was expected to die in his own continuum," Admiral Hoffman observed skeptically. "Despite the accuracy of the stories that Conan Doyle set down."

"He was, in THAT particular continuum," Skye affirmed. "He exists in several different continuums, with some differences in each. Those differences are necessary in order for the continuums to exist separately. Otherwise, they would collapse and merge into one continuum, or worse, create a multidimensional singularity."

"And you have proof of the presence of Mr. Holmes in multiple universes?" Connelly asked.

"Yes, sir," Skye averred. "Again, I refer you to the DVDs of our scans. In fact, I had to explain that to Sherlock—er, Mr. Holmes—shortly after his arrival. He had hoped to be able to return to his own continuum, but that proved impossible, as it would have failed the individuality test and caused continuum collapse. In between my other duties, I spent the equivalent of at least a solid two weeks working on the physics to send him back," here Sherlock blinked at the revelation of the time scale, then lowered his eyes to hide his pain, "but couldn't find a way to do it."

"Couldn't, or wouldn't?" Hoffman pressed. "Why else would you choose a continuum where he dies at Reichenbach? I submit that you intended the matter to begin with."

"On what grounds?" Skye demanded.

"Scientific curiosity," Hoffman fired back. "Admit it, doctor. You were curious to know how a brilliant man would fare, brought well over one hundred years into the future. In addition, it has come to our attention that the two of you are now married. It must perforce be questioned, then, whether or not you deliberately brought him here in order to seduce him."

Skye stood silently, stunned. She sensed the man beside her stiffen, as well, and grew even more concerned. *Sherlock —he doesn't BELIEVE that, does he?* she worried. Skye gathered her startled wits and prepared to defend herself.

"That is extremely offensive, Admiral, and I would like that formally noted in the record," she declared crisply, glancing meaningfully at the stenographer, who nodded while continuing to work at the classified computer. "In point of fact, several different subjects were considered for observation before Sh—Mr. Holmes was selected," Skye continued. "It was not a unilateral decision. Myself, my project manager Dr. Caitlin Hughes, and our team leads made the decision by unanimous vote."

Skye had, by this time, metamorphosed into Project Scientist Dr. Skye Chadwick, and her speech had likewise become precise and technical.

"Mr. Holmes was chosen for several reasons." She began to tick off fingers. "One—his high intelligence. Two—his known history, as provided in the Conan Doyle stories and verified via tesseract. Three—his known personality and responses, provided and verified by same. As to the choice of continuum, it was determined that investigating history that was already known would be a waste of the project, in both time and money," she declared. "It was therefore DR. HUGHES' stance that we should select a continuum in which the outcome was NOT known, and investigate it, collecting a record of events as we went."

"You cannot deny that you became romantically involved shortly thereafter," Air Force General Mackinaw declared, "nor that a man died in your bringing of Mr. Holmes to this continuum."

"If I may," Sherlock interjected, his voice betraying a hint of annoyance and anger in its stridence, "as I AM the subject of the discussion, it is only reasonable that my point of view be heard, and that my statements be for the record."

STEPHANIE OSBORN

"True," Navy Admiral Peter Kirkoff agreed. "You may speak, Mr. Holmes."

"First of all, in the matter of Professor Moriarty's death," Sherlock began, "it must be stated unequivocally that there was no stopping that. Each and every part of Moriarty's body was beyond the lip of the ledge, to include his feet, the soles of which pressed against the side of the cliff below. And it took every ounce of effort upon my part to counterbalance his weight and avoid joining him there. No one could have broken the hold he had upon me without his falling to his death, simply as a matter of physics. He knew he was about to die. His entire intent, at that point, was simply to ensure that he took me with him; a Pyrrhic victory."

"I've seen the classified video from the tesseract," Admiral Kirkoff observed. "Mr. Holmes is definitely right about that."

"In addition," Sherlock added, "if you have seen the video, you will know that Skye made an instinctive, if futile, attempt to catch him."

"Also true," Kirkoff agreed quietly. "She leaned perilously close to the point of no return herself, but Moriarty had already fallen beyond her reach."

"But WHY did Dr. Chadwick act at ALL?" the general pressed insistently.

"Dr. Chadwick-HOLMES," Sherlock corrected sharply, and the general nodded cursorily.

Skye drew a long breath.

"Believe me, gentlemen," she said, subdued, "I've pondered that matter for many and many long hours myself. I readily admit that I've been a fan of the literary Holmes since childhood, and finding him to be a real person, not merely a character on paper, was really...cool. But if you'll look through my dossier, you'll see that I had been a fairly active reserve policewoman, not so very long before. When you've got that kind of training, and been through some of the...situations...I've been through, sometimes it just...kicks in," she said, shrugging. "At one point during the fight, the understanding, the conscious comprehension, that we were in two separate universes...disappeared. I became a police officer looking at a murderous attack—a murderous attack upon someone I 'knew,' no less," Skye added, using her fingers to imply quotation marks. "The cop in me...stopped it."

"Literally," Sherlock murmured.

"But that instinctive reaction," Skye continued, "is exactly why we—note I said WE—shut down the project."

"And Skye was one of the most vocal team members on that matter," Sherlock pointed out. "Despite the fact that the project comprised her entire career."

There was a pause in the proceedings, while the officers absorbed this information.

———

"You had more to say on another matter, Mr. Holmes," the admiral recalled. "Please continue, if you would."

"With regard to our...romantic...relationship," Sherlock forged ahead, trying to ignore the heat that rose in his face, determined to defend his wife, "there are several matters to be noted. First of all, Mrs. Holmes, née Chadwick, was a model of decorum with regard to her deportment with me, from the very beginning. She is the epitome of a lady. It was that, combined with her intellect, AND her COMPLETE trustworthiness, which attracted me to her to begin with. She, quite simply, rang true at every point. It was many months after my arrival before anything developed between us greater than friendship. My awareness of my feelings began to surface when Skye nearly died in an attempt to prevent sabotage of her apparatus," he admitted, feeling his colour heightening. "And in every instance of the progression of our relationship, I, not Skye, was the instigator. And in every instance, Skye evinced decided, observationally verifiable, and very real surprise. Which surprise, given my reputation until that point, is quite understandable."

Sherlock moved forward to stand directly beside his wife, confident. "By way of example," he added, "shortly after I began to board at her ranch, we attended a social event together. It was the birthday party of a neighbour, and Skye brought me in order to help me acclimate to the modern social functions. While there, however, one of her acquaintances made amused and untoward remarks regarding the nature of our relationship—which at the time was purely that of a new arrival and his liaison. Skye became incensed and set the young man straight in short order. It was a decided dressing-down."

The tribunal sat silently, considering the couple.

"Let me also remind this tribunal," Sherlock declared firmly, even stridently, "that Skye did, indeed, nearly die in defense of Project: Tesseract. And in addition, she risked her feminine virtue, by disguising herself as a woman of EASY virtue, in order to obtain information which eventually led to the breaking of the spy ring. The second, in particular, did not come easily to her. And had it not been for our detailed preliminary planning, would have resulted in the loss of said virtue, when the scenario turned ill. It DID result in her injury. Both acts—the offering of her life, and her virtue—were completely voluntary."

Meaningful, impressed looks were exchanged among the Joint Chiefs at that declaration.

Sherlock paused and glanced significantly at his wife,

then observed, "And as Skye is a civilian, and not a member of the military, I submit that the jurisdiction of this tribunal is highly in question."

Skye continued without hesitation, following on smoothly from her husband's thought, "We must therefore ask what the true reason for this meeting is."

That brought several raised eyebrows among tribunal members. Just then, the door behind the Joint Chiefs opened.

The Commander in Chief walked through.

"Excellent deductive work, both of you," he said with a smile.

———

In short order, the Holmes couple came to understand that the entire scenario which had just ensued was a test to ascertain that all was indeed as it appeared, especially given the unanticipated circumstance of Sherlock marrying Skye. In reality they had been brought there in order that the President might present Skye with a medal of honor. Skye glanced at Sherlock.

"Déjà vu all over again," she muttered.

"Indeed," he said, trying not to grin. "You did so well with the Queen, that I shall keep silent and let you handle the matter, Wife."

"Gee, thanks," Skye said, heavy on the sarcasm.

———

The various military officers and the President took in the exchange between the married couple with some bemused amusement.

"Is there a problem, Dr. Chadwick-Holmes?" the President asked.

"Potentially, Mr. President," Skye admitted. "We had this same conversation with the Queen of England only a few weeks ago, when she knighted Sherlock." Eyebrows rose all around the room.

"Congratulations, Sir Sherlock," the President offered. Holmes held up a forestalling hand.

"I stand on no such formality," he noted. "Mr. Holmes will do nicely. It pleased the Queen to do the thing, and that is sufficient."

"But they had to create a whole new protocol for it," Skye explained. "Only a very limited number of people know that Sherlock was knighted, because of the potential for revealing that he's really THAT Holmes. Then the tesseract gets revealed too, and here we go 'round the mulberry bush again. Doesn't this," she gestured at the boxed and beribboned medal in the President's hand, "have the same potential?"

The President and his military officers smiled knowingly.

"This isn't the first time we've had occasion to do something like this, Doctor," the President noted. "And we already have the protocols in place, dating back to World War Two. That's why it's occurring in the Pentagon, under the auspices of the Joint Chiefs. This isn't a regular Presidential Medal of Freedom; it's a Presidential Medal of Honor."

"I've never heard of that," Skye murmured.

"Exactly," the President grinned. "In cases where an individual's service is above and beyond the call, but the awarding of a public medal would compromise national security—or, in this case, worse—the Medal of Honor is awarded in the presence of the Joint Chiefs of Staff, by the

Commander in Chief, in a suitably secure facility. The transcript of this entire meeting will be classified and filed with Project: Tesseract documentation, as well as an encrypted annotation placed in your personnel dossier."

He removed the medal from its case, handing the case to Sherlock. Then he placed the ribbon around Skye's neck.

"I hereby award this Medal of Honor to Dr. Skye Chadwick-Holmes," he intoned, "for service above and beyond the call of a citizen's duty; for the willingness to give her life, and more, in the protection of All That Is; and for her dedication to scientific ethics despite the cost to her own person and career. Congratulations, Doctor."

The President shook her hand, and the Joint Chiefs stood and applauded.

————

Agent Beaufort congratulated Skye as he escorted the couple out of the room; Skye's medal was now back in its case, safely hidden away in Sherlock's inside coat pocket.

"Sorry to have had to start the thing that way," a rueful Beaufort apologized. "I know you were tired and kind of upset, and I hated like hell to do it. But I had orders to handle it like that."

"We understand," Sherlock waved aside the apology, as Skye nodded agreement with her husband. "The Queen did something similar when we arrived in London."

"Would you like to stay in Washington overnight and celebrate?" Beaufort asked. "I have orders to set you up in a suite, with dinner reservations, if you'd like. Or if you'd rather, the plane that brought us here is still waiting with your luggage, and you can head straight home. Direct, private flight to CoSpr, no dealing with layovers."

The pair glanced at each other, and Beaufort could have sworn some unspoken communication passed between them.

"No, Agent Beaufort," Sherlock stated for them both, "I think we shall take advantage of your aeroplane and betake ourselves home to Colorado, if you do not object. No doubt the classified records of our most recent case will be shared with Skye's parent country very shortly, and you will understand that we are in some need of rest. Or at least Skye is."

"I'm doing okay," Skye demurred, "but I will be glad to get back to the critters. Our two-week trip to England lasted several months longer than I'd planned on."

12

Settling In

After a long, if fairly comfortable, flight and a drive up Ute Pass, the Holmeses found themselves at the ranch again. Their MI-5 caretakers handed over to them, and the pair started the process of unpacking and settling back into their first home. After a long day, they crawled into bed as the clock tolled midnight, and Holmes pulled out his journal, to Skye's secret amusement.

———

March 26
Midnight
One year in my new continuum, to the day. As I noted yesterday, how many things can change in a year's time: I now live in a completely different universe, in a completely different century. I have two homes, one in America, the other in England. I drive automobiles. I use advanced forensics equipment, computers, and other such electronics; I have a set of Irregulars spanning two continents, formalised by no less than a Royal Proclamation. I lost Watson, then found him again—after a fashion, at least. I bested two Moriarties; assisted

297

twice in the saving of All That Is. I have been knighted. And last, but possibly most important and amazing of all, I fell in love and married. I have a wife.

And that wife and I are, at last, home in Florissant once more. Little Anna-cat, the horses, and my bees are all well. Barwell, Billy's designated caretaker for the ranch, has officially turned over the ranch to us and departed down the mountain for Colorado Springs. The house and ranch buildings are intact. But although the first hints of spring were arriving in England, the spring thaw has yet to begin, here. There is still a thick covering of snow blanketing all, and likely will be for at least another couple of weeks, so Skye informs me.

And...the Watson dreams have ceased.

———

The pair settled in comfortably, greeted enthusiastically by their animals, though occasionally there was a vague expression of regret upon Sherlock's face when he watched little Anna. Their bills had been cared for in their absence, and the rest of the mail consisted of magazines and journals; they took their time going through those.

Several small cases awaited them from both Colonel Jones and Agent Smith; these were solved with due aplomb, sometimes without having to leave the ranch. One or two such matters floated across the Pond as well, washing up on their doorstep, and received equally successful attention.

Within a few weeks, the snow began to melt as winter in the Rockies gradually relented to spring. One afternoon shortly after the last of the snow had melted from the pastures, a pickup truck turned into their driveway. An open-framed, wooden crate was in its bed, with some sort of wire container inside that. Sherlock, who had been headed for the kitchen, detoured and peered between the curtains of a front window.

"Skye," he queried, "do any of our neighbours have a medium blue Ford lorry, some five years old?"

"Um," Skye said, looking up from her physics journal, "not that I know of, Sherlock. Why?"

"Because one has pulled into our drive. Ah! Billy and his friend Miss Tyler are getting out."

"Oh," Skye said casually, putting aside the journal and getting to her feet. "I wonder what they want. Probably a case."

"Most likely. They must have brought up a large piece of evidence. There is a crate in the back of the lorry."

Skye opened the front door as Tina and Billy got the crate out of the back of the pickup and carried it toward the house.

"Hi there," Skye called. "How are y'all?"

"Quite well, thanks," Billy grinned.

"Yeah," Tina agreed, beaming. "Billy just asked me to be his girlfriend. He's already solved any conflicts over the matter, work-wise, so there won't be issues, and the team's all for it, he says."

"Oh, that's WONDERFUL!" Skye exclaimed, as Sherlock smiled slightly. "And of course you said yes."

"Of course," Tina grinned. "Almost faster than he could ask." Billy flushed, but grinned back.

"And so what is the reason for this visit?" Sherlock wondered. "Surely it was not merely to inform us of your new romantic status."

"No, we have a delivery," Billy smirked, as he and Tina maneuvered the crate through the front door. A small whimper came from inside, and Sherlock cocked a curious eyebrow. "Here we go."

They put the crate down on the floor as Skye closed the

front door against the damp spring breeze. Then, with a flourish, Billy opened both a wooden gate and a metal gate with a single lever, and a fuzzy explosion ensued.

Suddenly Sherlock had an armful of wriggling, yapping fur, licking his face enthusiastically. Grey eyes blinked in surprised shock, and he pulled back enough to ascertain what had leaped into his arms.

"BRENDAN!" he cried. "Little fellow! What in heaven's name are you doing here?!"

"Coming home," Skye said with a grin, moving to her husband's side and putting a light hand on the small of his back. "Brendan, meet your new daddy."

"He..." Holmes glanced up in astonishment, "he is mine?"

"He is," Skye's grin grew even wider.

"Now THAT," Billy remarked to Tina with a matching grin, "is a rare sight: Sherlock Holmes, completely surprised." Tina grinned back, pleased for the detective, and decidedly amused by seeing him so taken aback.

The wriggling puppy licked Sherlock's face enthusiastically, yapping happily, and Holmes grinned from ear to ear. The sleuth could hardly get a word out for Brendan lapping his face frenetically. Skye giggled. A snort escaped Billy, and Tina snickered. Finally Sherlock held the pup at arm's length—then had to work to maintain his grip on the animal as it wiggled and writhed to get closer to its new master. Sherlock juggled the puppy while eyeing his wife.

"Scamp," he addressed Skye with mock sternness, then swiftly readjusted his grip on Brendan, who was trying to climb up his arm. "You are becoming quite impressive at pulling the wool over my eyes, my dear. No one has managed that so often nor so well in my entire forty years. And here I thought young Brendan lost to me, when all along, you were the purchaser."

"I was," Skye grinned shamelessly, as Billy and Tina stifled laughter at the pup's antics and Sherlock's efforts to contain them. "I figured we needed a good tracking dog, and when you told me how Brendan picked YOU out, then helped you find an important clue, I knew he was the one. Not to mention how you could hardly stop talking about the little sweetie." Brendan leaned over and swiped his tongue across Skye's cheek at that remark, and everyone laughed.

"You see, my dear?" Holmes observed, tucking Brendan under one arm before turning and leading the way into the den. "He is an intelligent one, our Brendan. HE knows upon which side his bread is buttered."

"Well," Skye said, gesturing the two MI-5 agents along, "I hope the Carvers trained him about cats and horses."

"Horses, I know," Holmes nodded. "And cows, and geese," he added with another grin, "for McFarlane kept all those. Cats..." Anna entered the den, "...may be another matter."

"Well, there's only one way to find out. Put him down and let's see," Skye said practically, the animal trainer in her emerging.

So Holmes set the dog on the floor and stepped back. Brendan immediately bounded eagerly across the floor toward the little Siamese. Anna responded by turning slightly sideways and arching her back, her tail going up stiffly.

"Oh, no," Tina groaned.

———

As the puppy approached, Anna fluffed herself. When Brendan was only a couple of feet away, Anna hissed a warning.

Brendan immediately dropped to the floor right where he was, nose between his front paws, and lay very, very still. He watched Anna closely, but did not move so much as a muscle. Anna eyed him warily for several minutes, but the dog did nothing. Slowly the cat's back lowered, her bushed tail growing smaller. When she had resumed an almost normal posture, though still watching Brendan carefully, Brendan dared one invitational tail thump against the floor.

Anna cocked her ears forward. Brendan wagged his tail eagerly once, twice. Anna took a very slow, deliberate step forward, craning her neck, sniffing in the direction of the puppy. Brendan continued to remain still, but emitted a soft whine. Anna stepped forward again, still sniffing.

It took nearly three minutes for the cat to cover the two feet to the puppy; during this time, the human inhabitants of the room scarcely breathed. Finally Anna and Brendan were nose to nose. Each sniffed the other; Anna moved the length of Brendan's head, sniffing carefully. Finally she licked Brendan's ear, then began grooming behind it. Brendan's tail thumped happily on the floor, and he gave Anna an enthusiastic lick upside the head.

Anna pulled back for a moment and gazed solemnly at the puppy. Then she very calmly licked her paw, set the fur on the side of her head in order, and gravely sat her down next to the dog. Brendan jumped up and frisked happily around his new furry friend, then scurried back to his master.

————

"Well, I'd say he's cat-trained," Skye remarked dryly. "That's the best cat-puppy introduction I've ever seen."

"Excellent," her husband exclaimed, delighted. "Brendan, my lad, you are indeed a bright youngster!" He crouched and scruffed the spaniel's head.

"I hope you two have a big bed," Tina murmured to Skye. "Two humans, a cat, and a dog gonna get crowded at night otherwise, luv."

"It's a California king," Skye grinned. "No problems there."

"They're good," Billy grinned back.

"Would the two of you care to stay for tea?" Holmes wondered. "We were about to put the kettle on."

"He's right," Skye agreed, "and we'd love to have you. Thanks for handling the import and quarantine for me."

"We'd love to, and no problem," Billy agreed, as Tina nodded.

———

One evening in very early May, the Holmeses were comfortably resting on the sofa in their den in Florissant, having finished a little problem for Colonel Jones that same afternoon. Sherlock smoked his pipe and channel surfed more in reverie than in interest, young Brendan lying contentedly on his beslippered feet; Skye leaned against her husband's side and absently petted a lap full of Anna while flipping through a scientific journal. It was altogether a peaceful, quiet tableau.

"That looks so nice, I hate to interrupt them," Skye's voice noted softly, a smile audible in it.

"Mm?" Sherlock removed the pipe from his mouth and roused himself from his reverie. "Did you say something, Wife?"

———

Skye looked up and focused her eyes on his face; she had been lost in an article.

"No," she said, bemused. "Did you hear something?"

"Indeed," Holmes' voice noted in response, distinctly amused. "And it is proving difficult to do so."

"Interrupt them, you mean?" Chadwick's voice grinned.

"Precisely."

The couple on the couch instantly sat upright, discarding all else.

"Is everything okay?" Skye queried anxiously, dumping Anna unceremoniously from her lap. The insulted cat moved to Brendan and curled up beside the pup. Brendan whined happily, and Anna settled down, purring.

"Calm yourself, my dear Mrs. Holmes," Holmes' voice replied. "All is well; we simply thought to pop by for a visit."

"Yeah," Chadwick added. "We wanted to fill y'all in on what's been happening here."

"Indeed?" Sherlock wondered. "So how are matters progressing over there?"

"Quite nicely, actually," Holmes responded. "The brane is rock solid; consequently, so is the continuum. The ranch, too, is well. Our ranch hands are now used to seeing us much more often, and little Martha Williams is delighted over that fact."

"Martha Williams?" Skye queried.

"Oh, that's right," Chadwick commented. "You don't know, 'cause it hasn't happened there yet. Er. Hm. Well, let's just say your Billy and Tina will likely only get closer as time goes by..."

"Ah," Sherlock and Skye both grinned in understanding.

"Therefore I may assume their offspring is quite taken with the two of you?" Sherlock added.

"Oh, yeah," Chadwick agreed. "'Unca Sherwock an' Auntie Skye' are two of her favorite people on the planet, I think. Especially Uncle Sherlock."

"Now, now, my dear, no more so than you," Holmes demurred. Skye and Sherlock grinned again.

"So have you returned to sleuthing?" Skye asked Holmes.

"Only armchair detecting," Holmes noted. "And some beekeeping at the ranch. My Skye and I decided that the investigations performed upon a properly functioning tesseract are highly enlightening, and absorb and stimulate the intellect without need for more dangerous investigations. Besides, it would be irresponsible of me, given our...other news."

"And what would that be?" Sherlock wondered.

"My dear, would you invert?" Holmes requested of Chadwick.

"Just waiting for you to ask, Hon," Chadwick answered eagerly.

———

The periphery of the cabin den faded away, revealing the pink granite of the Chamber. As it did so, both Anna and Brendan scooted under the sofa in fear and remained there.

Holmes stood in front of the seated couple, almost between two of the monoliths, only a couple of feet away; Chadwick still sat at the director's console several yards beyond, operating the controls.

"There," she noted in satisfaction.

"Good," Holmes said, turning and holding out his

hand to his spouse. "Then would you please join me, so we may properly share our news?"

As Chadwick stood, Holmes returned his attention to the couple on the couch. "After stabilising the brane and ensuring all was well, Chadwick and I duly filed our spousal paperwork with the state of Colorado, then decided to go upon a well-earned holiday. We took a leaf from your book, and went to London for a fortnight. And yes, Dr. Chadwick-Holmes, we did find our universe's Watson. It was altogether a delightful visit, and while we were there..." Suddenly Holmes stopped, flushing slightly.

For Chadwick was emerging from behind the console —with a decidedly swollen belly. She moved to Holmes' side and took his hand, smiling joyfully.

"I got pregnant," she finished for her spouse.

"That's wonderful!" Skye exclaimed happily.

"Capital, old man!" Sherlock averred. "So the two of you not only settled the continuum, but settled down together."

"We have," Holmes agreed, slipping a possessive arm around Chadwick. "She is due in about two months, Watson estimates."

"Ooo," Chadwick grunted, putting her hands to her belly. "And he's a lively one." Holmes placed his hand on his mate's belly to feel the baby kick.

"He is, indeed." The aquiline face glowed with pride. He reached for a nearby chair and pulled it over. "Here, my dear, sit down. You are carrying a goodly weight, and you know how your feet have been swelling."

"I was about to ask, boy or girl," Skye grinned, watching. "Boy, then?"

"Indeed," Holmes beamed before Chadwick could answer. "The sonogram was definitive on the matter."

Chadwick met Skye's eyes, and the two women shared a private smile.

"WATSON estimates, eh?" Sherlock noted.

"Indeed. For he has come to America to live with us," Holmes explained.

"Excellent! And have you determined a name?" Sherlock wondered.

"Yup," Chadwick allowed. "John David Holmes. Named for Watson—both of them—and my dad."

"Perfect," Skye purred.

"We thought so," Holmes agreed unassumingly.

———

"Quite so," Sherlock noted with a smile. "And now I see why you choose beekeeping, armchair detection, and working with the tesseract to the more active—and dangerous—detecting field work."

"Exactly," Holmes nodded. "Skye flatly refused to let me go out without her, and in any case, I should not like to put her in a situation where we might risk the baby having...no father to assist in child rearing."

"Very wise," Sherlock agreed. "I should make the same decision, were I in your situation. And someday..." he glanced aside at his wife, feeling heat flush his face, "will likely do so, myself."

Both Chadwick's and Skye's eyes sparkled with unshed tears; feminine lips produced twin wobbly smiles.

"I hope we can pop by to see that day," Chadwick said softly.

"I hope so, too, Sis," Skye smiled, as Sherlock hesitantly nodded, his innate reticence showing.

"Anyway, we wanted to tell you, everything's going

great, and thank you for..." Chadwick began, then her voice shook.

"For everything," Holmes said in a rough tone. "Both scientific and...otherwise." Grey eyes met identical ones. "You were completely right."

Sherlock nodded.

"Now we should go," Holmes noted, regaining control of his voice. "It has been a long day of research, and it is more than time to get my spouse up the mountain and fed. She eats like Silver Blaze these days," he declared, eyes twinkling with mischief.

Chadwick smacked him on the shoulder. Hard.

"Ow," Holmes exclaimed, devilment still lurking in his eyes. Sherlock stifled a snort.

"Well, she's eating for two, as the saying goes," Skye defended her other self, "and if the little one's as active as the two of YOU..." she indicated the Holmes men.

"She has a point, Brother Me," Sherlock grinned.

"She does, and he is," Holmes grinned back. "Well, Brother Other Me, we shall depart now, and let the two of you return to your quiet evening together."

"Okay," Skye said, still smiling. "Good to see you, and good to know that everything is going wonderfully over there."

"It sure is," Chadwick glowed from within. "'Til next time. 'Bye!"

"Goodbye!"

"'Bye!"

"Good evening!"

And with the faintest of hisses, they were gone.

———

Skye turned to Sherlock, gazing pensively at him. But he could see the happy glow in her eyes.

"They looked great."

"They did," he observed. "They smiled more in that single conversation than in the whole time you worked on the tesseract with them."

"I'm glad things turned out happily for them, too."

"As am I."

Skye glanced at the clock.

"It'll be bedtime soon."

"So it will."

"Any color preference?"

"Tonight? Pink. Satin."

"Okay."

———

May 3
11:23 PM

In all likelihood, this will be the last journal entry I shall make in this lovely little tome my wife gifted me last year. I have had no recurring "Watson" dreams since the resolution of the cross-continuum crisis weeks—nay, months ago now, and do not anticipate any in future. Perhaps my dreams lend data regarding how Conan Doyle obtained Watson's stories of our adventures, nearly verbatim, as they seemed to so eerily predict Skye's danger. But that is Skye's baili-wick to ascertain, not mine. At least not until I have an understanding of the science more like that of my counterpart in the other continuum we assisted. I am very glad, however, for their sakes as well as ours, that the continuum crisis—and other matters—ended so well.

Their visit this evening was thoroughly delightful. The time is not yet right to admit to it openly, but I found Skye positively adorable when she is with child. And my alter-ego was as proud and as protec-

tive as ever I should be, in similar circumstances. It is obvious they are happy together at long last. I am glad for them, in many, many ways.

"John David Holmes." It is an excellent name, that. Duly and properly honouring both friend and family.

I shall have to remember it. It may be...useful...one day.

About the Author

Stephanie Osborn is a former payload flight controller, a veteran of over twenty years of working in the civilian space program, as well as various military space defense programs. She has worked on numerous Space Shuttle flights and the International Space Station, and counts the training of astronauts on her resumé. One of the astronauts she trained includes Kalpana Chawla, who died in the Columbia disaster.

She holds graduate and undergraduate degrees in four sciences: Astronomy, Physics, Chemistry, and Mathematics, and she is "fluent" in several more, including Geology and Anatomy. She obtained her various degrees from Austin Peay State University in Clarksville, TN and Vanderbilt University in Nashville, TN.

Stephanie is currently retired from space work. She now happily "passes it forward," teaching math and science via numerous media including radio, podcasting, and public speaking, as well as working with SIGMA, the science fiction think tank, while writing science fiction mysteries based on her knowledge, experience, and travels.

http://www.stephanie-osborn.com

www.ingramcontent.com/pod-product-compliance
Lightning Source LLC
Chambersburg PA
CBHW051332020726
47501CB00007B/2043